GOLD, a lot of it, has been discovered in the oil-rich tropics of Sumatra. Or has it?

Why does a Frenchman want to kill Ray Sharp? Who's been shoved out of a helicopter and why? Is there a war breaking out in the massage parlors of a jungle boomtown? Can Ray get his estranged wife off his back and find her lost boyfriend?

From an American suburb incongruously set into a jungle clearing to the sleazy bars and high-rise offices of Jakarta; from a teeming neighborhood floating on a river to the dense, steaming rainforest — *Flight of the Hornbill* is a thrill ride through an exotic Asian landscape peopled with unforgettable characters; some desperate to make a buck, some willfully ignoring their past, and most unforgettable of all, Ray Sharp, expatriate corporate investigator, struggling to find his place as an outsider in someone else's world.

Flight of the Hornbill is loosely based on the facts of the real-life Bre-X gold fraud.

Also by Eric Stone

The Living Room of the Dead

Grave Imports

FLIGHT OF THE HORNBILL

FLIGHT OF THE HORNBILL

THE THIRD RAY SHARP NOVEL

BY ERIC STONE

Bleak House Books
Madison, Wisconsin

Published by
BLEAK HOUSE BOOKS
a division of Big Earth Publishing
923 Williamson St.
Madison, WI 53703
www.bleakhousebooks.com

This is a work of fiction.
Any similarities to people or places, living or dead, is purely coincidental.

Printed in the United States of America

Library of Congress Cataloging-In-Publication Data has been applied for

12 11 10 09 08   1 2 3 4 5 6 7 8 9 10

ISBN: 978-1-60648-021-2 (Trade Cloth)
ISBN: 978-1-60648-022-9 (Trade Paper)
ISBN: 978-1-60648-023-6 (Evidence Collection)

This book is dedicated to the memory of Mochtar Lubis, a great writer and one of the most remarkable people I've ever known. It was through Mochtar that I first came to know and love Indonesia.

Also to my father, Martin Stone, who introduced me—as he has to so much else and to so many others—to Mochtar on my first trip to Indonesia.

And as always, to Eva, my best reader and a truly great partner, in crime and life.

ACKNOWLEDGMENTS

Ben LeRoy, publisher, and Alison Janssen, editor of Bleak House Books, who are colleagues, pals and regular all-around smart and fun people to work with.

Janet Reid, my agent and sometime drinking buddy, who works hard for her (not very much so far) money.

Win Blevins who was the first person, other than myself, to read this book and who gave me some welcome guidance.

Madeira James, the world's greatest webmaven, and also a close friend and confidant. Check out my website at www. ericstone.com; check out hers at www.xuni.com.

Arian Ardie and Tim Jessup, two very good pals with whom I have spent many a happy hour exploring Indonesia, from its highest heights, to its seamiest underbelly.

Armelle, Imah, Marina, Santi and the real life Billy who let me into their heads and hearts, and who I let into mine. I learned a lot from them.

My ex-wife, KJ. We had some very good times together in Indonesia. I was, in many ways, a really lousy husband. She was in no ways at all like the character of Sylvia, Ray's wife, in this book.

Lastly, and there are too many to name, to the independent mystery and general booksellers that have welcomed me and my books. Without their support, publishing this would be a thankless task. One of the things I like best about my job is going on tour when a new book comes out. It's a pleasure and a privilege that I get to make the rounds of all the stores where I have made so many friends.

CHAPTER **ONE**

I recognize her by the click of her high heels on the cool stone floor of the porch. She's always had a distinctive walk. I'm loose, relaxed, an icy vodka cooling my right hand after a long day on a hot, crowded plane from Hong Kong to Jakarta. Hearing her walk up spoils my mood. I wish it was someone else. Irina's here, somewhere in the city. But it's not her.

"Hey, Ray, long time." Not long enough, I'm thinking as I turn to look at her. It's been a little over two years, since I moved to Hong Kong.

"How'd you know I was here, Sylvia? I just got into town."

"Is that any way to talk to your wife?"

"Ex-wife by now if I could've pinned you down in front of a lawyer."

"You used to like pinning me down for other reasons, Ray."

"Don't play cute, it's been a long day. What do you want?"

Sylvia sits on the arm of a large, rounded rattan chair across from me. Her skirt rides high up a great pair of legs and trim thighs. She's always worn expensive panties. It's been long enough that she almost looks good to me. Almost.

"Aren't you gonna offer me a drink, Ray? It's hot in here. I don't know why you don't like air-conditioning."

"You remember where the drinks are, don't you? Help yourself."

We used to live in this house. I'd turned it over to a friend when I left. He's out of town at the moment. It's a good place to stay.

"I'm not staying long, Ray. I need your help."

"Why doesn't that surprise me?"

"I want a divorce, Ray. I found somebody else and we want to get married."

That's a big relief. I've been trying to get her to agree to it since we split up. Divorce isn't easy in Asia. It takes a lot of cooperation from both sides, or years of waiting. She must have her reasons for giving me grief over it, but I've never understood them. We've still got a couple of bank accounts and a stock portfolio tangled up between us. It's not enough to make either of us rich, but my half would be enough to let me say "no" to some things and "yes" to some others. Freedom's one of the most precious things in life, and it can be expensive.

"That's the one thing you could ask. I'll be happy to help. You want to try and do this ourselves or do we need to get lawyers involved."

"I don't care, Ray, whatever you want. I'm not gonna give you any trouble." She looks around the room, at some of the furniture that used to be ours, and frowns. "You can have everything. I don't want any of this stuff anyhow."

"This isn't our stuff anymore, Sylvia."

"What, you let what's his name have it when you moved out? Why'd you do that, Ray?"

I just scowl at her, trying to look as cold as my glass while I tinkle the ice cubes and take a deep, slow sip of the vodka.

What's happened to her? Or is it me? I used to think she was so hot. She was fun. Crazy in ways I liked. At least in the beginning. Maybe it was just the great sex. And maybe that was the problem. It takes a lot more than great sex to maintain a marriage.

"There's one problem, Ray. He's disappeared."

I have no idea who she means. "Who's disappeared? Why should I care?"

She's misplaced her fiancé, Alex.

Alexander Lee Truscott, eldest son of a wealthy oilman from Texas had been sent for seasoning to Indonesia by his family. They wanted him to learn the oil business in the field. He'd been working as a minerals industry analyst for one of the largest brokerages in the country. Sylvia had met him at a party given by the U.S. embassy's trade attaché. They'd been going out for a while. Two weeks ago Alex proposed. The next day he'd gone to Sumatra to look over the operations at a recently opened natural gas field. He hasn't come back yet. No one knows where he is.

"As I said, Sylvia, why should I care?"

"You want a divorce don't you? You don't want any trouble over it. I can make trouble if I want. You've always been good at finding things, Ray. You help me with this, I'll give you what you want. I might even let you keep all the bank accounts and stocks, and you won't have to see me anymore."

"I wish I wasn't seeing you now." By the time we'd split up, we couldn't get away from each other fast enough.

"Let's not get into it, Ray. Are you going to help me or not?"

I want her out of my life.

She gives me his picture. He's pretty, of course. Maybe ten years younger than her thirty-six, with fair hair and weak blue eyes. By the time he's forty he'll grow a few more chins, but for the present he'd turn heads. I give her a pen and some paper and watch while she writes down the names and numbers of his friends and colleagues.

"I'll take that drink now, Ray."

"No you won't. You'll get out of here. I'll let you know if I find out anything. Leave me your number."

I close my eyes by way of telling her to get lost, then lose myself into another long pull at my drink. The sound of her heels fades toward the street.

Due Diligence International, DDI for short, is what's brought me back to Jakarta. I'm here to conduct an investigation for a Hong

Kong investment bank that's looking to hook up with Motex, a big oil and gas company I used to work for. Motex has recently climbed into bed with an Australian mining company, Lucky Break. The mining company claims to have stumbled across the world's biggest gold deposit somewhere around the oil company's fields in Central Sumatra. What the client wants to know is whether or not these guys are legit, or at least predictably corrupt in ways they can do business with.

There's paperwork to go over, planning for tomorrow's meetings. But my brain is sizzling with sorry memories and introspection. I'd been a lousy husband. Maybe Sylvia had been an even worse wife. Mostly, I wish I knew where to find Irina. I wish I knew if she wants to see me.

I need distraction. I pour another shot of vodka and tell Wazir, the cook, that I won't be home for dinner. A long shower later, I head out to find a taxi.

CHAPTER **TWO**

I've been standing at the bar a few minutes when I feel a hand in the pocket where I keep my wallet. I grab a slender wrist. Maybe I'm not drunk enough. Maybe she isn't good enough. I twist her around to get a look at her.

She's slight, almost but not quite underfed. Big round glasses amplify already big round eyes that are an unlikely shade of green. There's a Dutch colonist somewhere in her genes. The glasses sit on a pert nose, below a short bob of hennaed hair; above narrow lips brushed to look full with a singularly inorganic tone of red. She's wearing a man's button-down-collar Oxford cloth shirt, unbuttoned to expose what would be cleavage if she had any. Her skirt, unlike the mere wisp of garments hardly covering the other women in the bar, is long and pleated. It's got deep pockets that bulge suspiciously. She's more goofy looking than pretty. I like that about her.

I flop her wrist over to inspect her arm, looking for needle marks. Just for something to do. There aren't any. But there are slashes, short horizontal, raised scars, some of them fresh. I shake her arm to draw her attention to it.

"What's that?"

She smiles, but wry, like given a little longer it might work its way into a grimace. "Brrrrr-oh-kken hearrrrrt." She exaggerates the rolled *R*s, then coughs out a harsh laugh. There's something sad about it, but charming. I try not to be charmed.

I hold onto her, raking her up and down with my eyes, trying to figure her out. She doesn't try to get away, just stares back at me, not defiant, expectant or nervous, simply waiting for my next move. I decide to outwait her.

We're frozen in place, as a swirl of insanity is going on in the dark around us. Tanamur is crowded as usual, the typical sardined mishmash of expats, tourists, locals with money and other locals looking to latch onto some money. A riot of them are sweating on the dance floor, others shivering under the chill blowers around the bar. The place is loud enough that you've got to shout to talk and even then unless you're shouting directly into someone's ears, or they can read lips, they can't hear you.

I work at locking a blank look on my face but it isn't long before I crack a smile. She figures she's won and tosses me a dismissive look. She tries to pull away but I hold on to her.

"You're a lousy pickpocket. I should make you buy me a drink."

"You want buy me drink?"

"No, I want you to buy me a drink. You tried to pick my pocket."

She looks a little surprised, then shrugs and smiles. "No money, mister."

I reach into one of her skirt pockets and pull out a very fat man's wallet. I don't know how the guy sits on it. I split my cash into different pockets, as well as my wallet. She watches expressionless as I flip it open. I half pull a short stack of large denomination bills out and flick through them. A flap flops to reveal an ID card belonging to a Swiss banker I'd met once at a party. He was an asshole. I hand it back to her.

I'd gone out to clear my head. This isn't exactly what I had in mind, but it's working. I know she has other ways to distract me too.

"What's your name?"

"Annie. What yours?"

"Ray."

"You handsome man." She plants a broad smile on her face, the kind with a little chuckle behind it that says, I've got you now, and presses herself up tight against me.

I'm not ugly, but there aren't too many women twenty or more years younger than me who'd go out of their way to call me handsome. Not unless they want what's in my wallet or they've got more than their fair share of daddy problems. Still, I can be a sucker. Sometimes it's a fair trade. You know full well you're being taken, but it's the illusion that counts. So long as you can maintain it, it can be worth the price.

"Okay, what do you want to drink?"

Gin and tonic takes on a radioactive glow in black light. I don't know if it's the booze or the mixer. She puts away a few of them. I lose track after the third. I nurse a couple of vodkas.

She follows me out and into the cab when I decide it's time to call it a night. I don't want any company. I need to get up early and start work the next morning. And I'm not sure I can maintain the illusion much longer anyhow, maybe not even long enough. I barely know her. Maybe she really does like me for myself. At least a little. Stranger things have happened. Some other night, I probably wouldn't care.

"Where can I drop you?"

"We go your house, have good time."

"No thanks, I'm tired. I'll take you home."

She sticks an exaggerated pout on her face and strokes a hand high on my inner thigh. "You no like? I think you like me."

"I do. Not tonight though. Sorry."

"Too late go my house. I sleep your house, no problem?"

It's a big house. I show her to the guest room and go to bed. Sometime in the middle of the night she crawls in with me, wakes me up, makes a halfhearted attempt to get something started. I grumble at her, turn away and drift back to sleep.

In the morning I get up figuring I'll give her breakfast and a little more than is really necessary for cab fare. She's gone. So's my money and watch.

That's a shame. I liked her. I can't help but smile at myself in the mirror while shaving. She'd have done a lot better over the long haul if she'd simply tried to make friends.

I'm borrowing an office in The Pencil. That's the local name for one of the new high-rise tinted glass towers along Jalan Gatot Subroto. I stop for a coffee in the lobby branch of The Good Pain. It's not really called that. It's French, "Le Bon Pain," but an Indonesian friend renamed it.

Coming up with playful names for things is a Jakartan trait. "Pizza Man" is a heroically scaled bronze monument in a traffic circle. It's an "inspirational" statue of a muscular peasant, veins bulging from strain in his legs and arms, holding up what looks like a giant flaming platter.

"Hey Mister, You Want My Sister" is a mile or two down the street in another traffic circle. On top of a tall, narrow marble column an idealized bronze young man holds up the hand of an attractive younger woman.

The first thing I've got to do this morning is bury my nose in paperwork. I used to work for the public relations department of Motex. I quit that job to become a business journalist. Even so, I have a hard time making any sense of the oil company's reports and filings and even less of what little public information I can find on Lucky Break Mining.

At about noon the receptionist, Susi, opens my door, rolls a pair of disapproving eyes my way and announces that there is a "young lady" who wants to see me.

Before I can say anything Annie walks in and bounces down in the chair in front of my desk.

She fishes around in her fake Luis Vuitton handbag, pulls out my watch and tosses it on the desk. "Why you have cheap watch?"

I can't help but admire her moxie. I'd had a feeling about her the night before, something more than can be easily dismissed as vodka and hormones. "I used to have an expensive one. I lost it. Or maybe someone took it. I don't remember."

"You take me lunch?"

"You've got my money, why don't you take me to lunch?"

There's a street lined with *warung* at the back side of the building. Some of the more highly regarded small, family-run, rickety wooden food stalls have been in the same place for as long as anyone can recall. The one Annie parks us at offers two choices: fried rice or fried noodles. The second generation of the family to work there does the cooking; the third waits on the one picnic table and cleans up. When we sit down they greet Annie by name.

"Where'd you learn your English?"

"Not good English. With friend. Sometime school. Go school with her." She discreetly points with a thumb in the direction of the tired looking young waitress.

Annie speaks good enough English that in combination with my bad Indonesian we're able to swap life stories.

Her real name's Anika. She grew up in a small village on the fertile slope of an active volcano in Central Java. Her father is dead. He'd been a cop in a rural precinct. Her mother still lives in the village and tends just enough rice for the family and enough extra papayas to sell in the local market. When Annie was twelve they sent her to Jakarta to live with her aunt and uncle. They operate a small electronics repair shop out of the front of their two-room house, alongside one of the city's foul canals that bubble with methane and buzz with mosquitoes.

She'd gone to school until she was sixteen and has been scrounging, doing whatever she can to get by, for the seven years since. She doesn't always pick pockets or steal from the men who take her home or to their hotels. It depends on her mood at the time.

"So, why'd you steal from me? What'd I do?"

"You no want have sex. I think maybe you no like me, maybe big nose in air."

For a moment I consider explaining why I hadn't wanted to fuck her the night before. How I might some other night. How I've got all sorts of demons in my head ever since I got tangled up with the Russian mafia and the trade in women. How I'm in love with a woman, a Russian prostitute, who's probably somewhere in Jakarta right now. But I only consider it for a moment. I just shrug my shoulders instead.

We finish eating and she reaches back into her bag, digging around for money to pay for lunch. She offers me what's left of my money. "I sorry. You nice man."

I tell her to keep it. It isn't much to me. It's a lot to her.

The rest of the afternoon I stare out the window of the office into the thick haze, overlooking the disordered hodgepodge of modern glass towers. They rise up in strings along the broad boulevards. Behind them filthy urban *kampungs*—villages, but it's come to mean neighborhoods as well—spread like bruises, radiating out from the fetid canals that slice through the city out of sight of the Mercedes on the big streets. Annie lives in one of those poor neighborhoods.

Is her life hard? Of course it is. Is it any harder than it would be if it weren't for all those new tall buildings or the shiny expensive cars? Or is it maybe just a little bit easier because of them? I have no idea. It's just another of the many things that's tying my brain up in knots.

Maybe it's knotting up her thinking too.

I'd told Annie I'd meet her again that night. It's just shy of nine when I get out of the house and into a taxi. Outside the humidity is pushing the smog down to ground level and the heat keeps it roiling. The locally built Ford's air-conditioning pumps out just enough cool breeze that sitting in the front seat and directing the vent at my face I manage to travel without getting totally drenched in sweat.

I know Nasir, the cab driver, from when I used to live in Jakarta. He's been at the same cab stand for years. He's a great driver. He works too many hours, maybe eighteen or twenty a day. I doubt he's ever taken a day off. He once fell asleep at a traffic light when I was in the car. He was so obviously exhausted that I insisted we trade seats. I drove him to a park, found a shady spot where he could nap; paid him the meter plus a good tip and took another cab the rest of the way. He struggles to make enough money to keep his two kids in school. I get his cab whenever I can and overtip him when I do. He's a master of the *jalan tikus*, the "rat streets."

Nasir winds our way through back alleys so narrow that he has to pull the side mirrors in against the car's body to pass. Only once do we have to slow to a walking pace, so that a street vendor can pull his cart into a driveway to let us pass. I look at him as he impassively watches us creep by. He's walnut colored, hard and wrinkled, so thin that it seems like I can see his bones, and they're the color of the marrow inside them. The only thing that can possibly give a man like that the strength to pull his two-wheeled, heavy cart through the cracked, pitted and bumpy streets is the terrible choice between that or starvation.

An hour later Annie and I are entwined in a ratty, torn leatherette dark booth facing the pool table at Tambora. She's taking the night off, so she's being affectionate. I hadn't planned on it, but when she arrived she straddled my lap, kissed me, and my resolve to remain a platonic pal melted away.

Karla, a pool hustler I'd once had the pleasure of getting the clap from, winks at me as she sinks a two-cushion bank shot to take more cash from a Dutch stockbroker whose name I can't recall. The bar isn't crowded. It never is until well after midnight.

I'm beginning to think I'll ask Annie if she wants to leave soon, come home with me, when a narrow young man with long dirty hair, a very sharp face and dressed top to bottom in shiny black, slinks up to our booth and takes a seat practically on my lap.

Annie greets him in a rapid fire, slangy Jakartan street patois that I can barely follow. I catch just enough to know that she's telling him about me. He pats her on the head and puts a hand on my shoulder. "She *gila* girl, crazy girl. You lucky man."

He runs his hand down to mine, grabs hold and gives it a shake. "*Nama saya* Billy. You like boy?" He clings damply, hopefully, to my hand.

"*Nama saya* Ray. No thanks. I like girls."

"Annie friend. You friend. Maybe like three same time?"

"Two's fine. But I'll buy you a drink."

"Whisky cola."

Billy's the male equivalent of Annie—a hustler who also picks pockets. He'll pick up a tourist or visiting businessman, fuck or suck him to sleep and leave quietly with a wallet and watch. But what he really likes is burglary. "Big fun, go big house, man sleeping, maybe

lady sleeping, quiet quiet, slowly slowly, many good thing for Billy."
He laughs gaily. Just thinking about creepy crawling somebody's
house has brightened his mood. I worry a little about myself when I
find it infectious.

It's getting hot in the booth. Annie takes off her long-sleeved
overshirt. Underneath she has on a tube top. Beside the crosscut
scars on her left arm, there's a series of roughly tattooed black dots
along the left thumb. I hold it up to see it more clearly, then hold
her hand out to her.

"What's this?"

"Italy man catch me. Stupid. Go jail one year."

Things like that make me feel a little cut myself. Heartbreak of
my own pounds on my skull to get in. I know Irina's somewhere in
Jakarta. I miss her. I want to find her. I don't know what will hap-
pen if I do.

I look at Annie, maybe a little too long. It makes her uncomfortable. She pulls her hand away. Maybe I should ask to borrow her
razor blade, make a few scars of my own. I doubt that sort of thing
really works as therapy. Annie's well enough adjusted though, at least
in her own way, I think.

What about me? I'm in love with someone who isn't really all
that different from Annie. Irina's better educated, maybe a little
less self-destructive, we've got more in common, she's more
Western; but she's also a prostitute, another woman damaged by
the circumstances of her birth, her society. What is it between Irina
and me that's so powerful? What is it I find so attractive about
Annie and Billy?

Not too long ago I was in a hotel room in Russia, tied to a bed,
being burned with a cigarette by a Russian woman who planned to
kill me when she was done. At one point she asked, and sincerely
wanted to know, why I liked "bad girls," not "good girls." It's not
like she knew me well. Am I that obvious? I didn't know the answer
then. I don't know it now. I'm not sure I want to.

I want Irina. I enjoy the company of Annie and Billy. I could
spend years in therapy figuring out why. But right now I wave my
arm for the waitress and order another round of drinks. Distraction
is enough for the time being.

About a half hour of flirtatious chit chat later, Billy puts his arm around me, squeezes my shoulder and asks Annie something I can't catch.

"Billy say, 'Want go party friend house'?"

"Do you want to? If you want, let's go."

"Okay we go."

A *bajaj* is a terrible, fume-spewing, three-wheeled vehicle made in India. Thousands of them befoul the streets of Jakarta. When poor people have no choice but to pay for motorized transport, that's what they use, piling in dangerous numbers into the cramped backseats. *Bajaj* are responsible for a lot of the city's noise and air pollution and are frequently involved in horrific accidents.

It used to be that bicycle-powered pedicabs were the favored public transit for the poor, but the government decided they were a nuisance. They were too slow, clogging the streets that were fast becoming choked with automobiles. They were an embarrassment in a country that is trying to pass itself off as modern.

The government didn't really care about pedicab drivers, but the fact that they led miserable lives and died young gave the bureaucrats a humanitarian excuse to get rid of them. Despite pitched battles that erupted in the neighborhoods that relied on pedicabs, the police rounded up almost all of them and dumped them about a kilometer out to sea. The underwater reef they created was soon encrusted with coral, inhabited by fish and popular with weekend SCUBA divers who don't mind floating through all the other junk jettisoned by Jakarta.

We flag down a *bajaj* and bounce through the rat streets. The only light buzzes from low-wattage fluorescent tubes on the front garden walls of the houses we pass and the glow of the huge city reflecting off the low ceiling of smog. We stop at a small shop to buy some warm Bintang beer and finally pull up at a high wall next to a small mosque. The light beyond the wall glows blue and red and the rumble of heavy bass and drum dance music rolls out in greeting.

Billy slides open a gate and we follow him into a small garden littered with auto parts and overgrown with tangled vines of orchids clinging to the interior walls. A fat, pasty man is sitting on an engine block with a small, dark Indonesian girl who's costumed as an over-sexed girl scout. He wears a freshly plucked flower behind his ear, trying to cling to its place in his thinning hair. She's picking at something under his shirt on his shoulder. She's not working toward any merit badge I ever heard of. He gestures us toward the house with his beer bottle.

Things like that take my nose and rub it in all the ugly stereotypes of expats and local girls. Sure I'm younger than him. And I've got all my hair. And I'm a whole lot less out of shape. But still I… What I don't want to do is think about it. I need a cold beer.

The house isn't air-conditioned. A slowly turning overhead fan doesn't quite manage to push around enough of the heavy wet air. There are far too many people in the small front room. My glands shift into crisis mode and I immediately begin to pour sweat. Within moments I'm drenched, perspiration puddling in the folds of my clothes and dripping into my eyes.

Annie runs a hand across my forehead then looks at it like she's trying to figure out how to wring it out. It would be embarrassing, but she laughs in a way that diffuses it. She's accustomed to sweaty foreigners. It's one of the reasons she likes going with them to their hotels—good showers. She isn't sweating at all; as cool as if she were in the frosty lobby of one of Jakarta's deluxe new buildings. She spots some friends and excuses herself to go talk with them. She invites me along, but it's halfhearted. I don't want to make her friends feel they have to speak English or be polite for my sake. I tell her I'll catch up to her later.

I drift around in the currents of the crowd, finally pausing to lean against a strategically placed wall and take in the scene with a bottle of warm beer for company. When I first walked in it was just an indistinct, swirling lumpen mass. Then an eye here, a piece of jewelry there would glimmer for an instant, moving across one of the few narrow beams of light.

The mass begins to take shape. There are more men than women, mostly Indonesians in their teens or early twenties from the look of them. Some are dancing; most just swaying to the pounding music and talking. The air reeks of beer, sweat, clove cigarettes, perfume and the occasional faint but unmistakable vapor trail of

Sumatran pot. I enjoy watching, but it makes me feel old and the beer I'm drinking isn't doing enough to fight off the introspection that's been threatening me all evening.

Annie finds her way back to me, presses herself up against me and holds a large cold bottle of beer up to my lips. I take a quick, refreshing slug and catch her as she starts to flit away.

"Annie, who's party is this? If I'm drinking their beer, I ought to know."

She looks around, spots a slight, short man of about thirty in a bright red jogging suit and points him out with a discreet thumb. "Mochtar. He get job in big new shoe factory. Family happy, have party."

A Korean company that makes shoes under contract for U.S. companies has recently built a new state-of-the-art plant in a suburb to the south. "The Korean one?"

"Yes, very good job, pay two time more money than old factory. Have clinic for family."

The Koreans are almost certain to put an older, funkier, locally-owned factory out of business. There's been a lot of debate about it in the press.

I wonder if Annie ever thinks about that sort of stuff. It's the kind of thing Irina and I can discuss for hours, at dinner, in bed, drunk; maybe we'd be fooling around at the same time.

"What do you think about that, Annie? Good? Bad?"

She moves her face back from mine and gives me an odd look. I don't think many people ever ask her opinion about anything.

Her look works its way around to thoughtful, then cheerful. "*Tidak apa apa*. Is no problem. Job good. More money good. Mochtar happy. Family happy. Have big party."

She tosses off a light laugh, kisses me with a quick, sharp dart of her tongue, then moves away before I can ask any more questions. She shimmies across the living room floor and sidles up to a group including Billy, who's wrapped a possessive arm around a tall, light-skinned man.

Is there an answer to any of the questions about globalization in any of this? Damned if I know. Looking around, I'm probably the only person in the place bothering to think about any of this shit anyhow. Everyone else is just living their lives, getting by, dancing and drinking at the moment. If I want to write editorials I can go back into journalism. Fat lot of good that'll do any of these people at the party.

Like usual, the more I think about these things, the less I feel like I know about them.

I take a long, slow slug of beer. It's locally made, from an old Dutch recipe that the Indonesians have improved on. It's a very good brew. I take a deep breath, trying to clear my head.

I consider following Annie into the group, but one of the guys in the bunch reaches out a hand to cup her left ass cheek and pull her tighter into what looks like a closed social circle.

My mood's sinking. I'm looking for a place to put down my bottle before making my escape, when I see her across the room. Something punches me in the gut from the inside, pounds the breath out of me, sets off a rattle in my chest.

Irina looks like she did the first time I ever saw her. Maybe a little smoother, more refined around the edges, dressed in slightly more expensive clothes. She's cut her hair short to frame her face, to show off her long but sturdy neck. I don't know what to do. I freeze in place, feeling like I'm about to crumble to the floor.

She sees me and smiles in a way that doesn't make me feel like I've won the lottery, but about like I've won five bucks from one of those scratch off instant prize tickets. She turns to say something to the man standing next to her, then angles through the crowd toward me.

"Ray."

"I like your haircut." I reach out to stroke it, but she leans her head away.

"What is it you are doing here?"

It's been almost a year since I've seen her. It feels longer than that.

"I'm here for work. I've missed you."

"You here to write article?"

"It's a new job. I'm not a journalist anymore. I'm working for an investigations firm."

"Is it good job?"

"Yeah, I like it."

"How long do you stay in Jakarta?"

"I got here yesterday. I don't know, maybe a few weeks. Can I see you? Can we talk?"

"I miss you too." She touches my arm, lightly. I want to grab her, hug her tight. It's not the right time. It takes a lot of effort not to. "I have question I want to ask you."

I hope to hell it doesn't have anything to do with what happened to her friend, Sasha, or any of the mess I'd got into with the Russian mafia. I still don't have any answers for those questions.

"What question? What are you doing now? I was about to leave."

"Question is about money. You know about money. A man I know, stockbroker, he give me a good tip. I buy many shares of stock."

She's been saving her money since before I first met her. When was that? Four, maybe five years ago. Unlike most of the prostitutes I've ever known, she's always been conservative with money. She calls it her "independence day" funds. It's one of the things I like about her.

"A trick? What stock?"

She shrugs her shoulders to the first part of my question. She's never tried to hide what she does from me. She knows I don't judge her for it, but she's always avoided rubbing my face in it.

"Australia company, a gold mine, Lucky, Lucky... You know?"

"Lucky Break? Yeah, I know. I've heard of them." I can't tell her that I'm in Indonesia to investigate the company. I don't know enough about it yet to have any opinion. But I also don't know who she might talk to.

"I can't tell you much about them now. I'll look into them, see what I can find out. What are you doing? I'm about to leave. Want to come with me?"

"I cannot go now. I am here with a man. Where do you stay?"

I tell her where I'm staying. She remembers it from before, when I lived in Jakarta. I trade her the new phone number for her new mobile number and she goes back to work, back to the other man, a Japanese businessman by the look of him. I turn away to look for Annie, to tell her I'm leaving, alone.

She's in the kitchen, pushed up close against a flushed and flush looking short, round European with a rumpled, sweat-stained green suit. His lapels are gaping open and I can see the top of a fat wallet in the inside pocket.

"Pardon me, but I need to borrow her for a minute." I gently tug on her arm and pull her away.

"Be careful, I don't think he's drunk enough yet."

"You okay? I go his hotel, no problem?"

"*Tidak apa apa*, no problem. I'm going. See you soon." She smiles, kisses my cheek and gets back to her *bule* before anybody else can move in on him.

CHAPTER **THREE**

I spend a sleepless night and decide to get out of town, at least for a few days. I'd managed to pull together a reasonably useful background picture of Lucky Break in the office yesterday. And there's still people here who I'll need to talk to. But there's only so much I can find out in Jakarta when the gold mine I'm investigating is in Sumatra at the Motex compound.

Motex is practically a nation unto itself. It's a joint venture between a U.S. oil company and the Indonesian government's oil ministry. The company's cooperating with my investigation. It's not in the gold business. It's happy to make some money off a discovery on its land, but it's also happy to bring in other investors to spread the risk.

I hadn't worked at Motex very long. The company had brought me to Asia, got me settled. I gave it a good eighteen months before I just couldn't stomach being a public relations flack any longer and quit to become a journalist. I'd managed to keep good relations with the people I knew in the company.

I catch a cab to the Motex terminal, which is in the highest security sector of Jakarta's military airport. I bundle onto one of the company's no-frills DC-8s and squeeze into an aisle seat next to a pair of slim, quiet Indonesians. The burly, noisy American oil-workers all sit together at the back, close to the bathrooms and the galley, shoulders overlapping shoulders, forearms wrestling over the armrests.

The flight passes over the narrow strait between Java and Sumatra, over volcanoes steaming and smoking, over a dense canopy of jungle that from the air looks like an unbroken crown of broccoli. The plane follows the path of the Marinda River in from the east coast to its landing pattern, then rustles the tin rooftops of the river port town as it descends onto the steaming tarmac of a large, busy airport, set incongruously in the middle of nowhere.

Nowhere is where oilmen go these days to find their crude. It's been a long time since there's been any new oil or natural gas found on Signal Hill in Los Angeles or the suburbs of Oklahoma City. The easy-to-get-at oil was all combusted into smog by the early 1960s.

Oil and natural gas are found in the same places, or at least near each other. That's because they're essentially the same stuff. Made up entirely of hydrogen and carbon, oil has more carbon atoms that make it heavier and liquid, gas has relatively more hydrogen atoms, which makes it lighter and airy.

Motex has already pumped a lot of oil out of Sumatra and now the company's pumping the gas.

The Americans run the show and you'd know it from the look of the work site. There's something about us that makes us want to feel at home no matter where the hell we are, or what lengths we have to go to feel that way. Some of us at least—not me.

The company tore a gigantic clearing out of the forest, some six miles outside of Marinda, and built a compound. If you were blindfolded and dropped into the middle of it, you'd guess you were in a working class suburb of Dallas. Almost fifty square miles of fenced landscaping—tract homes with neat sprinkled lawns, schools, recreation halls and parks, churches, offices, workshops, a hospital, a motel and a shopping mall—is set down smack in the middle of one of the world's densest and most primitive jungles.

Along the edges an army of groundskeepers fight a constant

battle against creeping vines and mosses, poisonous snakes and dense clouds of insects. They're often pelted with shit by the troupes of monkeys that live in the trees at the perimeter.

There's a cluster of twelve once tidy, two-bedroom family houses that have been abandoned to a vocal family of *siamangs*, one of the lesser apes. About a month after the houses were built the nasty brutes took up residence in the trees nearby. Every morning they wake up, inflate their throat sacs as big as their heads and let loose a fierce onslaught of bubbling whoops topped off with something that sounds like a sonic boom. The noise can be heard several miles away. They like to spend their days lounging on the rooftops of the new houses. They make lousy neighbors.

One year there'd been a scare when a tiger found a hole in the fence. It slunk out of the forest and ate a matched pair of recently groomed, award-winning poodles and several pet Easter bunnies. For a week everyone kept their kids indoors and walked around carrying guns. Finally the poor, hungry beast was cornered, tranquilized and taken by helicopter to a preserve some several mountains and valleys away.

Eight thousand people live in the compound, only a few thousand less than in the nearby town. They come from the U.S., mostly the warm weather oil states—Louisiana, Oklahoma and Texas—and from all over Indonesia. The Americans, except for a few technicians on short visits, come with their families. The company promises them that their lives in Sumatra won't be much different than they were back home.

Their kids go to American-style schools. They have their pick of churches and the churches have regular bake sales. There's a bowling league. The supermarket carries eight different brands of laundry detergent and nineteen different breakfast cereals. If they want, they can eat steak and potatoes every night at the commissary while watching that season's football, baseball, basketball or the latest sitcoms on big screen TVs. Many of the expat workers and their families never venture beyond the fence.

The Indonesians are mostly young and single. They come from small villages all over the country and send the money they save home to their families. They don't associate much with the expats except for the occasional company social event, usually a picnic at which the Indonesians beat the Americans at soccer and badminton and the taller Americans get theirs back on the basketball court.

When I worked for the company I would stay in the Motex Motel, across from the mess hall and the Methodist church. It's free for employees or the company's guests. You can drink the water out of the taps and the cable TV plays the latest American shows and movies.

Alex, the missing fiancé, had been staying at the Marinda Palace, the only hotel in town with working phones and where the sheets are changed less than every hour, but more than never. The morning he was supposed to leave, he didn't show up for his flight. Sylvia called his room when he didn't turn up in Jakarta. The front desk told her that he hadn't checked out but he wasn't there.

Two days later he still hadn't checked out, still hadn't been in his room and hadn't picked up his messages. A day after that his boss called Sylvia and asked if she'd heard from him. Four more days went by before she showed up on my front porch.

The Palace, as it's known, is the sort of place in which a single man rarely stays unaccompanied for long. I'm just settling into my room when there's a knock at my door. Her nametag reads "Emmy." She's from housekeeping and wants to know if there's anything she can do for me. Anything at all. She takes hold of my hand to ask, brushing it against her chest.

She's light skinned, with a round face and long straightened hair. She's tall for an Indonesian woman, maybe in her mid-twenties, and acts more confident than subservient. I'm tempted, tired, and the thought of going back to bed for anything at all is enticing. I hold onto her hand longer than necessary and flirt as well as I can in my limited Indonesian. I invite her in.

Emmy comes into the room and sits on the bed. She reaches for my belt buckle.

"Not now. Maybe later." You can't just say "no" to an Indonesian, not if you're trying to be polite. I sit down next to her and take her hand off my pants.

"I want to ask you some questions. Is that okay?"

"No make love now? What you want mister?"

"I'm looking for a man who stayed at this hotel last week or the week before."

"Many man stay here."

I get up and pull Alex's picture from my briefcase. "This is the man. Did you see him?"

She frowns and pushes the picture away from her. "I no like. He bad heart, no good man. Too many girl, hurt girl, no good man, bad man. I no make love, no like. He friend you? Maybe you no good man." She gets up from the bed looking like she's about to leave the room.

"No Emmy, he isn't my friend. I have to find him for my job." She throws a suspicious look my way, but sits back down, a little further away than she had to begin with.

"I no see him maybe one week. He no check out, one day go. Leave bag room."

Alex's bags are stored in the manager's office. The girls he'd brought back to his room came from the disco in the basement of the hotel. Emmy agrees to meet me there after she finishes work at ten that night. She knows all of the girls who work in the place, and will introduce me to the ones who went with Alex.

Apparently she's decided I'm okay after all. She moves back up against me, puts her hand on my thigh and asks again if there's anything I want.

There is. But I have work to do. It takes some effort and deep breathing to turn her down.

"Maybe later. I'll meet you at the disco later."

I shouldn't send her away empty handed. I carry a lot of cash with me in Indonesia, as much as a million or more *rupiah* at a time. That sounds more impressive than it is. It's about four, at the most five hundred U.S. bucks. There isn't much in the way of street crime, especially against foreigners, and it isn't always that easy to find a money wall or a bank that won't cheat you on a cash advance.

I hand over twenty thousand *rupiah*, about eight dollars. Maybe it's a down payment for later, maybe it's for information. I don't know, but she takes it gladly. I walk out of the room with her.

It costs ten thousand *rupiah* for the manager to leave his desk, walk the ten feet to his closet and show me Alex's bags. He hangs around with his hand out, hoping to hit me up for more to look the other way while I paw through the bags. I send him back to his desk with a withering look.

I've got no idea what I'm looking for. Nothing is out of the ordinary. I check to make sure the manager's back is turned and pocket the small appointment book from the laundry bag filled with stuff that was cleared off Alex's desk, dresser and bathroom counter. I tell the manager I'll let him know what to do with the bags once I know myself.

By then it's too late to go to the compound and get much of anything done. Warner, my boss, isn't expecting to hear anything from me until at least the end of the week. He'll get annoyed if I bother calling without anything useful to tell him.

While it's still light I take a rattletrap, Indonesian-assembled Nissan taxi north on the only paved highway out of town. There wasn't much of interest in the appointment book. Just a few names I recognized from Motex; a half-dozen phone numbers, four of which had the Motex prefix; and the notation "Santo's truck stop— 8 km north," on the date before the day he was supposed to return to Jakarta.

Everybody who's spent any time at all in the area knows Santo's. It's in a clearing that's been burned out of the jungle alongside the highway. Every three months or so they fire the edges again to keep the forest at bay. It has a gas pump and a ditch that Santo crawls into to work on car and truck undercarriages. There's a small *warung* where you can eat fried rice or noodles and cut through the grease with a burning toxic rice wine that Santo brings in jugs from his village in the mountains.

The real business is in back. There's an old dairy cow barn broken up into dirt-floored stalls and lit by kerosene lanterns. It's a massage parlor. At least that's what the police license by the door says it is. Women of all ages, sizes and shapes rent the stalls. They live and work in them. They make okay money servicing the guys from the compound. Santo makes a lot of money.

The Christians at the compound try to shut Santo down just about every other month. But the local police captain is a regular customer and they don't stand a chance.

Depending on who's there, it's also as good a place as any to pick up local gossip. There's bound to have been someone around the place talking about a big gold find in the vicinity.

CHAPTER **FOUR**

Santo's gone to his village for some Muslim holiday or another, or maybe just to get more rice wine. An old woman is standing at a huge, blackened wok. She grunts when I show her the picture of Alex, shrugs when I ask about gold. She lets the ash drop off the end of her cigarette into the frying noodles, then lifts and tilts her head in the direction of the barn. I grunt back and walk through the muddy lot.

To get into the barn you have to buy an overpriced beer or soda as a sort of admission ticket, at a short bar in front of the door. Once you've paid, the bartender raises the hinged part of the counter and you collect your drink as you pass through. I pick up a can of Bintang beer. It's cold in my hand, even better on the back of my neck before I open it. It's also good going down my throat.

I slowly walk along the center aisle of the dimly lit barn, listening to the dull slap of bodies, low grunts and groans, and *oohs* and *aah aah aahs* coming from stalls closed off with shower curtains drawn across the front. Most of the curtains are floral print. There's one with an outdated map of the world. I used to have the same one. A group of women are seated at a picnic table at the far end. As I approach they put down their sodas and tea and arrange themselves for my inspection.

It's not the A-team. Either the young and pretty ones aren't working yet or they're occupied in the closed stalls. The women are uniformly dressed in frayed batik sarongs with a variety of t-shirts on top. One particularly wizened old crone attempts a fetching smile with her few remaining, dull yellow teeth. She's wearing a wash-worn purple Motley Crue t-shirt. That earns her a smile from me.

I'm about to pass around the photo of Alex and then flee in terror when a young woman in her mid-twenties, with short cropped, dyed blond hair and a square muscular build, emerges from a nearby door carrying a steaming bowl of instant noodles. I smile at her, and when the other women notice who I'm smiling at they all slump, allowing their posture to announce "game's over."

The Motley Crue woman says something to the others in a Sumatran dialect and they all laugh. She fixes her gaze on me. "Young girl. Pretty. Massage no good. No strong." She makes a muscle with her right arm. Everyone laughs again. Me too.

I put my hand out to the young woman anyhow. She sets down her noodles and takes it, leading me to a stall about halfway up the aisle. She pulls aside the bright yellow Hello Kitty shower curtain and gestures me inside.

There's a cold-water sink at one end and a small refrigerator with bottles of lotions and oils and a pile of towels on top. A metal bar, hung by wires from the ceiling, has clothes hung from it. A full-length mirror takes up most of the wall facing the single bed, but only a small center part of it isn't covered with pictures from her village. The pictures are of her sisters and brothers and parents and grandparents and a lot of other people who she would describe, if I asked, as also being her sisters and brothers and parents and grandparents. Like a lot of Indonesians from rural villages, almost everyone she grew up with is her family and she wants them there with her.

"What's your name?"

"*Nama* Lili. No *Ingirris*."

Lili does, however, speak enough English to let me know that it's going to cost fifty thousand *rupiah*, about twenty dollars, whatever I want to do.

I just want a massage. I take off my clothes and lay face down on the bed. She wiggles out of her Pepsi Challenge t-shirt, exposing her breasts. She crosses her arms over them when she sees that I've raised my head and am looking at her. She unwraps the sarong from around her waist and rewraps it higher, covering herself from the breasts down to mid-thigh.

She hikes up the sarong, tucking the bottom of it into her crotch, and clambers onto my thighs. Leaning over she pulls at a couple of hairs on my back. "Monkey man," she giggles, and then goes to work.

The old woman was wrong. Lili has strong hands and before long some of the grunts and groans coming from the stalls are coming from me. By the time she's done with my back and has moved onto my legs I'm dozing, puddled onto the thin mattress. Finally she yanks my toes, cracking the joints, then gets off the bed, slaps me on the ass and says something that must mean "turn over."

I turn over. Lili pouts her lips and flicks at my limp cock with a fingernail. "No like Lili?"

I tell her that I do like her but that all I want's a massage.

"*Nanti?*" She wants to know if I'm going to want something more later.

I just close my eyes and let her finish the massage.

When she's done I show her the picture of Alex. She doesn't recognize him. While I dress she takes the picture to show it to the other women around the table at the end of the barn.

Lili returns with a woman I hadn't seen before; a short, fat, long-faced woman in her late-twenties or early-thirties whose huge breasts are almost falling out of a torn Metallica t-shirt. Her name's Rina.

"I see him. No good man, no good heart."

"When did you see him?"

"Maybe one week, maybe ten day; don't know."

"Why was he no good? What did he do?"

"He go my sister. Take hotel. Hurt her, take dress and kick out, no money. Bad man."

I'm beginning to get the distinct impression that Alex is no sweetheart. I don't like to think that Sylvia has such bad taste in men. After all, she'd been with me all those years. Has she fallen so far that his money's enough? There has to be something more, doesn't there?

"Do you know where he went? Do you think your sister might know?"

"Sister go village, Sulawesi. No come back. He go way other bad mans. Go forest. No see."

There isn't anything else to get out of her. There's a whole lot of forest around and Alex's having gone away into it with some other bad men could mean a lot of things, or nothing at all. If I can find out what he was working on, I might get some new ideas. Looking for him is getting interesting.

On my way out, I stop at the table where the masseuses sit and wait. I ask what anyone's heard about gold being found nearby. They've all heard about it. They've heard it's a lot of gold. Most of their customers have talked about it. None of them can remember anything more about it than that. Why would they? If I start tossing some money at them, some of them might recall something more. Or they might not. I don't bother.

The taxi's waiting for me. The driver smirks knowingly when I get back in and tell him to take me to the hotel. It's not late and I'm not in a hurry, but I do need to take some time to figure out what to do at Motex tomorrow. The case of the missing fiancé is looking like it might be a lot more fun, but Due Diligence International and its Hong Kong Investment Bank client is paying the bills.

CHAPTER **FIVE**

Getting information on Motex is no problem. It's a huge international company that's listed on three different stock exchanges. Most of what my client needs to know about Motex is already available to the public. It's a simple but tedious matter of digging it all out to write up a report from annual reports, financial filings and press clippings. I need to interview a few people locally, to make sure the company operates on the up and up in Indonesia. But unless things have changed drastically since I worked there, they do. Well, at least as much as any big oil company ever does anywhere. Bill Warner, my boss, has hired a forensic account-ant to take on the big headache; shuffling through the mountain of numbers. My eyes go out of focus and my brain begins to strobe when I try to do something like that.

What I don't know are the specifics of the big gold find: where, when, how, what, what's it all mean, what's this Lucky Break Mining company all about? That's the bigger part of the job. I spend the early part of the evening jotting down notes, coming up with questions to ask, figuring out who I need to ask those questions, things like that. By ten I've had enough and go downstairs to the coffee shop for something to eat.

I dawdle over a plate of *nasi goring*. The fried rice is greasy; the fried chicken that comes with it is pretty good. I try tamping it all down with a couple of cups of truly terrible, grit-filled, weak coffee. It's one of the mysteries of Indonesia that the coffee is so bad. The country grows some of the very best coffee beans on earth, yet most people prefer instant Nescafé to the real thing. Considering how they roast and prepare fresh coffee in the country, it's no wonder.

Trying to brush some of the bitter grains out from between my teeth with a finger, I walk through the lobby and down the stairs to the basement disco.

There isn't as much light as the name implies in the Twilight Disco. A few red and green bulbs glow from behind cigarette tar-coated potted palms that cling miraculously to life in the sticky smoke and deep gloom. A large mirrored ball rotates precariously low over the dance floor, spotlights hitting it from two sides then ricocheting in shrapnel around the room. The shards of light catch a small swirl of people, indistinguishable as individuals, undulating en masse in sync with a stomach churning bass line.

I step inside. The carpeted floor is spongy and malodorous with spilled beer; the air pungent with the sharp, cloying reek of clove cigarettes and cheap perfume. I stop just inside the door, waiting for my eyes to adjust. I'm beginning to think they won't, when a shadow glides off the dance floor and takes hold of my hand.

"Mister, hello." It's Emmy.

From what I can make out in the gloom, she's changed into a translucent white blouse, a short skirt and plenty of makeup. I almost don't recognize her. She grabs hold of my arm and guides me like she's helping a blind man across the street, along the edges of the pulsing parquet to a seat in a booth.

"Mister, you want drink? Give money I go bar."

I fish out some bills and hand them to her, tell her I want the usual, a vodka, and to get whatever she wants. I fall back against the leatherette, swivel my eyes toward the dance floor and am relieved to find that I am beginning to make out a few details.

The crowd is mostly young women. There's a table of four very drunk oilmen who've attracted a flock of a dozen or so brightly colored girls. They flutter around the men in competition for their attention and whatever's in their wallets. Otherwise, as far as I can see, I'm the only other foreigner in the place.

My eyes settle on the women leaning against the bar. They eye me back. Three of them detach themselves from the group and sidle languorously in my direction. They look around while they do, wary. They had to have seen me walk in with Emmy. There are strict rules of territory in bars like this. The peace is kept only when they're obeyed.

Emmy returns with my drink and a friend, Tommy, who is carrying a drink of his own. The three approaching girls look at each other, one of them tosses me a "maybe later" look, and return to their places. Emmy sits down, handing me a small, wet wad of bills.

"My friend. No worry, I buy drink my money, no steal you."

Tommy's a little weedy guy with a thin lopsided mustache and a ballet dancer's moves. He looks not much more than fourteen but it turns out he's twenty-six. He sits down on one side of me. Like almost all the Indonesians in the bar, he's a hustler.

Young Indonesians go to bars and discos now more than ever. As the economy grows and people get more money, there's just no keeping young people at home. Somewhere in town there's undoubtedly a place that the locals go with their dates, or with their friends, just for fun. But the basement bar in a businessman's hotel isn't that place.

I stick out my hand to shake but Tommy stretches out his and strokes my face.

"You nice looking man. Maybe no money with you. We go your room, have fun."

It's funny. I'm never cruised by gay Western men. Maybe there's something subtle about me that screams "straight guy" at them. I'm not nervous around gay men, so I don't think it's my body language or anything like that. I wonder about it sometimes. I've asked gay friends about it and they can't figure it out. But none of them are interested in me, either. I'm not interested in Tommy that way, but I'm not unfriendly about it.

Emmy and I talk as well as we can in the din. She's twenty-seven, which she thinks is old. In Indonesia most women are married with children by her age. The hotel doesn't mind that she spends time with guests, just so long as she gets her work done. It's even encouraged. Most of the women who work in the hotel are young and attractive. Management and security take a cut of any extra money they make in the place.

She's a little shy at first. Maybe because I turned her down earlier in the day she isn't sure how to act with me. After a couple of drinks she loosens up and eases her legs over mine. Tommy can't help but see what's going on. He lets out an exaggerated sigh, brushes my face with his hand again as if to say "too bad," and heads across the dance floor. I barely notice him leaving. Emmy has taken a firm grip on my attention, burrowing tight into my side, her fingertips lightly stroking at the crotch of my pants.

I pick up her hand and hold it in mine between us. "Emmy wait, remember, I'm trying to find one of the girls who went with the man I'm looking for. Are any of them here?"

"You no like me?"

"Yes, I like you very much. But I need to do this. Please help me."

She doesn't particularly like that but gets up to make a circuit of the disco. She's back in about five minutes and hasn't seen anyone who can help. She says that a friend of hers had spent time with Alex. She'll probably be in the disco tomorrow night.

After that, Emmy pulls out all the stops. There isn't a trace left of the shy girl. And it's just what I need. I've been avoiding sex. It's been locked up in my head with everything that went wrong in Macau. For an instant my conscience tells me to slow down, think about this, what's it all mean? Then a loud shout of just plain old-fashioned horniness tells my brain to shut up. And it does. And it's a huge relief.

She leans back into me, takes my hand, brings the middle finger to her lips and laves it up and down with her tongue, looking at me from under heavy eyelids. She puts it in her mouth and sucks gently, bathing it in a warm wash of saliva. She's got plenty of effective cheap tricks and I can't think of any good reasons why I shouldn't be falling for them.

She farts, loud enough to be heard over the roar from the dance floor. She blows my finger out of her mouth with a pop and lets loose a husky laugh. She shrugs her shoulders into my chest. "You want go?"

The hotel elevator, filled with Taiwanese businessmen, stops at every floor. Emmy and I stare at each other across their gray suits. She teases a finger across the ridge of her red lips. The Chinese are uneasy and silent between us.

In the room she won't let me turn on the light. There's just the faint red and yellow glow from a neon sign across the street. She pushes me to the bed and takes control, undoing my belt, unbuttoning my pants and pulling them down. She pushes up her skirt and before I can perform any of the niceties, she throws her legs on either side of me and pulls me into her.

Once I'm settled where she wants me, she reaches behind her and unhooks her skirt. She pulls it away and in the scant light I can make out her hairless lower lips, opening and closing around me like the mouth of a big lazy fish at feed. A small tattoo of what looks like an Indonesian shadow puppet would be covered with pubic hair if she hadn't shaved.

She doesn't make a sound, just watches me with brightly glazed wide-open eyes. I try watching her face but my eyes keep returning to where we're joined. Every time I look up she grins down at me. I push my hands up under her shirt, catching a glimpse of what looks like another tattoo, but then she leans forward and holds my hands down at my sides. She rides me slow, with a circular motion, and it doesn't take long.

She lies on top of me afterward, hugging me, for just a little while before getting up and going into the bathroom. I can hear her humming a pop song in the shower. Before she comes back out I turn on one of the bedside lamps.

She emerges damp, patting at her hair with a hand towel, wrapped in a bath towel, with another bath towel draped over her shoulders.

"Would you like to stay tonight?"

"Yes. I wash shirt. You have shirt?"

I get up to get her a t-shirt from my suitcase. When I come back with it I reach for her and pull us down onto the bed, kissing her neck and running my hands over her body. The towel on her shoulders slides off and I can see her tattoos. We're kissing but she notices me trying to look at her shoulders.

"No. *Malu.*" Now she's shy again.

"Please. I like them. I think you are very beautiful. I think they are beautiful. Please let me see."

A resigned look comes over her, she goes limp and still underneath me, allows me to look.

She's got a dragon on each shoulder, large, scaly creatures with wings that curve down and into her armpits. They're inked so that when she lifts an arm one of the wings flaps as if in flight.

The dragons stare down at her breasts as if to guard them from harm. A cobra curls around her right breast, spreading its hood, baring its fangs and flicking its tongue at the nipple. Her left breast is enmeshed in a spider's web that has trapped a naked man. The spider, a voluptuous half-human female, is coming toward the man from under her breast.

It's good work, clean lines, recent enough that the colors pop out from her skin. I kiss the tattoos and then trace a line with my lips and tongue down onto her belly and then further down. She tries pulling my head back up but gives up easily. She tastes fresh, of soap and water until her lips open and a trickle of salty brine washes over my tongue.

It takes her a minute, but then she relaxes and not long after that she tenses again, then shuddering, pulls my face hard into her for a few moments, before lightly convulsing, going limp and gently pushing me away.

I make my way back up her perspiring body, kissing the spider on her breast, stroking her nipple with my tongue, kissing the dragon on her left shoulder, snaking an arm around and underneath her neck and taking in the sight of her face.

When Emmy sees me looking at her she smiles and buries her head in my armpit. "*Malu.*"

"No, no reason to be shy. You are a beautiful woman. I like being with you very much." I speak to her as much as I can in Indonesian. It makes her smile.

She looks at me and laughs. "You talk *Bahasa* same baby." We fall asleep in a tangle.

CHAPTER **SIX**

I wake up the next morning after nowhere near enough sleep. Emmy doesn't ask for any money, that's not how it's done. When she's in the shower I slip a hundred thousand rupiah, about forty bucks U.S., into her purse. If I don't, she might want to see me again anyhow, or she might not. It'd be the same if I was an Indonesian man of about her same age. Even before she looks in her bag, we've made plans to meet in the disco later tonight. She'll bring her friend who'd been with Alex.

By ten-thirty in the morning I'm already fed up with work. It's too hot and I'm getting cranky. When I worked for Motex I had an office in the compound. It's hardly been used since I quit. The company's let me set up there, which is fine, but the air conditioner's busted, possibly sabotaged. The overhead fan works, but only sporadically. I have to keep the window open and the screen's broken too. I've spent my morning slapping at the bugs that are clamoring for a blood donation, drinking cloyingly sweet, gritty coffee and going over reams of jumbled papers: assay reports, extraction projections and something called "heap leaching projections" that I barely understand. I keep at it until noon, though.

At lunch the mess hall is abuzz. A fire gutted the barn at Santo's early that morning. No one had been hurt, but the place had gone up and come down fast enough that nobody got out with much more than their lives either. A group of oilmen, hiding themselves as best they could behind old dish and hand towels, which the old lady in the *warung* sold to them for an extortionate price, had slunk back into the compound near dawn.

Once I get him to own up to having been there, one of the guys tells me that he smelled gasoline just before hearing a loud *crump* from one end of the barn. He'd run out the other end, pausing only to get his shoes where he'd stuffed his wallet and watch.

By three the heat, insects and technical jargon have reached unendurable levels. The sun's pounding on the back of my head through the window. I give up when I hear a loud pop from the overhead fan and look up to see it motionless, a wisp of smoke rising from its motor. I wheedle the loan of a company car from an old friend in the motor pool and drive out to Santo's.

The old woman's standing in her usual spot, stirring cigarette ash into her wok as if nothing's changed. I walk past her, out to the field where still smoldering black rubble wafts undoubtedly toxic fumes into the air. Three women are sifting through the debris. One of them, dark and lanky with a cubist face of indeterminate age, I recognize from the day before.

"We close mister," she yells when I approach. The women laugh and go back to inspecting the charred remains.

I walk up, squat by her side and speak softly. "What happened?"

"Maybe bomb. Maybe bad mans. You go Lili yesterday. Lili say you no like her."

"I liked her fine. I want to find out what happened here."

"Why you want mister?"

"I'm trying to find a man. He was supposed to come here."

"Same man Lili show photo yesterday?"

"Yes, do you know him?" I pull out the picture and show it to her again.

She turns away quick, too quick. "No see him."

It's plain that she's hiding something. But just as plain that a direct approach isn't going to get me anywhere.

Her name's Irma. She's got two kids and a husband who's gone to Malaysia to find work.

"What are you going to do? Where will you work?"

"Babies no be hungry mister. I find job city."

"Maybe I can help. I will give you some money, you can tell me where you live."

"Why you help mister?"

"Maybe we can help each other."

I give her twenty thousand *rupiah*, enough to see her family through for at least a few days. She looks around to make sure that the other women aren't listening and tells me how to find her sister's house in the city. She's staying there. I tell her I'll come by the next day. On the drive back to town it's all I can do to stay awake and on the road. I get back to my room, turn on the TV and fall asleep before CNN can depress me about the state of the world.

Emmy shakes me awake about eight. She used her passkey to get in when I didn't respond to her knock on the door. She wants me to take her to dinner. I take her to the top of the hotel.

There are big picture windows up there, but not much to see out of them. Green hued fluorescents and a few dim yellow bulbs illuminate some shops in the streets below. Otherwise there are the bright white pinpoints of kerosene lanterns set out on the tables of the *warungs* and hanging off the front of food carts. The carts are called *kaki lima*, "five feet," after the one wheel and two pegs that hold it up and the two feet of the man who pushes it around. In the distance there's a large flame, a gas flare that lights up the surrounding trees, picking out a small flickering circle of forest in the darkness.

Emmy points out a table across the room from where we're sitting. Three Chinese men and two white men are seated in front of glasses, an ice bucket and several bottles of brandy and whisky. They look drunk. The Chinese are dressed in dark, expensive suits that even there, in the swankiest restaurant in Marinda, look out of place.

The white men look rough, with awkward haircuts and ill-fitting shirts with loosened collars. Under the table I can see that one of them is wearing muddy boots that have been given no more than a quick swipe with a cloth to remove the wettest gunk.

The guy with the boots is talking, loud, in a thick Australian accent.

Emmy tells me she's heard they're here because they've found gold. A couple days before, she'd cleaned one of the white men's rooms. It was full of lab equipment and the people in it wouldn't leave while she was there. They watched her carefully.

There is a note in Alex's appointment calendar; no person's name, no time, just the date—a couple days before he disappeared—and "Lucky Break," the name the mining company involved in the gold find. It's a connection between my real job and what I'm trying to do for Sylvia. Maybe the guys at the table across the room know something about it.

Emmy and I order. Then I walk over to the table with the five men.

"Hey fellas, sorry to bother you. I'm Ray Sharp. I'm doing some work with Motex." They all look up but none of them says anything. News of the gold find has been trickling out, but there haven't been any big stories yet, so I'm not sure what I should let on. "I'm writing up a report for an investment group on the company, what they're up to, new developments, that sort of thing. I'm just talking with anyone I can, trying to find out what's going on around here."

The Chinese lean into a huddle and begin whispering. It sounds like Cantonese, what they speak in Hong Kong. It's a loud, sharp language. It doesn't whisper well, but I don't speak enough of it to catch what they're saying. The Australian guy with the boots stands up and thrusts out an oversized hand that looks like it's been badly sewn back together a few times. He tries to strangle my hand with it.

"Hal, good t' meetcha. Yeah, we might have a little scuttlebutt for ya. Me and my mate here're gonna be downstairs in the lobby bar after a while, why don'tcha you and the pretty lady you're with join us then." The Chinese glower at him and then offer polite smiles in my direction.

"Thanks, I'll see you later." I walk back to my table resisting the urge to turn around and catch them staring at my back. When I sit down and do look, the five of them have pushed their heads forward into a group.

I'd have rather eaten Indonesian food in one of the small restaurants in town, but Emmy is overjoyed with the faux European fare. The waiter fawns all over us, making me a little uncomfortable. She likes it though. She sits totem pole straight in her chair, smiling and flirting and practicing her table manners.

After dinner Emmy frowns when I tell her that I need to meet with the guys from the other table. She perks up when I give her fifty thousand and tell her I'll see her in an hour or so in the disco.

Hal and the other Australian, whose name is Gary, are in the lobby bar. We order drinks and make a little small talk. I trot out some gossip I've gathered from old friends in the company about Motex, hoping it'll get them to do the same about their business. Hal does all the talking. Gary looks into his drink, occasionally raising his head to take his eyes for a walk around the room. He rarely settles them on me.

After what I hope is a friendly enough interval, I get to the point. "What's this I keep hearing about gold around here?"

"Ya know mate, our Chinese partners don't want us to talk about it with you."

"What else is new? Those Hong Kong guys always keep everything close to the vest, unless they want to ramp up the stock price or something. I'm just curious. I'm supposed to know what's going on around here. It's part of my job."

"Surprisin' you don' know already. No harm in tellin' ya, 'specially since you guys are in on it." I haven't let on that I'm not actually working for Motex. I haven't lied, exactly, though. "Yeah, we found gold, a lot of it."

"I heard that. There's been at least a couple of small stories about it in the press. Some people are saying it's the biggest find ever."

"Maybe it is, maybe it isn't, mate. It's a bucketful, any ways you cut it."

"Why'd you look around here? I've never heard of gold being found around oilfields before."

"Gary here, he's our chief geologist, he was just lookin' over some of the satellite maps and thought he saw a good formation.

Somethin' to do with one of the rivers 'round here, ain't that right, Gary? Way it fans out below a mountain or somethin'.

"So we nosed around some, took ore samples and they come back plenty rich."

"You're not doing too good a job of keeping it quiet. People're talking. Aren't you afraid of setting off a rush?"

"Nah, we got it all straightened out with the army already. That and we cut you guys in on it with us. Motex's the big stink around here."

"What do you mean by rich? Come on, how big you think this thing's gonna be?"

"Big. You know Freeport out there in Irian? They say they've got the biggest deposits there are. This might be bigger'n that."

"When're you gonna start mining?"

"Already are on a small scale. But soon, maybe couple a months, we'll bring in the big 'quipment. This is a bugger all place to work ya know, gotta bring in everything, train the locals what to do with it, get security set up, all that."

I ask if they've heard of any financial analysts poking around and they haven't. I show them the photo of Alex. Hal's seen him. He'd been at this very bar one night with Lucky Break's CEO, Tony LeClerc, a Frenchman who's lived in Hong Kong for a lot of years. LeClerc's in Jakarta, but he'll be back in Marinda later in the week. Gary hasn't said a word, but I get the impression he isn't happy with Hal talking so much. Finally he nudges Hal with an elbow and gives him a look.

They want to talk about rugby after that. I don't know anything about it. I buy the guys another round of drinks then head downstairs to meet Emmy and, hopefully, her friend who'd spent time with Alex.

Emmy and another woman are squeezed into a booth with a couple of sloppy drunk oil guys who're draped all over them. I make sure she sees me as I walk past to the bar. I pull up a stool, order a vodka and soon attract a covey of women wanting to know if I want their company. After a few minutes Emmy shoulders her way through them and stands by me.

"*Selamat malam.* I miss you." She takes a cautionary look back at the booth that she's come from and gives me a quick kiss, flicking her tongue into my mouth.

"Me too. Are you busy?"

"Go there," she points at the far end of the bar, to a booth dimly lit by a low blue light. "Friend, she go man you look for. We come ten minute."

She orders drinks, then turns and speaks rapidly to the women surrounding me. She orders drinks for two of them as well and they follow her back to the booth.

It's more like forty-five minutes, what they call *jam keret*, "rubber time" in Indonesia, before Emmy and her friend sit down on either side of me.

Emmy hasn't told her friend anything about me and she isn't sure what to do when she meets me. She's probably thinking I want to take two girls up to my room. I kind of like the idea, but when she sits down and puts a hand on my thigh, Emmy leans over and whispers something that causes her to snatch it away like it's been burnt.

I take Alex's picture out of my pocket and hold it up to the low, flickering candle for her to see. She moves away from me and gives Emmy a look that says, What've you got me into?

She doesn't speak much English. But between Emmy's bad English and my feeble Indonesian, I manage to explain things and get my questions answered.

"Yes, she say she go with him. Say no good man. Take money, say bad words security. Make trouble."

Near as I can make out, Alex picked up Emmy's friend in the disco. He'd taken her upstairs to his room, was rough with her and in the morning refused to give her any money. Then he got the hotel security guards to throw her out.

I make a mental note to ask Sylvia what the hell she sees in him when I get back to Jakarta. Then again, maybe I don't want to know.

When Emmy's friend met him, Alex had been in the disco with Gary and a guy named Tony who had a different accent. The three of them were looking at some papers, using small penlights in their dark booth, and laughing. She'd sat with them for a drink or two.

She thinks they were talking about gold and the forest and some other men from Hong Kong. She can't be sure but she remembers hearing all those words. Alex was handsome. She thought he looked like a movie star. He bought her champagne; she'd never had it before. He flirted and was nice to her. She'd been happy to go to his room, at least until the next morning.

It's not much, but what little of it there is sounds fishy. Alex is obviously up to something with Lucky Break. And he's definitely missing. It's getting interesting.

CHAPTER **SEVEN**

Motex's chief geologist is an old-fashioned Scotsman in his mid-fifties, tall and fat with a tousled full mane of white hair and very thick glasses that keep sliding off the tip of his nose. I go to see him the next morning.

He's sweating profusely despite the air conditioner being cranked up high and the fan blowing straight at him. He's either one of those people who associate freezing cold air with fresh air, or his size keeps him overheated. It takes a lot of effort to keep my teeth from chattering.

Motex sent out a memo asking its people to cooperate with me. They want the due diligence to go well and the Hong Kong money to flow in. We make polite chit chat for about thirty seconds before he asks me to just get on with my questions.

"Is it all just oil and gas around here? Are there any other minerals?" He peers intently at me from between two large stacks of professional journals on either side of his desk. He doesn't look happy. His response, when it comes, is barely short of shouted.

"Bloody hell, is gold, that shite, the only thing anyone bloody well thinks 'bout 'round here anymore? So what if the buggers think they've found gold. Can't be much or we'd've found it now wouldn't we? What with all the bleedin' holes we drilled 'round these parts before we found what we were lookin' for."

"I only heard much about it last night. Some people were talking. There are some guys from Lucky Break Mining at the hotel. It's an Australian outfit. I don't know much about them. Does it make any sense? I can't recall ever reading about gold fields anywhere near oil or gas fields."

"Anythin' is bloody possible ya know. Times you see a bit of gold around coal, but mostly it's hangin' out 'round copper or silver, different sorta substrata than what we want in our business. But maybe those boys from Down Under know somethin' I don't."

"If there is a big gold deposit around here, how's it gonna affect Motex?"

"It's gonna be a pain in the bloody arse is what it's gonna be. It's not like ya have to worry 'bout ev'ry Tom, Dick and Abdul runnin' 'round drillin' for oil or gas—it takes plenty o' 'quipment and money. But gold, screamin' Jesus, ev'ry fucker with a big pan and a stick of dynamite figgers he can get rich. The bastards're gonna be crawlin' all over the bleedin' place and then the army, those f'in crooks, are gonna wanna get bought off to keep 'em away. It ain't what we need kiddo, I'm tellin' ya."

"Any idea where these guys are poking around?"

"Fucked if I know. Somewhere out there in the bleedin' trees. Do spend a fuck of a lot o' time over at Santo's from what I hear. Come outta there all poxy if they don't watch out. Ask me, bloody good luck that fucker's burned down."

I spend the next couple of hours dropping in on anyone else I can think of who might know something about gold. No one knows anything, or so they tell me.

By three I've run out of ideas. I check with my friend in the motor pool that it's okay I'm still using a Motex car, and head into town to visit the woman from Santo's.

At the eastern edge of the city I park on a small patch of dirt in front of a wooden archway outlined with bare fluorescent tubes.

White and purple orchids are knit through a trellis tacked up on one side. Painted on a board nailed crookedly to the top of the arch is the name of the neighborhood, Kampung Sungai. There isn't much creativity in the name "River Village," but it's descriptive.

A pack of young boys and men stand around smoking clove cigarettes in tattered shorts. Two of them kick a not-fully-inflated soccer ball back and forth. They look like they could be trouble, if the inclination strikes. I figure it's best to buy them off before it does.

I approach the one they all looked at when I drove up. I tell him I'm looking for someone and suggest that he and his pals might want to keep an eye on my car for two thousand *rupiah*.

He smiles and holds up five fingers. It isn't worth haggling over. I give him the five thousand. He offers me a cigarette. I nod "thanks" and put it in my pocket. I don't smoke but it would be rude to turn it down.

I walk through the arch and down a gangway into River Village. The neighborhood floats on rafts tied up just off the bank. Narrow wooden walkways run between houseboats, dirty water sloshing over them in the places where the larger under-timbers have rotted away. I stroll around for a while, not quite sure how I'm going to find Irma's sister's house. There're places where I have to turn sideways to make my way through the thin passages between houses and stores. There's a floating mosque across from a small restaurant with a picnic table out front that takes up half the walkway.

It's steambath hot and humid. Salty fluids puddle on my body, then form rivulets and following the demands of gravity run from my head, down my torso, along the inside of my pants legs, over my shoes and onto the boards underfoot. My sweat mixes with the river water and is carried east out into the Malacca Strait.

The kids are even worse than the climate. Before long I'm being hounded by a gaggle of thirty or forty children, all shouting "Hey meester, hey meester!" and "Bic, Bic!" the universal cry for a ballpoint pen. Every so often I pass a house or a shop where an adult stands out front. Sometimes they take pity on me and shoo the kids away, scattering them briefly. But there isn't really anywhere for them to go other than into a house or into the water. Every time they get chased away, they return in greater numbers.

As tempting as it is, I know better than to try and get rid of them, or yell at them, or even to hurry up my pace to get away from them. Like all vicious predators, packs of children can sense the slightest weakness or fear in their prey and turn it to their advantage.

I've got a camera with me. It's a holdover from when I was a journalist. Scant seconds before I reach my breaking point, our parade comes to a charred, empty raft, loosely attached to the walkway. It looks like any vacant lot where a house has recently burned to the ground, except for where the river peeks through as it gurgles by underneath.

Inspiration stops me. I make a show of suddenly turning around. I yell, *"Anak anak nakal!"* which means "naughty children," to get their attention. It does. It stops them in their tracks and sets them off laughing like it's the funniest thing they've ever heard. I point at the blackened timbers. *"Mau photo?"*

They do, apparently, want me to take their picture. They jump onto the burnt raft, all forty-five or fifty of them, pushing and shoving and jostling for position in the front of the crowd. A few of them fall into the water and others, still laughing, fish them back out. The big ones bully their way to the front so I put the camera down and yell, *"Besar belakang, kecil depan!"*

Surprisingly, they pay attention and the big ones move to the back, the little ones to the front. I lift my camera to my face and start counting to three. A bunch of them strike kung-fu poses that they've seen in the movies. They want more and I oblige with a few extra snaps.

After that they don't go away, but we've apparently come to an unspoken understanding. They're a whole lot less obnoxious. Every so often one or two of them dashes ahead and strikes their kung-fu pose, yelling, "Photo! Photo!" I don't take any more though. It's not anything I want to encourage.

I've been walking around for a half hour and I'm no closer to finding Irma. Sooner or later, though, word will get around and she might come looking for me. Foreigners, other than aid workers and missionaries, are rare visitors to places like River Village. I decide to sit somewhere, let somebody know who I'm looking for, and wait.

The main walkway runs parallel to the riverbank, about thirty feet out into the water. I haven't turned off of it so I turn around and head back to the small restaurant across from the mosque.

I park myself at the picnic table and ask for a cold Bintang. They've got a warm bottle and ice that they chip from a large block and put into a plastic cup. Once past the arch with its fluorescent tubes, there isn't any electricity in the neighborhood, other than a couple of dim lights at the mosque that are run off a small gas-powered generator.

You're not supposed to drink the water in places like Indonesia. Maybe there's something wrong with me but I've never had any problems. Even if I had, it's too hot and sticky for warm beer. A little dysentery might be worth a cold beer, even one with ice in it.

Irma shows up about halfway through the bottle. I offer to buy her a beer but she doesn't want to drink there. I buy three bottles, get another plastic cup filled with ice and trail behind her down a small side alley where the buildings tilt in at the top and the eaves hang over so that only a narrow sliver of sunlight pokes through. There are a couple of inches of water underfoot and we splash through it until we get to a freshly painted green stucco wall with a raw plywood door in the middle.

Irma knocks three times. The woman who opens the door looks a lot like her, only younger. She's wearing a brightly colored, floral print sarong and a black lacey bra. Her hair is piled in a high bun on her head. She leans out to Irma and they whisper back and forth. Then Irma steps inside and beckons for me to follow.

I've taken just a step inside the door when something quick moves in the corner of my left eye. Everything twists out of focus, fast. An instant later there's a thud and I'm not sure what it is, or even if it's happening to me or someone else. My eyes act like they've come undone in their sockets, jiggling around the room uncontrollably. They can't get a fix on anything. Somewhere higher than it should be above me, the ceiling is a brightly lit tunnel that I can't see the end of. The walls of the room are far away too; they just go on and on to the horizon.

I'm picked up by the shoulders and flung through the air. It takes a while, in slow motion, before I crash land onto something soft. But it's only soft for a moment before it gives way underneath me and becomes much too hard.

I lie there, not moving, trying to take stock. I close my eyes and feel myself breathe. It hurts, but not so much as it did the time I cracked my sternum falling off a cliff. After a little while my ears clear and I can hear myself panting. Hot spots are forming on my elbows and one of my knees, the sort of hot spots that I know are going to hurt like hell later but haven't started to yet. I squeeze my eyes tighter to clear them before opening them.

I wish I hadn't. My vision is filled with a big guy. He has a pale face and a very bad haircut. He sports a large bandage, a little pink in the middle and frayed and yellow at the edges, on the side of his neck. I don't really mind any of that. I do object to the gun poking out from his ham of a right hand. It's a small gun, but it doesn't need to be any bigger.

My head's clearing, but I figure I'll let him get in the first word.

"Why the fuck you askin' so many questions?"

The voice is a lot smaller than he is. It's a voice you'd expect from a jockey, or a pimply kid behind the counter in a convenience store. Still, the pistol lends it authority. Guns do that.

I try to answer but my own voice is sticking in my throat. "Uh, I, um, Motex, doing work for Motex."

"So the fuck what? Why're you nosin' around? My boss don't like that." He kicks me in the knee and the hot spot gets hotter.

"Who's your boss?"

"No more questions, fuckwad. None, zero, zilch. Got me?"

"Uh, okay. No problem. I'm also trying to do a favor for a friend. Well, not a friend, my ex-wife. Well, she isn't my ex-wife yet but if I can find her boyfriend for her then she'll..." My nerves dial my mouth to its blather setting.

The big guy doesn't have any patience for it. He kicks my other knee and that one gets its own hot spot. Then he screws the gun up into my nose. The sight at the end of the barrel pokes into the top and makes me want to sneeze. I scrunch it back. I'd hate to get shot because I sneezed.

"Shut the fuck up. There's a lot a fuckin' trees out here, 'lot a river. I hear there's tigers and snakes big enough to make you lunch. No one'd ever know where you gone. Get it?"

I get it. I carefully nod yes.

He yanks the gun back, kicks me again in the newly hot knee, turns and walks out the door.

The room got a lot smaller while we were talking. The ceiling's come back down to its normal height. Irma and her sister are gone. The place is empty other than the thin, stained mattress I'm sprawled on. Two of my three beer bottles are lined up neatly next to the door but the cup of ice is missing. I slither over to them, trying to stay off my knees. A friend once showed me how to open a bottle with a car key. I've never had to do it before. The first sip, warm and viscous, is the best taste of beer I've ever had.

CHAPTER **EIGHT**

It feels like miles back to the car. My camera and a bottle of beer weigh a ton. It takes only a minute after I stagger outside, for the parade of kids to fall back in line with me. Once they get a good look though, they mutter among themselves for a little while and then drift away. Maybe it's the way I'm walking, like my knees aren't quite attached at the joint. The hot spots have begun to cool and a raw scratching pain is settling into their place. Not walking hurts as much as walking does. Sitting or lying down might be better, but neither is going to get me to my room at the hotel. If I stop to take the weight off, I'm not going to want to get back up again until my knees have healed. That's going to take a whole lot longer than I want to spend in River Village.

The car is unmolested where I left it. The big kid with the cigarettes walks up to me. I think he's going to ask for more money but when he gets a close look at me he just silently offers up another cigarette. I take it, lean against the car and light it from the smoldering butt he holds out.

I take a deep drag. It should launch me into a spasm of coughing. Its mentholated sweetness mingled with the cloying taste of clove is awful, but the smoke burning in my lungs clears my head.

"*Apa kabar?*" Is he just making conversation, or does he really want to know what's up?

"A big man, a *bule,* did you see him?" I use the derogatory slang for a white man even though I'm one, hoping it might win me a point or two.

He had seen him, and thinks it's strange that the guy drove off in a police car with a local police captain. It's even stranger that they'd driven away from town, toward the forest or the Motex compound where the local police don't usually go.

I thank him with the remaining bottle of beer, get into the car and drive to the hotel. I barely make it to my room. The bed looms up in front of me looking like everything I want in life, and I fall onto it.

There's no missing the fulgent mane of red hair, or the brilliant, loose light brown eyes, or the high, flushed cheekbones, or the fire engine red fat lips. By half a foot at least, she's the tallest woman here. Dancing by herself, she makes broad awkward movements, taking up a lot of room, arching on her wide feet, throwing out her arms and embracing as much space as she can. At one point she spins out of control and I'm worried she's going to fall over. But she recovers at the last possible moment and almost makes it look deliberate. She stops then, maybe to regain her balance, but she doesn't fully stop. She's grinding her hips in slow counterpoint to the beat. She fucks the air around her. Just watching her dance is to feel her, to smell her, to taste her, or at least want to.

I can't take my eyes off her. Finally she moves off the dance floor, to the bar. I walk over, trying to be nonchalant. I offer my bottle of beer. She takes it with a nod and a smile. She presses it against the back of her neck, then against the sweat drenched front of the light sweater she's wearing, then lifts it to those swollen lips, wraps them around its neck and takes a long swallow before handing it back to me.

I can hardly speak but I have to say something, anything. "Ray."

"Irina."

"Where're you from?"

"Moscow." Her voice is deep, heavily accented. She leans toward me, standing splayed, an open invitation. Her eyes wash over me.

"Are you visiting or do you live here?"

"Mmm."

"How long have you been here?"

"Two years."

"What do you do?"

She reaches for my beer, takes it and smiles over the bottle. She runs her tongue around its neck, tilts her head back and takes another deep gulp. "We go my room."

Emmy shakes me out of it. I'm not happy about that. I know where that dream was heading. She must have used her passkey again to get into my room. I'm not sure how happy I am about that, either. She's been there a while. I can vaguely remember falling onto the bed, fully dressed. I wake up naked and neatly tucked into the sheets, Emmy's sitting on the side of the bed, holding a damp washcloth to the side of my head. When I open my eyes she takes the cloth away and leans over me, a concerned look on her face.

"*Apa kabar?*"

"Not so good. What time is it? How long have you been here?"

"Friend front desk say you hurt, go room, knock door no coming. You blood, head. Stop now." She shows me a bloodstain on the washcloth. "*Ada mimpi?*"

"Yeah, I was having a good dream. What time is it?"

She holds up an oversized Swatch. It's a little before nine at night. I haven't been out all that long, just a few hours.

"Thank you for taking care of me." I reach over to stroke her face. She takes my hand and holds it down on the bed at her side. She looks serious.

"Why you hurt? You trouble?"

"Yeah, I'm trouble. It's because I'm looking for Alex, the bad man. Some people don't want me looking but I don't know why. I'll find out though."

"Why you want find bad man? Maybe more trouble."

"Maybe, but I promised I'd find him."

"Maybe bad promise."

"Probably, but I've got to keep it, or at least try."

"Good, you good man. If bad man, no good promise."

It's plain that she's had more than her fair share of experience with people not keeping promises. I smile and try to hug her but I don't have much energy for it.

"Have you had dinner?" I'm beginning to feel better, although my knees hurt like hell, my head throbs and there's a stitch in my side that makes breathing a lot more painful than it should be.

"Me no eating. Sit here, watch TV." The TV is tuned to Asian MTV with the sound down low. That and Mexican soap operas dubbed into Indonesian are the favored viewing of all the girls I've met in the country. Some early pubescent Cantonese pop singer, barely covered by a Union Jack dress, is cavorting with a litter of bulldog puppies on the screen. It makes me nauseous, but a perverse fascination with it takes over and gets me past that.

I call room service and order a bowl of *soto ayam*, a rich, thick chicken soup. Emmy wants *nasi goring*. A drink would go down perfectly, but I figure I'd better lay off until my head fully clears. It hurts to get out of bed and stand up, but I force myself to take a long, hot shower. By the time the food arrives I'm starting to feel a lot better and plenty mad.

I don't like being hit in the head, or threatened with guns, or having my knees screwed up. I'm trying to do my job, just ask some questions. Someone must think I'm onto something if they're sending goons after me. I had no idea that I was getting in the middle of some good guys versus bad guys kind of deal until the big guy laid into me. My knees and side, the gun up my nose—that should be enough for my common sense to kick in. If I'm smart, I'll take the big guy's advice and butt out.

But I'm not so smart when I'm angry. And I'm too damned curious about what's going on. And it's my job. And quitting isn't going to get Sylvia off my ass. There are a lot of good reasons to keep looking. And after being beaten up, I want someone else to suffer before it's through.

Emmy turns up the sound on MTV. An entire rural Indian province is performing a Hindi version of the Macarena. It's kitsch, and strangely riveting and among the most awful things I've ever seen on television, but I can't tear my eyes away from it. I wait until it's finished before asking, "Do you think you can get me into the room where all the lab equipment is?"

"Why want more trouble? *Sudah* trouble. Stupid promise." She looks worried.

"Yeah, I know I've already got trouble, but something bad's happened, maybe something really bad. I'm not even sure what it is yet. I don't know if I can fix it or stop it, but I want to try."

"You crazy man. Maybe *bodoh*."

"I don't know, maybe I am stupid, but I've got to do it. If you're worried about your job or anything, I'll find some other way to get into their room."

"No, no worry job, worry you. No like you hurt."

Finally she agrees. The men with the lab equipment usually go downstairs to the coffee shop for breakfast early in the morning. When they do, she'll come and get me.

I change the subject and ask about her tattoos. It takes a little prodding, but she tells me about them.

"Before, boyfriend Jason, he want. He say he like very much, he make picture tattoo, pay money. He say we marry, go back live Germany. I very happy. But he go away another girl, no come back.

"My father, he very important man, Imam of *masjid* my family village. He angry me, no want me go with foreign man, no want tattoo. He lock me in house, say never go out again, stay house, take care family only, grow old lonely.

"My brother get big fight with father. I try stop fight, my brother fall down, hit head, he die. Father screaming, crying, he say my fault brother dead. I run away, come to city, get job. Never see family again."

It's another case of "brrroken hearrrt," a fucking Greek tragedy. There's a lot of that going around. At least Emmy doesn't cut herself, not that I've seen.

It hurts but I hug her. She pushes me down on the bed and is very gentle. When we finish it's still early, but I fall into dreamless sleep without the usual struggle. It's been a long couple of days.

Six-thirty comes way too soon. Emmy's shaking me awake again and telling me I have to hurry. I get dressed, splash water on my face and am out the door in no more than three minutes. She lets me into one of the rooms on the floor above mine and busies herself in the hallway to act as lookout.

The Australian mining guys are staying in three connected suites, and it's too much to search thoroughly in a short time. One of the sitting rooms is taken over by two long tables; the rest of the furniture pushed to the sides. There's a lot of lab equipment on one of the tables and the other is covered with what look like ore samples.

There are five coffee cans filled with gravel and dirt and a dozen irregular-sized chunks of rock, some no bigger than a thumb and a couple about the size of a basketball. I don't see anything that looks like gold, but then I've never seen it in any form other than jewelry or pictures of gold bricks. I heard somewhere that real, unprocessed gold doesn't actually look anything like the stuff you see in rings.

On the equipment table there's a one-liter beaker about half-full of what might be gold. It's a dull yellow dust of some sort. It looks pure. Looking around I can't see any evidence of what they might have done to extract it from the samples. I have no idea if that means anything or not.

I paw through a few drawers in the bedrooms but there isn't anything useful. In the third bedroom a suit is hung in the closet, just one dark, faintly pinstriped suit and nothing else. It's out of place. All the other clothes in the bedroom are flung on the bed and the chair, or still in the suitcase, and they look like what Gary, the quiet mining guy, would wear.

The label is from a very fancy tailor in London. Years before, when I was a journalist, a man I was interviewing dodged my questions by telling me in too great detail about the five thousand dollar suits he had made by the same tailor. The wallet in the inside jacket pocket belongs to Alex.

Emmy's getting nervous. I've been in the room for almost a half hour and she wants me out of there quick. I poke around a little more but don't find anything of interest. I'm wondering what else to look at when the elevator rings down the hall.

Emmy, standing watch by the cracked open door, goes out to look. The elevator's around a corner to the left from the room and she moves fast to head off whoever's coming out of it. I wait and listen. I can hear her talking, making something up. It sounds like babble, half-Indonesian and half-incomprehensible English. I slip out, taking Alex's wallet, and move to the right down the hall, just making it into the stairwell before anyone can see me. I lean against the wall and wait for Emmy.

She shows up in about a half minute. I kiss her on the cheek, say thanks and make plans to see her in the bar after ten that night. She heads up the stairs to get back to work. I go down to my room.

Alex has bad taste in wallets. It's undoubtedly expensive and really ugly: mottled brown, red and black, and tanned from the skin of some endangered reptile. I turn it over in my hands thinking that Alex is the real snake.

I can't figure out what Sylvia wants with him or for that matter, what he wants with her. His driver's license tells me he's eleven years younger than her. He's filthy rich and has at least ten to fifteen years left in which he can milk the golden tit of his good looks. Sylvia can be fun, she's smart, wears well on the arm at fancy parties, knows all the right people and gives great head, but none of that's much trouble to find for a guy with his looks and money.

There isn't much in the wallet. I'm about to give up on it when I feel a small lump in the lining. An uncle once gave me a wallet for Christmas that had the same hidden compartment. I wondered what's the point? If someone steals your wallet, they're just going to take it. They're not going to carefully empty it out and politely hand it back to you having failed to find whatever else you're hiding. Alex, obviously, hadn't thought of that. It takes me a bit of fumbling to find the seam and get it open.

Inside there's a folded up thousand dollar bill. The only time I've ever seen another one, it was on display with 999 others just like it in a downtown Las Vegas casino. Grover Cleveland is on it. He was the only bachelor ever elected president, but that doesn't tell me anything I need to know. It could be a windfall, but I put it back.

In the hidden compartment with the bill, there's one of Gary's business cards with a scribbled note on its back: "T—Santos—10p W."

There's also a credit card, and that gets my interest. It's a platinum American Express corporate card with Alex's name on it. There isn't anything so unusual about that except that the card isn't for his brokerage firm, it's for Lucky Break Mining. Who's he working for anyhow?

I order breakfast from room service and take a shower and shave while waiting for it. I can't eat much. I'm still a little out of whack from yesterday's beating. I collect the company car from the hotel valet and drive out to the Motex compound.

CHAPTER **NINE**

I close myself into my sweltering old office and call a friend in Jakarta who works for Liberty Harbor, an American company that runs a nickel mine in Kalimantan, the Indonesian part of Borneo. Tim's an environmental geologist who used to work for a gold mining company in New Guinea.

"You know a lot about gold mining. What do you make of this Lucky Break find up in Sumatra?"

"So much for the pleasantries. Where the hell are you and why do you ask?"

"Yeah, sorry I'm a little distracted. I'm up here at Motex in Marinda and everyone's talking about it."

"Okay, but next round of drinks are on you. As for this gold business, I've heard about it. I'm skeptical."

"Why?"

"It's just not the sort of place you'd expect to find gold. The geologic structures aren't right. You might find a little, but certainly not the quantities I've been hearing about."

"Maybe it's unusual, but is it possible?"

"I don't know. I guess anything's possible, but I wouldn't have thought so."

"Could they be faking it?"

"As I said, anything's possible. It's not hard to fake. Hell, it's an old tradition. Salt your samples, scatter a few bribes around to make sure the assaying work falls into line, dummy up some maps. I don't know anything about Lucky Break; I'd hardly heard of them before this."

"You will now, their stock's gone wild. The company's listed in both Sydney and Vancouver. I wish I'd bought shares about three weeks ago. They've gone from a buck and change to eighty something. I could sell today and retire."

"I guess the word 'gold' still has that effect. I'm sick of the stuff myself. In my business all the word conjures up is people harassing me about arsenic in rivers."

"Do they need to do anything special to register their claim?"

"Not really. From what I hear it's on Motex's land and they've cut them in on the deal. Just so long as someone pays the army enough to keep them quiet, there's not going to be any problems. The main worry's gotta be the banks and analysts. Any smart finance people are going to want independent paperwork. Then again, banks and brokerages being what they are around here, a crook doesn't need to do much to put the fix in. They need to file reports with the government. Since it's at Motex, the state oil company's gotta have copies."

"From who?"

"There're some mining consultancies, geologic survey outfits, groups like that. You can pay the government to do it but I'm not sure how much good that'll do. You can pay this government to do anything and everybody knows it. No one in the know takes the government reports very seriously. Some of the brokerage and accounting houses have consultants who they try to pass off as independent. That might work."

"You ever run into a guy named Alex Truscott?"

"Oh Christ, you're not involved with that schmuck are you?"

"No, not yet. I started out looking into Lucky Break as a simple due diligence job for a client in Hong Kong. Then Sylvia shows up and suckers me into trying to find Truscott. He's her fiancé. Next thing I know my job and Truscott are getting all tangled up together."

"What'd Sylvia ever see in you anyway?"

"Yeah, right, thanks. Why's he a schmuck?"

"Standard issue rich kid stuff. Mommy and daddy sent him out here to lay on a thin veneer of credibility when they bring him back to Texas and turn him into a senior executive or something. Couldn't find his ass with both hands tied behind his back. I don't know how much the family has to pay Purdy & Dabs to let him play analyst. He could be just the kind of patsy a crowd like Lucky Break would want. He's handsome, they say. Knows the right things to say at cocktail parties, I hear."

"Charming."

"Not in any way that I can see. For some people I guess good looking and glib are good enough."

"Whatever it is, it's worked on Sylvia. You seen copies of any reports?"

"I haven't been looking. I imagine we've got them around somewhere. I'll see what I can dig up."

"That'd be great. I'll be back in Jakarta tomorrow. Drinks at B.A.T.S.?"

"You got it. You're buying."

B.A.T.S. is the "Bar At The Shangri-La" hotel and it's where the expense account guys like to meet. It's got the most beautiful collection of available women in the city. A lot of TV and movie starlets and models pick up extra spending cash working the bar, but the money's handled subtly enough that everyone can pretend it's no different than any other pickup scene.

I'd been there once with some friends when the chairman of one of the biggest foreign companies in Indonesia had strutted in. Dressed in hand-tooled snakeskin boots, a sharkskin suit that must have cost somewhere in the low five figures and a blindingly white Stetson hat, he'd spent hours trying to buy the attention of one of the only women in the whole place who wasn't looking to be bought.

He didn't succeed. He did walk out later with two models from Madura who work as a team, cost plenty and are famous for having given the clap to, and emptied the wallets of the entire expat male staff of a Belgian bank.

I rarely go to B.A.T.S. I can afford it, but it's not my scene. Sylvia once accused me of "having a penchant for the low life." I smiled awkwardly and replied, "I guess you're right." What I really wanted to say was, "Yeah, so what?"

B.A.T.S. is plenty sleazy in its own way. But I prefer my sleaze without pretensions.

I spend the rest of the day going over paperwork and making calls to find out what I can about Lucky Break. I manage to talk with some of the people in Motex who might have a shred or two of information. They don't tell me much.

Emmy and I meet up later as planned, in the hotel bar. A few drinks there led to a few more in my room.

In the morning I slip two hundred thousand into her purse while she's in the shower. I give her my phone number in Jakarta, but we both know she isn't going to call. She'd be crazy to waste her money on those sorts of niceties. I'll see her when I come back to town. I get back to Jakarta with just enough time to drop off my stuff and change clothes on my way to meet Tim.

I almost call Irina from the taxi on my way in from the airport. I start to dial her number, then think better of it. I want to see her, bad. She's gotta know that. But I should give her the room to make that move on her own. She's the one who stopped seeing me. Maybe she came by while I was away. If she did, then I'll call.

Annie and Billy are at the house, watching a Mexican soap opera that's been dubbed into Indonesian. Wazir must've let them in. I try not to look disappointed that it isn't Irina waiting for me.

Annie springs off the sofa to kiss me hello. It makes me a little nervous having them just show up, especially when I'm not home. I'll have to take inventory later, see if anything's missing.

When she finally takes her tongue out of my mouth Annie erupts into a broad smile. "Tonight Billy, me, pay you." She turns her head to direct my attention to Billy. He's holding a large wad of cash and grinning. I don't want to know where he got it.

"Thanks, but you don't need to do that. I'm the rich foreigner, remember?"

"No, Billy have good luck yesterday. Big good luck. No problem money today." Annie gestures at him, like she's introducing someone on stage.

Billy laughs and fans the bills at me.

"Okay, okay. Just don't tell me what kind of luck. I don't want to know."

He must've robbed someone. Where else is he going to find that kind of score? I hope it wasn't anyone I know.

I invite them along to B.A.T.S. "We're meeting a friend of mine and he's sort of straight. Please don't let him know about any of this, okay?"

Of course Tim will know what Annie does. There are mostly only two kinds of Indonesian women who go to bars: rich ones who've spent a lot of time overseas and working ones. Anyone with the faintest eye for style or an ear for spoken English will know that Annie isn't one of the rich ones.

He'll know the same about Billy unless he's so homophobic that he can't imagine such a thing.

Prostitution is part of the social fabric here. I guess that's true in a lot of poor countries. It's so normal that most men, and even a lot of women, don't give it much thought. On the level that expatriates or tourists come across it, it takes conscious effort to even think about it in terms of one person selling, or to be precise renting, themselves to another. In the bars at least, it's more like a fair trade, an exchange between two people who each have something the other one wants.

Maybe there's something wrong with it. I don't know. I haven't made up my mind. But that's irrelevant. It's just one among the many different ways people in this country find to get by. It pays better than subsistence farming or a low-wage job in a factory. And for most of the women who meet foreigners in bars it's easier work, at least physically. As for what it does to their mental state, I couldn't say. I guess it's different for everybody.

As for my own mental state, I've spent a lot of time over the past year worrying about it. Am I exploiting Emmy and Annie? Are they exploiting me? Am I just trying to avoid facing my feelings about things?

The movie producer Don Simpson once said that he didn't pay women for sex, he paid them to go away afterwards. Is that what I'm doing?

If I am, I'm not very good at it.

Annie, Billy and Emmy are what's known as "pro-ams." Sometimes they'll go to bars and meet men to have sex with for fun, like sexually liberated people anywhere. Sometimes it's just a better alternative, a more comfortable place to spend the night than at home. Usually they'll expect something for it, whether it's money, a small shopping spree, a particularly nice dinner, whatever. But isn't that the way dating often works in most places? Sometimes it's only for the money. There aren't any set rules to the game.

Burglary and picking pockets, however, is something else altogether. I like Annie. She's becoming a friend. Billy's a pretty good guy too. It doesn't bother me that they're pro-ams. I'm not sure how I feel about them being thieves.

I've known criminals before. But my friends in the past were on the wrong side of laws I didn't agree with.

One of my girlfriends before Sylvia was a stripper who hooked a little on the side and dealt cocaine. She was exciting. We used to take her guns and go shooting in the desert outside of L.A. I woke up one morning, rolled over expecting to bump up against her and she wasn't there. She'd taken all of her stuff and some of mine too. I missed her more than I missed my TV.

Laws against theft are fine with me, but I keep coming up with excuses in my head for Annie and Billy. They're poor in one of the world's poorest countries. They're impoverished in ways I can only glimpse and hope to never really know. And they're poor in a place where there are beginning to be a lot of rich people around.

I don't agree with the anarchists. Property isn't theft, stealing it is. But in Indonesia, where the government does almost nothing to help the poor, maybe stealing from the rich is a form of taxation. The rich in this country, in most countries, find more than their fair share of ways to exploit the poor. So if Billy and Annie find some less than savory means to help themselves, who am I to blame them?

None of those are questions I'm going to come up with answers for in the time it takes our taxi to get to the Shangri-La. It's a beautiful, modern high-rise hotel overlooking a horrible, polluted, stinking canal lined with railroad tracks. Until the hotel was built, there was a shantytown strung along the tracks and both sides of the canal. It was famous for its transvestite prostitutes. When they built the hotel they chased the poor people away and planted trees. They haven't cleaned up the waterway though. Its thick, black, oily surface bubbles with pockets of methane gas. The stink of it drifts onto the front portico of the hotel. But it stops at the doors.

The lobby always smells of fresh cut flowers, orchids and gentle notes of clove. Enormous five-story windows showcase beautifully manicured gardens, a crystalline turquoise swimming pool and a dramatically lit, Mogul-style mosque in a field of wildflowers just beyond the hotel grounds.

The community that worships at the mosque used the hotel to its advantage. The Imam of the mosque said that hotel guests looking down on the religious building would profane it. So the owners of the hotel paid to renovate the mosque, provide funds for its maintenance and to install floods to bathe it in soft, warm light.

Indonesia has the world's largest Muslim population, but other than a few fanatics of the sort that can be found in any country, in any religion, Islam here is a moderate, peaceful practice. When the hotel was built, everyone got something they wanted. The Muslims are happy to have people appreciating the powerful architectural beauty of a mosque. The Chinese owners claim that the huge windows looking out over a religious building are good *feng shui*. The hotel guests like the view.

Or at least that's what everybody tells themselves. The poor people who were tossed out of their homes in the shantytown aren't so happy about it. They had to find somewhere else to live, in some other slum or back in their villages. And like almost all the workers in any business in the country, the hotel's employees, even though they're paid more than the usual local rate, still aren't paid enough to raise themselves very far out of poverty.

And yet they're thankful for the jobs. They're better than no jobs. The work's cleaner, easier and less dangerous than a lot of other work. And there's always the possibility of interacting with foreigners and expats, and that comes with opportunities.

It's complicated, this globalization business. I've worked for Motex, a huge international company. As a journalist I covered a lot of the world's biggest businesses. And now I'm investigating them. And I'm still not sure what to make of it all. I'm suspicious of the big multinationals and their factories, hotels and fast food restaurants in poor countries. But basically I'm for it. Most of the time it does more good than bad, at least a little more.

CHAPTER **TEN**

The three of us walk into the Shangri-La lobby, the swimming pool glowing blue-green ahead, the mosque blindingly white behind it, the tinkling of a piano in the lobby bar, the scrape of salad forks against bone-china plates in the lobby café. The suddenly chilled air mixing with the practiced unaccented tone of the doorman saying "Good evening," laps at our faces in greeting.

We take the sweeping marble staircase down to B.A.T.S. and I pay the cover charge. Tim's already at the bar, deep in what appears to be serious, or at least intent conversation with a tall Indonesian model who has been poured into a highly polished, micro-thin, black latex catsuit. I could count the wrinkles in her skin, if she had any. She can't be more than eighteen and probably photographs younger. She's got surgically fattened, ludicrously red lips and the catsuit bulges improbably at the breast for an Indonesian. I look down along her legs and see that a good five or six inches of her is platform heels. She's got to be an acrobat to balance on them. I hate to interrupt.

"What's this about me buying the drinks?"

Tim turns around looking a little put upon by the intrusion. Then he sees Annie on my arm and smiles. Then Billy on the other arm and he raises an eyebrow.

I introduce them and he introduces us to Candy. I buy a round of drinks, and after lingering just long enough for etiquette's sake, Annie and Billy wander off, gin and tonics in hand. I ask Tim if he has time to talk. Candy stands by him, posed like a statue, a possessive hand on his waist. He gets off his barstool and pats it for her to sit. She does, making sure I see her pout, and we move a little way off.

"Sure you're going to be able to peel that thing off her?"

"I imagine I'll find a way."

"Better keep her in air-conditioning—a minute or two outside in that get-up and she's going to just melt away like the Wicked Witch of the West." It's hot and humid, always, in Jakarta.

"Yeah, and I'd like to get back to her before she does. I found a report. It's a bunch of the usual broker nonsense, talking up some stock no one's ever heard of, a few modifiers thrown in here and there to hedge the bet. Sylvia's squeeze, Alex, wrote it.

"I also talked to a few guys in the office. My company's got at least a fingertip in it. Something big's going on, but they're playing it close to the vest."

"Is that strange? Don't you usually know where all the bodies are buried?"

"Some of them, not all. You know our guys, not exactly the world's chattiest bunch."

"So I guess you didn't find out anything."

"Not a lot. Just that Motex's got some money in it as well as the land. We've thrown some money at it and I think we loaned them some hotshot young geologist. The mining minister is sniffing around and it's the usual to-ing and fro-ing about how big a slice he can cut for himself and how little everyone can get away with giving him."

"That's no surprise."

"No, but it's funny, he's being a bit more circumspect than usual. He's generally a bull in a china shop but he's tiptoeing around this one. Everybody is."

"Do you think there's really any gold? Is this just a stock swindle or what?"

"Smells bad if you ask me. Wouldn't be the first. I've brought you a copy of the report. It's glowing, of course. If your boy Alex isn't in on it he'd have to be thicker than a brick."

"Well thanks. Is this your round?"

"Buy your own damn drink. I've got Candy to consume."

Tim hands me a large manila envelope then turns back to his catsuit lady. She pouts again and whines a request for a drink, something radioactive pink with an umbrella and what looks like an entire fruit plate in it. I order a vodka for myself and two gin and tonics and go to find Annie and Billy.

They're at work in a booth with a florid faced, sweating fat man sandwiched between them. He barely notices when I walk up and stand next to Annie. He's focused on something far off in the distance. Both her and Billy's hands are busy in his lap.

I don't want to disturb them so I set the drinks down in front of them, bend to Annie's ear and whisper "later," then leave to make a circuit of the room.

I nurse my drink. At twenty-five thousand *rupiah* it's the most expensive shot of booze in town, and I want to make it last. I'm about to leave when I spot Ron Raymond walking in the door. He's an oil analyst for a big French firm, a disgruntled Yank bound by a huge salary to a corporate culture he doesn't much care for. We used to drink together sometimes when I lived here. He likes to gossip.

Making my way through a gauntlet of enticing smiles and exposed flesh at the bar, I stick a hand out at him.

"Hey, Ron, out hunting?"

"Ray. Just browsing, what about you? Long time no see."

"Strictly business. Can I buy you a drink, I've got a couple of questions."

"At these prices, sure, even on my salary a freebie's always welcome."

We make our way to a couple of barstools that have just been vacated by a matched set of game show hostesses. They've got up to double-team an elderly banker who has tottered into the bar. The seats are nice and warm.

Ron orders an overpriced Jack Daniels.

"Anything us lowly analysts ought to know about what's up in Marinda these days?"

"You tell me. I don't work for them anymore."

"That's right, moved to Hong Kong, back to journalism or something like that."

"I was, but now I'm with Due Diligence International. I'm a corporate investigator."

"Where's your fedora? Here on a case?"

"As a matter of fact, yes. I'm looking into this gold business up in Marinda. Hear anything about it?"

"Yeah, it's gotta be a crock. There's no gold in Sumatra other than what's in a lot of people's teeth and the cops' wrist watches."

"That's the impression I'm getting. How do you think these guys are getting away with it?"

"There's always enough morons out there ready to believe anything. That and they bought themselves an analyst."

"Alex Truscott?"

"He'd be the one. What do you know about this?"

"Young Mr. Truscott is missing."

"That's interesting. I'd heard he was about to be canned. Maybe he just went home to mommy and daddy."

"Why's he on the block?"

"The usual, indiscreet insider trading. It goes on all the time, but even in Indonesia you've got to exercise at least a little discretion."

"He didn't?"

"Not that I heard. Rumor has it he made a personal bundle off that gas find in Irian and his timing was suspiciously perfect. I also heard P&D was embarrassed about his Lucky Break report. They got a lot of flack along the lines of 'what's this kid know about gold.'"

"So you figure he's in on this thing?"

"He's gotta be. The stock's gone apeshit in both Vancouver and Sydney. Chances are good he's cashed out and gone off to count his spoils."

"Do you know anything about these Lucky Break guys? I was asking around about them in Marinda. I'm pretty sure they set a gorilla loose on me."

"I do recall hearing that they play rough. Maybe you oughta be careful. What's in it for you anyhow?"

"Job and freedom. It's what I'm being paid to do. And Sylvia's got her hooks into Truscott. She says she'll get her foot off my neck about the divorce if I find him for her."

"She'll have to give you the divorce sooner or later anyhow, you know. Why not wait?"

"She can make it expensive and difficult. I'd rather have it cheap and easy."

"Wouldn't we all. The girls in here aren't cheap, but they're easy. You done with me? Hope you don't mind but I think I'll go rustle up some more convivial company. Thanks for the drink. If I hear anything new I'll give you a call."

Annie, Billy and the fat man are gone. I don't know if it's the smart thing to do, but I call Irina. She agrees to meet me at the house.

CHAPTER **ELEVEN**

I rina beats me there. Wazir let her in and sat her down in the living room with a pot of tea, but she'd gone into the freezer, found the bottle of vodka and has finished off a couple inches of it fast. She's drunk and depressed. I want to throw myself into her arms, kiss her for a while, take her to bed and spend the rest of the night making love like nothing bad ever happened between us.

I don't. I kiss her on the cheek, open a beer, sit down next to her and drop a hand onto one of hers. "I'm glad you're here. I've missed you."

"I missed you too, Ray, but I am not knowing how I feel."

"About me?" I know that's not really it, not really.

She gives me a look that doesn't let me off the hook. It's a question I dread, as much for myself as with Irina. But sooner or later it has to get answered. It might as well be now.

"Do you still blame me for Sasha?" About a year ago a close friend of hers was killed in Macau. I'd been trying to help the brother of a colleague get the woman he loved away from the Russian mafia, and Sasha'd been trying to help. It had all gone horribly wrong. It was my fault. At least some of it was.

"I am still not knowing, Ray. I want to forget."

"I wish we both could." The other night with Emmy was the first time I'd even wanted to have sex with anyone since everything'd gone so bad in Macau. I enjoyed it, and that should have been enough. It was at the time. But it's not enough to shut my brain up now.

Irina grips my hand and leans into my shoulder. We sit there quietly, not sure where this is going. I don't know what she's thinking. I'm remembering the second night we ever spent together, another night when she was drunk and depressed and we were sitting on the same sofa.

She'd taken me out to dinner, told me she wouldn't take money from me ever again. It was already clear that there was something strong between us, something the money she took from men could-n't possibly ever buy. She told me her life story.

It spilled out of her; sad and sadly typical. Irina grew up in Moscow. Her father was a low level scientist in a government pharmaceutical lab, her mother a clerk in the housing office. She was an only child and her parents doted on her. She'd studied hard, aced all of her tests, and gone through university then medical school. Life wasn't easy, but it was easy enough. Her mother got them good housing and could always trade bureaucratic favors to put meat on the table.

She was about to start her medical internship when the roof caved in. "My mother, my father, we all think we live in developed country. Maybe not so rich like America, but good country, strong country. Then come Gorbachev, then Yeltsin. Big surprise to every-body, we live in poor country, poor like China, poor like Indonesia. No more communism. We need money but we have no money."

Her medical internship didn't pay enough so she got a job in a bank. One of the customers, a handsome man with a big account, asked her out. A few weeks later he set her up in her own apartment. He gave her money, enough to give some to her parents as well, and to buy the fancy clothes he liked seeing her wear. She stopped work-ing. He took her to nightclubs and swank restaurants and he was a good lover. She knew he must be married. She only saw him two or three times a week and he never spent the night. But he was good to her and she was happy and living was a lot easier than it would have been without him.

But one evening a friend of his came to the apartment and told her that he'd left. He'd gone away to America and she had to get out of the apartment. She didn't know what to do. The friend consoled her, fucked her, then gave her a phone number to call. A company he knew was looking for attractive women to work as entertainers.

Irina wasn't naïve. She knew what kind of "entertainers" the company was looking for. Some of her school friends were doing it. One of them came home from a year in Japan with enough money to open her own small nightclub in a suburb. She was getting rich.

"I live in poor country. In school, before, I read about poor countries and how capitalism makes poor girls be prostitute. Philippines, Thailand, poor girl have no freedom. So I think, what difference? I am poor girl too, the same. So I call number, talk to man, go to office. I give him blowjob and he give me job."

A week later she and five other women arrived in Macau. The man who met them took them to a small apartment that all six of them shared. He introduced them to the *mamasan* of the nightclub in the Lisboa Hotel. He took their passports and said they could get them back when they paid him for the plane ticket, rent on the apartment and a lot of other expenses. If they worked hard, didn't spend too much money and were popular with the customers, maybe they could get free in three or four months, then they'd be working for themselves for the rest of their six month contract.

Irina went to Macau three times. She made enough money that she was able to buy her parents' now-privatized apartment and set her mother up with a small sewing supplies shop. Then she came to Jakarta. She worked for eighteen months at the huge nightclub in Ancol, the amusement park near the waterfront.

It took her a year to buy back her passport and the other six months to come up with enough money to get out of the contract that would have forced her to go back to Russia.

She likes Indonesia. She likes the people and speaks the language fluently. She only needs to pick up men a couple nights a week to make more than enough money. She practices medicine, illegally, giving examinations and advice to bargirls and "hostesses" who can't afford or don't trust regular doctors. She never wants to go back to Russia.

When we met, she'd been here for two years. We fell in love hard and fast. She didn't want to quit what she was doing, she liked the independence. She saved her money and thought about what it could do for her in the future.

When I moved to Hong Kong I asked her to come with me, but we would have had to get married for her to get a visa. I'm still technically married to Sylvia and Irina didn't want that anyhow. We saw each other as often as we could, until Sasha died and she didn't want to see me anymore.

It starts out quiet, gentle. Irina turns her face to mine, her lips moist and slightly pursed. I kiss her tentatively, brushing my lips softly against hers, letting the tip of my tongue lightly trace along them. She responds hesitantly at first, uncertainly, cautiously.

But then we fall into it, the familiar old heat and want erupting between us, mashing us together. We sink sideways, horizontally onto the sofa. She kicks off her shoes and with her toes pries off mine. Her legs snake around my thighs. Her tongue works wonders from my mouth down to my neck and she pulls hard at my skin with her lips. I push her head away and bend my mouth to suckle on her neck. I yank aside her shirt and move down to her shoulder. I brush it lightly with my teeth.

She's panting, speaking in muffled bursts of Russian between rapid shallow breaths. The sounds she makes blend with the low hum and soft ticking of the overhead fan and the occasional snap and sizzle from a glowing bug zapper that hangs outside the window. We pull at each other's clothes, opening them where we need to for access. I slide into her effortlessly; aching flesh into a warm, soothing bath. My ears pound with the base sounds that belch from us.

The sofa shifts and then rocks underneath us. As our rhythm speeds to meet our need, the couch scratches across the hardwood floor. I hold to her; a shipwrecked sailor clinging to flotsam on a swollen sea. I lose myself in a torrent of heaving and grunting and pungent salty odors.

We fuck until almost every part of us is raw and sore. When we finish we lie there panting, the drying sweat cooling our bodies.

A while later I wake her up and half carry, half walk her to my bed. It doesn't take long before we're asleep, spooned together. It's better than any sleep I've had for a very long time.

In the morning we're still entwined. I need to get to work but I don't want to wake her. I want to watch her sleep; to go away, then come back and find her still there. I don't know what last night meant. I'm afraid that it might not have meant anything. I want the last year back, for it to have never happened.

I wiggle out from underneath a leg and an arm. Irina's awake when I get out of the shower. I sit down next to her on the bed, not knowing if I should reach out to touch her or not.

"Good morning. I'm happy you're here."

She smiles and takes my hand, pulls it to her breast. "I am happy too, Ray. But also, I am sad. Still, I do not know. Maybe last night, maybe it was only vodka and old memories. I want to forget, but I cannot."

I can't really expect everything to be miraculously better between us after last night, can I? Making love is good for a lot of things. But no matter how good it is, there's only so much it can do.

I change the subject. "I looked into that company for you."

"What do you think, Ray?"

"I think you ought to sell the stock, quick, today if you can."

"Why, Ray, is there problem?"

"I'm not sure yet, but I think there might be. It's risky; better to put your money in something safer."

"What is problem?"

"I can't say yet, not until I'm sure. But, Irina, really, I think it's a good idea to sell your shares now."

"Okay, I call stockbroker today."

"Who is he? Do you want me to check him out for you?"

"I cannot say. He is a client." She's always been discreet.

"If you have any problems, let me know. I'll see what I can do to help. What are you doing tonight? I want to see you again."

"I do not know, Ray. Maybe. We talk later."

CHAPTER **TWELVE**

The Good Pain is as good a place as any to read Alex's report on Lucky Break. While going over it I nurse a large, weak coffee and nibble at what passes for a toasted bagel in Indonesia. It's a poppy seed bagel. If I was in Singapore, I could be thrown in jail for eating it. The government there imagines that you could plant one and raise opium. Or something like that.

The report is written in the usual over-exuberant analyst-speak. Smart investors would skim it and toss it straight into the trash. Most investors aren't that smart.

"...likely to be the greatest gold find in history...the seam is so pure and accessible that the extraction cost is minimal...only downside is that the company must act cautiously in selling its refined bullion or they could flood and depress the market." There's only one reference to an assay, and that's from the company's own geologist. There aren't any independent assessments of the gold find and the history of the company and its financial statements are sparse.

According to the report, Lucky Break is three years old. It was founded by Anthony LeClerc, a French mining engineer who lives in Hong Kong. The company is registered in the British Virgin Islands and despite its sparse record of profits, losses or any sort of activity at all, it is listed on the stock exchanges of Sydney, Australia and Vancouver, Canada. I can't figure out how it got listed in Sydney, but anything's possible. Vancouver, well, that's the wild west.

I toss the report on the table and pick up the now cold coffee. I take a slurp and am about to throw it away when I look up into the wide, bright gray-green eyes of Juli Samsudi, the local correspondent for *Asian Industry*. I was deputy editor of the magazine before quitting to work for Due Diligence.

Juli is sporting a slightly wavy helmet of shiny jet-black hair. Those remarkable eyes are magnified behind thick, serious looking glasses. She always dresses conservatively from the neck down to the waist where the look comes to a crashing halt against the hem of an impossibly short skirt that shows off athletic legs. She'd be of average height if it wasn't for the three-inch heels she routinely wears. But she wears them well, striding rather than walking, with nary a wobble along the way.

Juli's from a very well-connected, wealthy Javanese family and exudes the air of self-confidence that growing up privileged can give someone. But when she opens her mouth to talk, everything relaxes. Any upper-class starch she might have had was knocked out of her by twelve years of high school, university and then graduate school in San Francisco. Her English is pure, unaccented, impeccably colloquial American.

I've always been a little intimidated by her. That's good. If I wasn't I'd make a fool of myself and in this case that could be very bad. She's married to one of my best friends. She's definitely off-limits.

She picks up the report from the table and waves it at me.

"Hey Ray, catching up on the bullshit over breakfast?"

"Juli, buy you a bad coffee?"

"Sure, I guess my professional ethics will permit that. So what's up these days?"

"Business or pleasure? Is this on the record?" I'd called Ben, her husband, to let him know I'd be in town for a few weeks. I'd told him why, but it's not something I ought to be talking about with the press. He must have told Juli. She's got a sharp nose for stories.

"Nah, let's just call it friendly for the time being."

"Well, as for Motex, nothing that's gonna turn your crank. Hardly anything's changed since I worked there. Same old shit. As for me, Sylvia's got me hunting for her latest conquest. He's gone missing and that's getting interesting."

"You mean Alex? That little shit. If he's gone missing, good riddance."

"He wrote that fiction you were just waving at me."

She leafs through a few pages and drops it back onto the table.

"What the hell has this got to do with you and why the hell are you doing anything for Sylvia?"

"If I hunt down the boyfriend she won't give me any grief over the divorce. My 'fuck you money's' at stake."

"Who do you need to say 'fuck you' to?"

"No one at the moment, but I'll feel a lot more secure when I know that I can."

"Feeling insecure lately?"

"No more than usual. It's also looking like Alex is at least hip deep in this Lucky Break gold find business. That's my real job, due diligence on that deal."

"Not surprising. Those guys are crooks."

"What guys?"

"Lucky Break. I guess I shouldn't say they're crooks, but I smell a rat. I can't dig anything up on them. They came out of nowhere and in the last few weeks their shares have been going berserk over a gold find that nobody thinks exists."

"I'm pretty sure it doesn't and I'm pretty sure our boy Alex is in on it."

I make her promise not to write anything about it until I've pinned it all down and located the missing fiancé, then I cough up everything I know. She turns pale when I tell her about the big guy with the little voice and the gun at River Village.

"Jesus Christ, Ray, you've gotta be careful. Is it really worth the risk?"

"It's my job. It's interesting. I'm pissed off enough that I want to get back at the guys who sent the goon after me. And it's gonna get Sylvia off my back. What's not to like? How's Ben?"

Ben's an environmental consultant who does a lot of work for the World Bank. We met about a month after I moved to Indonesia, when I took a few days off to finish a freelance writing assignment left over from before I got the job with Motex.

I had traveled upriver in Kalimantan, the Indonesian part of Borneo, to an orangutan preserve that was the fiefdom of a world famous, reputedly mad, Frenchwoman, Sophie Lemoge. I was there to write about the delicate balancing act between conservation and development. Logging concessions and mines surround her encampment.

It was the rainy season and no one who didn't need to be was anywhere around. I'd taken a small plane from Jakarta, three and a half hours to a squalid little port town. When I stooped out of the hatch onto the tarmac, the air slugged me like I'd opened the door to an overheated steam bath. It was a half-hour crawl on dirt roads in a nicely chilled Nissan taxi to the river. The driver pulled to a stop in front of a wooden walkway that disappeared into a tall thatch of reeds. He pointed and said that was the way to the boat.

I was drenched in sweat within ten feet of leaving the cab. The walkway squished underfoot, supported by a wet bed of moss. I waded through the thick, liquid air, taking short gasping breaths. When the walkway entered the reeds they lashed at me like coarse strands of damp hair. It felt like hours before I got to the river taxi but it couldn't have been more than a couple of minutes.

I climbed aboard and looked for somewhere comfortable to park myself. There wasn't anywhere. A throaty diesel engine belched black smoke, the wooden boat shuddered enough to cause concern that the caulk in the seams of the boards wouldn't hold, and we moved away from the floating dock.

Once we were underway there were two bad choices: I could sit in the shade in the hold; there were huge bags of rice that made comfortable enough seats, but the air was still and dead and added to the dense, wet heat was the stench of the diesel fuel. Or I could climb on top of the boat and sit on the poached-wood top-deck, the equatorial sun scraping me as effectively as sandpaper, but at least there was a breeze and a view.

I sat up top. It took six hours during which I was alternately fascinated and more miserable than I'd ever been. It took very little time for the boat to move into the narrow river channel where the jungle closed in on it. At times I had to duck and turn my back to the front as giant Nipa palm fronds swept the deck. Huge birds and proboscis monkeys with their Jimmy Durante-style noses watched our progress upriver. Occasionally I could make out a small bit of the bank through the dense foliage. Sometimes there'd be a slight rippling in the water ahead, a fish maybe, or a caiman or a python getting out of our way.

About an hour before sundown the boat pulled in at a high, wooden dock. In the dry season passengers would have to clamber up onto it from the top-deck, but with the river swollen from rain I had to step down to it from the lower deck. At the end of the dock, on the same level as the boat, there was an office. A hand lettered sign on the door said "Hotel." Scattered along raised wooden walkways there were fifteen or so one-story wood huts with tin roofs.

Everything sat up high on stilts, a good eight or so feet above the usual level of the river, but that time of year it looked like it was floating.

I was shown to my room as the sky grew prematurely dark, then sparked into intermittent strobes of lightning. The thunder sounded like an approaching rumble of tanks supported by heavy artillery. The already soaked air swelled like a sponge that couldn't possibly absorb any more water. The heat packed in tight around me, choking me at the pores.

I put down my bags and got to the door of the hotel's bar and restaurant just as the downpour started drumming on the tin roofs.

An attractive young woman in a batik sarong and New York Yankees t-shirt ran past me, out into the torrent. I paused under the eave to watch her. She ran to a small shed, went inside and almost immediately I heard the sputter of a gasoline engine. A few light bulbs strung on wires that looped over the walkways flickered on. She came out and ran back toward me, her hands held over her head like that could somehow protect her from the water that was pouring as if from a burst dam.

She ran past me and into the bar, shaking herself like a wet puppy. I followed her inside. There was a tall, rumpled looking man sitting on one of the stools. He didn't even look around when the woman and I came in. He looked like someone who'd got through prep school and an Ivy League college all cool and tidy, then started sweating when he got to the tropics and wasn't about to stop anytime soon. He had wavy, light-brown, gray-edged hair that still held a hint of what had once been an expensive cut. He was dressed in Brooks Brothers casual clothes that had gone limp with fatigue. He was staring somewhere into space, hunched over a glass of beer with ice and a plate piled high with freshly fried *krupuk*, the tasty shrimp cracker that is inescapable in the country.

I sat down a couple of stools from the man as the woman slipped behind the bar. She brought me a vodka with ice and my own plate of *krupuk*. I'd taken a sip and a nibble before he turned toward me.

"Looks like it's just us staying here at the moment. I'm Ben Phillips."

"Ray Sharp." I stuck out a hand and he gave it a well-practiced shake, not too strong, not too soft, and not too long or short either. The kind of shake that has to be bred into someone.

"I've heard the name. You're the new PR flack for Motex. What brings you out here?"

"I used to be a writer. This is just a last fling before I'm subsumed by the corporate culture, or something like that. I'm doing a story on Sophie Lemoge and the local loggers for a business rag back in the States. What about you?"

"I'm an environmentalist, at least that's what the degree says. The World Bank sent me here to see how she's treating her apes."

"I thought she was treating them well. That's the point isn't it?'

"I've heard some things. I'm headed up there tomorrow. You too? We can swap stories after we've poked around some."

Ben was from Boston but had been in Indonesia for the past five years. I hadn't been in Indonesia long, but we knew a lot of people in common. We drank and talked, the downpour battering the tin roof overhead. Netty, the woman behind the bar, disappeared for a while and came back with large steaming plates of *nasi goring* and enormous grilled river shrimp that snapped and squirted hot delicious liquid into my mouth when I bit into them.

At about eleven the rain slowed to a trickle and I figured it was time to go to bed. The boat to Sophie's camp was scheduled to pick us up at six the next morning and I had some notes to prepare. Ben was, unsuccessfully I guessed, trying to coax Netty back to his room with him. I said goodnight and walked the wet planks to my hut.

The sun came up about fifteen minutes before six. Steam rose from every surface. I walked through the vapor on the slippery boards. Through the mist everything was a blur of green. Netty greeted Ben and me with Styrofoam takeaway containers of breakfast; last night's *nasi goring* reheated with a fried egg on top. The boat was waiting. We clambered up top and sat silently eating, watching the jungle slip past as we headed upriver.

Sophie Lemoge was known for two things: her work with orangutans and her temper. When we arrived at her dock she was shouting in Indonesian at someone we couldn't see who was apparently wading in the thicket of reeds by the water's edge. Her face was bright red and purple with swollen veins and it blended almost seamlessly with a huge mane of unkempt hennaed hair. She was wearing a loose white shirt, tied in a knot just under her breasts. She wore baggy, thin-khaki shorts. Her legs were pocked and swollen from insect bites.

She stopped yelling long enough to turn and scowl at Ben and me as we stepped onto the dock. "You are the journalist and the man come to put his nose into my business. One minute."

She turned back to her yelling. We walked up the boards to the nearest building and stood in the shade under the eave. It was only eight in the morning and it must have been a hundred degrees with humidity fast approaching total immersion.

After about five minutes she abruptly stopped screaming, shook herself as if to rid her body of pests, turned and walked toward us buttoning her shirt. She was tall and had a surprisingly kind and unlined face, once it regained its relaxed shape and natural color.

"Bonjour. I am Sophie Lemoge, who of you is the journalist?"

"Ray Sharp, Ms. Lemoge." I held out my hand and she took it. Her nails were, incongruously in that setting, perfect, clean and polished an organic shade of red that matched her hair.

"Please to call me Sophie." She cracked a smile that must have been practiced on dozens of reporters before me, but I bought into it anyhow. She held onto my hand and turned to Ben.

"And you are the, how do you say in English, the meddler from the World Bank."

She ignored Ben's outstretched hand, turned around and tugged on mine.

"Come to my office; there I will explain my work, later I will take you for a tour."

All day long she was friendly and flirtatious with me and hostile to Ben. She deftly danced around any questions about her relations with the local logging and mining companies and she flatly refused to answer any of Ben's queries at all, telling him only to see for himself.

Late that afternoon the boat took us back downriver to the hotel. The darkening sky swarmed with huge bats, big, hook-nosed proboscis monkeys chattered at us from the trees, and we compared our impressions while waving our arms in a futile effort to ward off the swarms of mosquitoes.

Ben wasn't impressed. "She's a piece of work."

"She was nice enough to me. I guess she doesn't like you eco-types. Think I've got a shot at her?"

"She'd let you fuck one of her apes if she thought it would get her a good write up. Maybe a ménage-a-trois with her favorite if you were from National Geographic. You might not have noticed, but she was so nice that you didn't get anything worthwhile out of her."

"I noticed. I'm not too worried. I have other people to talk to and her question dodging will make for some good quotes. I'm going to have to write it under a pseudonym anyhow—Motex doesn't know I'm here and I don't think they'd approve."

Ben wasn't impressed with Sophie's operation. The worst part, he said, was that there wasn't a good enough quarantine system for orangutans that had been returned from "civilization." In close contact with humans, as pets or in badly run zoos, the apes are susceptible to all sorts of diseases they don't encounter in the wild. There aren't a lot of wild orangutans left in the jungle near the camp, but there're some and they show up every so often to scrounge meals.

When one of Sophie's females comes into heat, bellicose males show up at the camp to fight over her.

Sophie allows the rescued and wild apes to mingle. The idea is that it helps reintroduce the "civilized apes" to the forest. Maybe it works, maybe not, the jury's still out, but it could be spreading disease. One of the things Ben was doing in the area was tracking down the source of a rumor that a wild male orangutan had been found dead in the jungle, of tuberculosis.

The next day I was planning to go further upriver, to talk to some of the people at the logging and mining camps, after which Sophie had invited me to dinner. Ben would spend another day being ignored and given the runaround at the orangutan reserve.

Nothing much ever came of either of our visits to Sophie's camp. Ben never was able to pin down enough solid information to come up with any sort of well-informed decision about what she was up to. Neither was I. We both had our suspicions, but those were all.

I did eat Sophie's cook's feeble attempt at a French dinner in the jungle. The Frenchwoman and I got along very well over the first bottle of wine. I was beginning to think that the evening would finish up in her bedroom, until I asked the wrong question. I'm not even sure which one it was. In any case, she clammed up and shooed me out the door and into a small speedboat that took me on a scary, pitch-dark ride back to the hotel.

Ben was at the bar. I joined him.

"So, no jiggy-jiggy boom-boom with the ape woman huh?"

"That's for sure. Guess I asked one question too many."

"I'll drink to that."

I didn't get my story, but I made a lifelong friend. I'd also contracted malaria, apparently another lifelong companion. Not a life threatening case, but one that comes back to visit every now and then. When it does, it causes little more than one or two fever-ridden bad nights complete with very scary dreams and the occasional awake hallucinations.

"Ben's fine."

"You don't look so sure."

"Well, he's a little frustrated. This isn't an easy place for an environmentalist. And there's always my family."

"That's right, he's not good enough for you, is he?"

"He's not a Javanese prince, happily. Anything new with you, other than your new career as a detective that is?"

Over another bad coffee I tell her about Irina.

"How come we never met her when you lived here?"

"I don't know. Irina and me, it's complicated."

"And all those other bargirls aren't?"

"No, that's the point. They're just welcome distractions."

"From what?"

"Myself, I guess."

"And Irina isn't?"

"No, I can't get away with anything with her. She's my equal. More than. She keeps me honest. She's smarter than me, funnier. Sometimes we sit up all night just talking and laughing about books and politics and art and it's all I can do to keep up with her. All that, and she's sexier than hell, too."

"So she's the perfect woman. I'll bet Ben and I like her, if I don't hate her."

"You never liked Sylvia."

"We could never figure out why you did."

"There was a time when things were good between us. And when we moved here, it was all new and interesting and fun. We didn't know anybody. I guess at first we clung to each other for security and were distracted from finding out how little we've got in common."

"I'll say you don't have much in common. You two are screwed up in totally different ways."

"That's nice. Thanks. At least Irina and I are screwed up in some of the same ways. I don't know if it's gonna work out. I hope so."

"Give her some time, space. One of these days I want to meet her."

CHAPTER **THIRTEEN**

I consider going upstairs to the office, but there isn't anything for me to do there. Purdy & Dabs, Alex's company, is nearby. I've had drinks a couple of times with Susan Benigno, one of the directors. We aren't friends, but we're friendly enough.

The taxi lets me off across the street from P&D's office building. Crossing Jalan Rasuna Said in the middle of the day is a daunting task. During rush hour the traffic is slow enough that a pedestrian can safely dodge between cars. Late at night the drivers are bombing along at maximum speed, but they're few and far between. At midday they cruise along at a rapid and unpredictable clip. The only safe way across is one of the overpasses. The nearest one is about a quarter mile up the street.

In most places a quarter mile isn't very far. On Rasuna Said it's along a narrow, pot-holed, rutted sidewalk with an open sewer at the edge. A steady stream of pollution-belching vehicles slips by too close for comfort. Exhausted looking laborers push heavily laden stiff-wheeled carts through the traffic, urged on by the incessant bleating of horns.

Modern buildings loom all around, set back from the street behind walls of plants and long driveways. The few remaining spaces between them are taken up with construction sites from which emit ear splitting hi-torque whines and stomach churning, earth shaking booms.

Vendors block the approaches to the pedestrian overpasses; food carts, newsstands and tables overflowing with counterfeit music cassettes. The steps are lined with beggars, some silent, some shrill, some with children tugging at their clothes or yours or suckling on a breast. The crosswalk at the top is an open-air marketplace of household goods and *jamu*, traditional medicine, spread out on blankets or laid out on the concrete.

I slowly make my way up the street to the overpass, cross and head back on the other side in the direction I'd come. It takes longer than it would in most places, even with the same obstacles. If I walked at my normal pace I'd need a shower by the time I got halfway there.

Susan has a corner office that overlooks red terra cotta tile roofs, broken only by the occasional white dome of a mosque, the glint of the sun on a tree-lined canal, or the stands of tall palms that make up the aerial view of Jakarta behind the façade of the tall new buildings on Rasuna Said. I hadn't called ahead for an appointment, and I haven't seen her in over a year, but I get in without waiting. We make small talk for a couple of minutes while I stand and admire the view.

She's Italian but has lived most of her life in Asia. She's beautiful in a Sophia Loren in her forties kind of way and has a well-developed knack for either inflating a man or bursting his bubble with one look. One of the few women who's broken into the management boys' club of the region's brokerages, Susan got where she is through a string of remarkable, prescient research calls and a no-nonsense but fair way of doing business. Known for her honesty in a business that often isn't, she works harder than almost anyone else I know.

At night she plays harder too. So of course some of "the boys" say she slept her way to the top. That makes her laugh. She likes to trot out a quote from an old interview with the actress Sharon Stone:

"You can only sleep your way to the middle." Once, after a few drinks, she confided in me that she likes being underestimated, she uses it to her advantage.

"Enough with the little talking, Ray, what can't wait until we see each other somewhere?"

"I'm looking for Alex Truscott."

"So am I. I want to fire him."

"Can I ask why?"

"You tell me first."

"You know, Sylvia, my wife? She's engaged to him. She won't give me any trouble over the divorce if I can find him for her." I'm not about to spill anything about my due diligence on Lucky Break to a stockbroker. Not yet at least.

"That is stupid."

"I know, but there's some money involved and it'll save me a lot of grief. So, your turn, why do you want to fire him?"

"He is taking money from Lucky Break Mining. I find that out after already he writes a report for us on them. Bang, he is dead for me. They can have him, if they want him."

"When'd you last see him, or speak with him?"

"Before I know about Lucky Break. I send him to Marinda to visit Motex. I call three days later, he is not there. He has not checked out of the hotel, but no one knows where he is."

"How'd you find out he was working for Lucky Break?"

"I have little birds. I cannot say."

"Do your little birds tell you anything about Lucky Break?"

"I hear they are bad men. After the report from Alex I send a note to our clients saying to ignore the first report. Do you think maybe he is in danger? I want only to fire him. He is too handsome a boy, maybe even a little bit charming also. To have him hurt, I do not like to have that."

He apparently has a way with women, some women, at first, that I just can't see.

"So far he's only missing. Some people suspect he took the money and ran. If I find out anything I'll let you know."

Susan's secretary buzzes her. She has a meeting. I promise I'll buy her a drink when we next run into each other. We're bound to sooner or later if I'm around Jakarta for any length of time. She's one of the few foreign women I know here who enjoys some of the same low sleazy dives that I do.

I go back to the office after all and spend the rest of the day making notes, some calls, reading all the press reports I can find on Lucky Break and the gold find. But there's only so much I can find out from secondary sources. The useful information's in the field. I book myself onto a Motex flight back to Marinda two days later.

When I get back to the house Irina is still there. It's not easy to keep from wagging my tail and barking like an excited puppy. She's been reading a banned novel in the original Indonesian. I read it in translation. It was too dense for me. Maybe I can get her to explain it to me.

We kiss hello and the sparks fire between us. She drops the book to the floor. We tangle, wrapping ourselves into each other. It's unbearably hot at first, then it passes into something beyond reason, something extra-sensory. It's the same old fucking, but it feels like new territory.

Afterward, I don't want to ruin anything by bringing up our relationship. I'm waiting for her to tell me if all this means anything or not. I have to accept that. But I have to say something.

"I didn't expect to see you. I'm glad you're here."

"Me too. When you leave, I go back to sleep. Wake up late. Wazir made me lunch. I started to read book. I am happy too."

I pick the book up off the floor and leaf through it. She's under-lined passages, made notes in the margins. It's a habit of hers that I've always found both endearing and a little irritating. "I heard a lit-erary critic call this guy the Dostoevsky of Indonesia. I thought he was full of shit."

"Is a very good book, but no, is not Dostoevsky. You never learned to read Russian language, only knowing bad words." I'd learned a lot of swearing from Sasha and the Russian gangsters I'd been involved with the year before.

"Did you get a chance to call your broker friend, sell your shares?"

"I call him, but he is in Singapore for two days. I will call again day after tomorrow."

"Isn't there anyone else at his firm who can take the order?"

"I do not know. I am not wanting to make problem for him. I call in two days."

I can't push her any further. We'd agreed that I wouldn't ask her about her business. If she wants me to know something, she'll tell me. Something like this, I'm not sure where the line is, but I don't want to risk crossing it. Not when things are still unsure between us.

"Are you busy tonight?"

She isn't. We make plans for dinner. She wants to go home first to change and make some calls.

We're meeting at a deluxe Indian restaurant not too far from the backpacker hotel that Irina has lived in as long as I've known her. It's as good, if not better, than any Indian restaurant I've ever found in India. But that's not so strange. In India, as in Indonesia and most other really poor countries, anyone who can afford to go out to eat can afford to have a cook at home. So, when they do go out they want Chinese food, or Italian, something that they don't get at home. There are few really great Indonesian restaurants in Jakarta, at least not ones where you'd want to have a romantic dinner. If you want great Indonesian food, get yourself invited to someone's home.

I get there early and lean up against the bar for a drink while I wait. Ben and Juli are there, waiting for a table.

"Hey Ben. Juli, are you stalking me?"

She kisses me on the cheek. "We were here first."

"If you stick around, you'll get to meet Irina."

Ben smirks. "You always did work fast. You've only been in town a few days."

Juli puts a protective hand on my shoulder and turns to Ben. "I started to tell you in the car, Ray's in love. But it's complicated."

"Isn't it always." Ben's brow wrinkles for a moment. He looks skeptical. In the past we'd spent a lot of nights together cruising Jakarta's bars and nightclubs in search of temporary companionship.

"Wait a minute, Ray, is this that Russian babe, the one from when you lived here? I didn't know you were still seeing her."

Juli looks miffed. "Hey, how come you never told me about her?"

Ben throws me one of those "sorry, I didn't mean to blow your cover" looks.

I shrug my shoulders at Juli. "Sorry, I guess it just popped out in one of those guy-talk moments. But after this morning you know more about it than Ben does, anyhow."

Ben tosses me another look. "About what?"

"She'll be here soon. Let it rest. Juli can fill you in later."

"You guys want to join us for dinner?"

Juli rolls her eyes and punches Ben lightly on the arm. "I think they probably want to be alone."

"No, I don't know. Let me see what Irina wants to do when she gets here."

As usual, Irina is dressed to impress. She's stitched into a tight black dress, slit and cut in all the right places. She's perched on heels that even her up with Ben's six feet two. It's a struggle for him to keep his jaw from dropping open. I'm sure Juli hates her on sight. A lot of women do.

The restaurant is one of the expatriate hot spots in the city but it's also known as a good place for discreet encounters. Most of the tables are screened behind thick potted plants and there's an unspoken rule that whatever you imagine you're seeing around you, you aren't.

We haven't been seated long when I'm surprised by Sylvia parting the palm fronds that hide our table.

She's never liked Ben or Juli and the feeling's mutual. They exchange stiff greetings. She merely tilts her head curtly at Irina, without looking at her.

"I see you haven't classed up your act, Ray." The years I'd spent cheating on her hadn't done much to foster tolerance on her part toward any other woman in my company. Then again, I never cared who she cheated on me with. Just another of the things we didn't have in common.

"Did you come over here to insult my friends, or is there something on your mind, Sylvia?"

"Can we talk for a moment? In private."

I apologize to everybody and get up to follow her into the bar. She makes a beeline for a small table in the corner, away from anybody else. She sits. I remain standing.

"Oh sit down, I don't bite."

"Depends on what you mean by 'bite.'" I straddle a chair, putting the table between us.

"What've you found out, Ray?"

"Lover boy's missing all right. You're not the only one looking for him."

"Do you think he's okay?"

"I don't know. He's deep into what looks like a gold scam and involved with some pretty nasty people. Maybe he's okay, maybe not. Maybe he's cashed out and disappeared with the loot. The one thing everyone agrees on is that he's one of the bad guys."

"Not to me."

"Why not? I don't get it. You don't have that bad taste in men, at least I hope you don't."

"Unlike you, he's always been a perfect gentleman. He knows the best people and takes me to the best parties. In Singapore we stay in a suite at Raffles. We stay in the best resorts in Bali. He's got money and he's not afraid to use it. He doesn't make me feel small, Ray. Not like you did. He cares about the finer things. He doesn't want to hang out with low lifes. I don't know if he's faithful or not, but he's discreet and has real class."

"No comment. Sorry I asked. Anyhow, he might be in trouble."

She looks concerned, puts a hand up to her throat. "What do you mean? What sort of trouble?"

There's no telling why anyone wants to be with anyone else. I can't understand what she sees in Alex, but still, it softens me a little toward her. I thought I'd been in love with her once, too. I was wrong. It'd been a lot of things other than love, but I hadn't known it at the time.

"Like I said, he's mixed up with some bad people and now he's missing. I don't know how deep into it he is, but if that's the reason he's disappeared, you might not like what I find out."

"It's not just me, Ray. I'm having dinner with someone else who wants to find Alex, someone else who's worried about him."

"Who's that?"

"Tony LeClerc. He's the head of a company Alex was doing some work for. I'll introduce you."

She wants to make small talk after that, but I tell her I don't have time for it. I get up and go back to my friends. The four of us watch Sylvia sashay across the room, doing a pretty good job of attracting every eyeball in the place. She sits down facing a man with his back to me and leans over to tell him something at close quarters. He turns, looks my way and smiles when our eyes meet.

Irina puts a hand on mine. "She is your wife?"

"Ex-wife soon, I hope. I'm sorry she's such a bitch."

Ben waves a hand to get my attention. "What's she want?"

"I'm trying to find her missing boyfriend in exchange for her being friendly about the divorce."

He raises an eyebrow. "You sure it's worth it?"

I change the subject to dinner. While we eat Ben catches me up on his new project in Kalimantan and I catch him up on my new career as a corporate investigator. I'd worried about Irina and Juli getting along, but they're deep in quiet conversation, speaking Indonesian. From what little I overhear and understand I gather that they've swapped life stories and moved on to discussing Indonesian literature. I reach for one of Irina's hands and give it a soft squeeze.

We're waiting for our coffee when Sylvia drops by the table again, this time with Tony LeClerc in tow. He looks enough like a stereotype of a Frenchman that you'd think he'd be embarrassed by it. He's medium height and has a slender build. Not many people in Jakarta, and no one else that I know of in the mining business, wear a three-piece suit. The one he's got on is impeccable, sporting a neatly folded pocket hankie that matches his tie. He's wearing a starched dress shirt, the kind with different color collar and cuffs than body, and a tastefully understated but very expensive watch. His coal black hair is perfectly imperfect and he looks down at me through flat eyes set far back from the tip of his finely chiseled nose. He offers a limp handshake.

"You are the Monsieur Sharp I hear about, no? You are investigating my company on behalf of investors, no?"

"Everyone's talking about your gold mine."

"Yes, it is good fortune."

"Is it? For you, I guess, in any case. I hear you'd also like to find Sylvia's boy, Alex. He's a popular guy."

"Perhaps we will talk more."

"I'll be in Marinda day after tomorrow. You planning to be around?"

He pulls out a slim gold case and carefully extracts an embossed card on cream-colored rag paper. He reaches into an inside jacket pocket and comes out with a matching gold pen that he uses to write a number on the back. He extends the card to me, held out between his index and middle fingers. There's something prissy about it. I almost laugh, but I restrain myself.

"Please call me."

Sylvia tugs on his sleeve and they leave.

"What the hell was that all about?" Juli puts a concerned hand on my arm when she asks.

"He's the grand poohbah at Lucky Break. I'm pretty sure it was one of his thugs who clocked me in Marinda. He knows I know it."

"Clocked you? That's quaint. You mean beat you up. Why's he worried about you?"

"I think he figures I'm not buying this whole gold business. He's afraid my poking around might blow it up."

"Be careful, I don't like him."

"Me neither. But don't worry, I'll give you the story when I get it."

"I'd rather have you healthy."

"Me too. I'll see if I can manage both."

After dinner the four of us walk down the street to an open-air bar where we toss back a couple more rounds of drinks before heading home. As Irina and I get into a taxi, Juli pulls me aside.

"I like her. I really do. I wasn't sure I would. I hope it works out, Ray."

"Me too."

Irina and I make out like teenagers the whole way back to my place. I overtip the driver to make up for the annoyed looks he's been giving us in the rearview mirror. We get in the door but then only as far as the front sitting room. An hour or so later we make it to bed.

CHAPTER **FOURTEEN**

Irina and I lounge in bed until lunch and then she has to go. She's got a date this evening, a paying one.

I don't know why her work doesn't bother me. It even sort of appeals to me. I don't think I'm very good at relationships, and Irina's job helps guarantee our independence. I don't know that anyone else is going to understand that. Hell, I'm not sure I do. I want to be with her. I don't want to tell her what to do, how to live her life. That's her business.

The rest of the afternoon I work at the house, trying to come up with what to do next.

I'm settling in for a quiet night at home for a change when Annie and Billy show up at about seven-thirty. They insist on taking me out to dinner, then to something they'll only describe as "Indonesia dance, surprise, you like lot." They're dressed down, in street rather than work clothes, trying not to call attention to themselves. Annie suggests I do the same.

We take a taxi to Jatinegara, a poor neighborhood that radiates out from one of the city's main train stations. The station is engulfed in a riot of food, *jamu* and household items vendors. They're everywhere and they're mobbed with customers. Some of them place their carts across the tracks. When a train pulls in or out of the station they'll get out of the way, but slowly, as if to show who's really got the right of way.

We cross the tracks and walk down a rutted dirt street, one faint streetlight and kerosene lanterns on the porches of small houses lighting our way. We cross an open sewer on a wobbly wood board. Billy takes my hand to steady me, but almost throws me off balance instead. We turn down a narrow lane, tall vine- and orchid-covered walls rising high on either side of us. It's a little scary at first, but interesting.

From around a corner I hear the hum and see the greenish glow of fluorescent lights. They're coming from a small restaurant, more of a *warung* with plasterboard walls and a corrugated sheet metal roof. There's a window at the front, piled high with small plates of fried, oily food. A tiny plastic fan stirs the air just enough to keep a squadron of flies at bay. Inside there are three rickety card tables, an ice chest and a shelf with a small black and white TV tuned to a Muslim prayer station.

The tables are full but a stout, elderly woman in a plastic floral-patterned apron welcomes us with a big grin that exhibits a mouth dotted with about half as many teeth as the standard allotment. She waves us inside, brings out three folding chairs from behind a batik cloth curtain hanging at the back of the room and bullies the two men sitting at one of the tables into squeezing closer together to make room for us.

We sit down and she brings us plates of food from the window display.

I've eaten in *nasi Padang* restaurants before, but none quite so down and dirty as this one. It's a style of cooking and presentation from West Sumatra and it's popular all over the country. Each person is given a plate of rice and then anywhere from eight to as many as two-dozen small plates and bowls of food are brought to the table. In a big spread there can be three or four different dishes each of chicken, beef, lamb or goat, fish, shrimp, vegetables, tofu, eggs and *sambal*, dishes in which chilies are the main ingredient. *Padang* food is the spiciest in Indonesia. That, and the fact that it's mostly fried or dried, helps it to hold up all day against the elements as it sits in the window attracting customers and flies.

One of the reasons that the restaurants are so popular is that they're cheap. A poor person can pay only a few *rupiah* for a plate of rice and then spoon the sauce from the dishes onto their rice for free. So long as you don't eat the main ingredient of a dish, the meat or the vegetable, you don't have to pay for it.

West Sumatra is one of the more devout Islamic parts of the country, so a lot of *Padang* restaurants only have water or juice to drink. Without us asking though, the woman pulls two large, wet, cold bottles of Bintang beer and three glass mugs from the ice chest. She offers me a fork and spoon, but everyone else is eating with their fingers so I wave them away. The food is delicious, some of the best I've had.

When we walked in the other customers looked at me with a mix of curiosity and concern. There's an almost audible sigh of relief when my pleasure becomes apparent. The stout woman is astonished and pleased when I ask for more of the spiciest *sambal*.

Billy, looking concerned, pours me more beer. "You crazy man, too much chili."

Annie watches me eat with something like a possessive sense of pride. She whispers something to the men sitting next to her. They all laugh. I raise my mug and the whole place toasts to something. I'm not sure what.

After eating we walk back the way we came, but before getting to the main road we turn left down a wide dirt path beside the railroad tracks. There's a highway overpass ahead, under which there are flickering lights and from which I can hear a loud, deep drumming, a high, melodic screech and something that's either singing or a cat in a high-speed blender.

As we get closer I can make out groups of people in the dark, some sitting at picnic tables in front of food carts, others standing in the shadows. A few rundown *warung* are selling a variety of sweet and salty snacks and drinks.

A higher-pitched, Indian sounding drum and a gong join the deep drumming. The screech takes form, sounding like a scratchy out-of-tune violin. Finally the singing takes on tone and color and I can distinguish words, though they aren't in Indonesian and I can't understand them.

Directly under the overpass there's a small stage built of salvaged wood lashed together with wire and lit by one fluorescent tube with a tattered black-light filter. On the stage are two drummers, a gong player and a man playing an upright fiddle with only two strings. In front of them sit eight women. They wear brightly colored, but not matching, starched dresses that exaggerate their hourglass shapes. There must be an intricate web of construction underneath them.

The women are heavily made-up, their hair piled up in extraordinary rat's nest coifs. They range in age from sixteen or seventeen to somewhere in their sixties, but it's hard to make an accurate guess through all the make up. One of the younger looking women is holding a microphone and the extraordinary but not altogether awful singing warbles out of her. The others sway in time to the hypnotic beat.

In front of the stage on a swept patch of dirt, six men are dancing or practicing a martial art in time to the music. They move all four limbs, one at a time in broad motions, up and down and out and around. They dance separately, only on occasion shifting their stance to briefly confront each other for a short burst of sharp moves. Every so often one reaches into a pocket, pulls out money and hands it to the oldest of the women on stage. She smiles and nods her thanks and stuffs it into her accomodating cleavage.

Across the street from the stage there's a dirt slope on which people sit and watch. At the back, where the slope runs into the underside of the concrete overpass, in the deepest shadows I can faintly make out more people, discreetly coupled in the dark. There are picnic tables at either side of the stage, laden with bottles of beer and orange soda and plates of *krupuk* and boiled peanuts.

We sit on a bench at one of the picnic tables. A young girl sets down thick, chipped glass mugs filled with large chunks of ice broken from a block on the ground nearby. Annie picks up a bottle opener that's on the table, opens a couple bottles of beer and fills our glasses. We all wait a minute for the ice to cool the beer, then gulp it down fast before the ice melts and dilutes it.

One song winds to an end and Annie nudges me with her elbow, pointing out the men who're giving money to the woman on stage. I get out a five thousand *rupiah* note and take it up to her. She pulls my hand along with the money, clasping it to her sweaty bosom and smiling. The other women on stage laugh and one of the young ones licks her lips and winks. That makes them all laugh more.

The next song starts and Billy gets up to dance, pulling me along with him. I'm a lousy dancer even when the moves are familiar. I do my best to imitate him. After a few minutes of providing clumsy amusement for the onlookers, I sit down next to Annie and pour myself another glass of beer.

While we watch, Annie explains that the music and dancing are called *jaipongnan*. It's from Sunda, West Java, and the language of the songs is Sundanese. It originated in brothels. The women sing and dance to attract customers and the men show off their macho dance floor moves. It's a mating ritual of sorts.

Though it's a poor rough crowd that gathers under the overpass in Jatinegara to watch it, *jaipongnan* has become respectable and even shows up in theaters. When the Indonesian government sends cultural dance troupes overseas, it's often included in the program. That's not to say that they don't still dance it in brothels in West Java, or that the women I was watching weren't prostitutes.

The women on stage though, aren't necessarily available for sex. Some are, but it's a lot less formal than in a brothel. Anyone who's interested would have to be a regular, get to know the woman they're interested in, woo her, take her out to dinner, buy her small gifts.

Maybe it's all very simple if you're born here. You can understand the place without giving it too much thought. Or, more likely, you don't feel the need to understand it at all. But for me, on the outside looking in, it's the most confusing and complicated place I've ever known. Nothing is ever completely what it seems. That's one of the reasons I like it here so much.

Annie and I sit and watch Billy dance, our legs rubbing up close against each other. It's comfortable, nice, hanging out with a friend, maybe a lover. But once again I'm not satisfied with just leaving it at that. I catch myself thinking about what Annie is or isn't to me. About Emmy and Irina. But not for long. Thinking too much is a disease.

Drinking isn't a cure for thought, but it helps relieve the symptoms. We finish our beers and Billy suggests we move down the street to the second stage, on the other side of the overpass.

The women on the other stage are *banci*, either transvestites or transsexuals. They're all bigger than the women on the first stage, but some are even more attractive. About half are obvious in the way that souped-up drag queens can be. The other half would require close inspection, in a couple of cases very close inspection, before you could tell that they weren't born women. As we sit down at the picnic table next to the dancing area, they lean in our direction and amp up their flirting.

Despite the rarified and sexy world that expats live in, Indonesia is not the most sexually liberated place on the planet. It's generally pretty conservative. Yet *banci* are easily accepted as just another part of society, as are gay people—so long as they don't make waves about it. No matter what someone does sexually in the country, whether straight, gay or something in between, they're expected to be discreet about it. Outward or aggressive displays of emotion or sexuality are frowned upon and repressed. It's one of the things about Westerners, especially us demonstrative Americans, that bewilders a lot of Indonesians.

We sit and watch the *banci* singers and drink more beer. It's still relatively early when I want to go home. I'm leaving for Marinda the next morning. We flag down a taxi in front of the train station and take it back to my place. I give Billy twenty thousand *rupiah* for cab fare, and he continues on out into the rest of the night. Annie insists on coming in to help me pack. That involves her nagging me to buy new clothes. She doesn't think I dress well enough for a rich foreigner.

Then she wants to have sex. Once again I'm tempted, but I tell her no. I want to get a good night's sleep. I've also got a slight hope, even though I know she won't, that Irina will come over.

So, once again Annie starts out in the guest room and ends up in my bed later trying to get something started. This time she succeeds. It's fine, sleepy and lethargic, comfortable, but nothing special for either of us. It tires me out, makes it easier to drift off, at least for a little while. Annie talks and squirms a lot in her sleep. At one point her arm flails into my nose and wakes me up. After that I can't stop from doing some tossing and turning of my own. I wish it was Irina with me.

I'm not all that well rested when I get out of the house the next morning to go to the airfield. I manage to sleep a little on the plane, squeezed into a narrower than usual middle seat between two over-sized oil guys from Louisiana.

CHAPTER **FIFTEEN**

When I worked for Motex's PR department, I had to fire Iris. She was good at her job, I liked her, but she'd been the most recently hired and the company was cutting back. I haven't seen her since. She's driving the Motex van that's come to the airport to pick up passengers. I get in the front seat, next to her.

She recognizes me immediately. It takes me a minute. She's nondescript; medium height, medium build, dressed in neutral colors. She used to wear glasses but she's switched to contacts. Her one distinguishing feature is her hair; it used to be very long, jet black, straight and lustrous. She's cut it to about shoulder length and given it a jaunty wave on both sides of her face.

"You cut your hair. I didn't know you could drive."

"You thought I was *ayam kampung*, didn't you, Boss Man?"

"Village chicken?"

"Figure it out. I went to school in the states, Cal Riverside.

Didn't you ever wonder why my English was so good?"

"I didn't really think about it."

"You didn't think about much did you? Why did you fire me? Why not one of those other clowns?"

"I hardly remember. That was a long time ago. I think it was because those other clowns had been there longer than you."

"I liked that job. I miss it. I think the department might be hiring again soon. Do you know anyone you can talk to? I write better than I drive." As if to make her point she swerves and barely misses a *satay* vendor pulling his cart along the side of the road.

"Keep your eyes on the road, okay? It's been a while, I'm not sure I know anyone who gives a shit about anything I have to say anymore."

She makes the circuit of the compound, dropping the other passengers off at various points, making sure I'm the last one left as she pulls up in front of the motel. "This is you."

"No it's not. I'm staying at the Palace."

Iris turns to look at me and exaggeratedly raises one eyebrow. It looks like something she might have copied from Groucho Marx. "A girl?"

"You're a smart ass, you know that?"

"Yes, I'm better at that than driving too."

"None of your business, but maybe you can help me with something."

"I'm a good girl, I don't do that."

"I didn't mean that. I meant something else."

"Something to do with that man you're looking for and why you got beat up the last time you were here?"

"I guess word gets around."

"Not so much, but I hear things. I see things. I listen and look better than a lot of people. Also, Emmy is my friend. You be good to her."

"I thought you were a good girl?"

"So is Emmy, but she never went away to university. She's got a bad family. I have a lot of friends."

"Okay, okay. If I get a company car can you get some time off to help me out? I'll pay you."

"I don't need time off, I'll just get assigned as your driver. I can make the boss of the motor pool do almost anything I tell him."

I know him. That doesn't surprise me.

We stop at the motor pool and check out a Land Rover. Then Iris drives me to the hotel. When we get there she tells me she's called ahead and we're meeting Emmy for lunch.

I check into my room then head downstairs to meet Iris and Emmy in the coffee shop. They're in a booth, laughing. I sit down across from them. Iris looks up and gives me the Groucho treatment.

"So, Boss Man, Emmy says you are hot stuff." She puts on a heavy Indonesian accent that she doesn't normally have. "You big trouble *bule* man, no? Why no like Iris too?" She and Emmy bust up laughing. My face gets hot and I can sense it turning bright red. The two of them look at me and laugh even harder.

Finally they settle down. "Sorry, sorry, none of my business, right?"

I glare at Emmy.

"*Maaf, maaf,* I sorry. Iris same sister, no secret."

It would be stupid for me to be angry. And counterproductive. It's not polite to show anger in Indonesia. It's not smart either. Doing so is the quickest way to make sure that you don't get what you want. In America you can raise your voice and shout and get things done. In most of Southeast Asia people will just figure you're crazy and quietly ignore anything you have to say.

I laugh also. Just a chuckle at my own expense, but I mean it.

We've eaten most of our lunch when one of the guys who works the front desk comes to the table with a folded note for me. Tony LeClerc wants to see me at his operations office that afternoon. I think it's safe enough. There'll be people around, people who know where I've gone, and he didn't strike me as the sort of bad guy who's willing to get his own hands dirty.

I make plans to meet Emmy that evening. Then Iris and I head out of town, past the Motex compound and into the forest. The note came with a detailed map, as the place isn't easy to find. We turn off the highway about a half hour past the compound, about twenty minutes after passing Santo's, onto a barely visible track that leads into the trees.

About a hundred feet through the dense forest that fronts the highway, it opens onto a wide, newly graded red, dirt road. The jungle's been hacked back another twenty or thirty feet, but is still there, a high, unbroken green wall on both sides of us. The road, compacted from the native clay, is absolutely flat and straight. It's been blasted through small hills and large boulders to form a straight bright red scar on the landscape.

We drive several miles until the road crests a small hill and makes a sharp turn to the left at the bottom on the other side. There's a clearing and three huts built from roughly hewn local wood with tin roofs. The sun pummels the metal and beats into our eyes. About a dozen small motorbikes and one large pickup truck are parked in the clearing out front.

Hal, the talkative Aussie I met at the hotel, comes out on the porch of the largest of the three huts and waves us in. Iris says it might be a good idea for her to stay in the Land Rover and keep the engine running. She needs the air-conditioning in any case. I get out, walk up the three steps and, thinking it's best to play friendly, shake Hal's extended hand.

"G'day, mate, isn't that what we Aussies are supposed to say? Howzzit goin'?"

"LeClerc inside?"

"Sure is, come on in out of the heat. Your girlie gonna be okay out in the Rover?"

"Yeah, fine. You first."

Hal tosses me a smile that doesn't make me feel any too secure. I watch him closely as I follow him inside, ready to make a quick move if I see anything suspicious. I instinctively duck as I enter through the door. No one hits me. I look up to see LeClerc rising from behind a desk, something between a smile and a grimace pasted on his face.

He makes a circular gesture with a hand at a chair in front of the desk.

"Monsieur Sharp, thank you for coming. Please, sit."

I sit. He sits too, makes a tent out of his interlaced fingers and stares at me over it. "Why, monsieur Sharp, do you wish to make trouble for me? I am only a businessman. Gold is my business."

"Right. Look, I don't give a shit what you're up to out here. I'm just looking for Alex Truscott." It's not the right time to be asking questions about his gold operations. I doubt he'd tell me anything but lies, anyhow.

"Why do you care to find him, monsieur? Is he so important?"

"I might've given up by now if I hadn't been pushed around by one of your thugs."

"Please, Monsieur Sharp, I have no need to employ thugs."

"So the big guy with the little voice and the bandage on his neck works for somebody else? I doubt it."

"I cannot permit interference with my business."

"Help me find young Mr. Truscott and I'll get out of your hair."

"Yes but, I also do not know where he is. How can I help you, monsieur?"

"I'm tired of dancing. Let's sit this one out and talk. You might not know where he is now, but I've got an idea that you know where he was."

"Perhaps he does not wish to be found."

"Tough shit. I just want to find him and get this all over with."

LeClerc tilts his head and turns up his palms. He nods at Hal, who is somewhere behind me. I assume that means our meeting is over. I'm about to say something else, something smart I'm sure, when a rag is shoved tight up against my nose and mouth. It smells of sweet chemicals. It isn't bad. It's the last thing I remember before waking up with a pounding headache, my head cradled in Iris' lap.

I look up into her face. She looks concerned, or mad, I can't tell which. "You're back."

I reach up and press my knuckles hard against my throbbing temples. "I wish I wasn't. Where are we?"

"I don't know. They put a blindfold on me and put me in here. They threw you in here about a half hour ago. We're locked in."

If I squeeze my head while slowly turning it, it doesn't hurt too much to look around. There are some tools and a few wooden crates. It's a supply shed.

"What time is it?"

"I don't know, maybe late afternoon."

"I'm sorry I got you into this."

"Can you sit? Your head is heavy."

Iris helps me sit up and slowly. As I scrunch my eyes and move it back and forth, my head begins to clear.

"Is anyone around?"

"I heard a truck start about fifteen minutes ago. I haven't heard any voices."

"We need to try and get out of here."

"Good idea, Boss Man."

I get up and walk around the room. It's small and doesn't have any windows. A little light filters in through cracks and knotholes in the cheap plywood walls and one hard beam shoots through a seam in the ceiling. The door is solid enough but it doesn't fit that well and I can see that it's latched with a flimsy piece of flat metal, no doubt held in place with a padlock I can't see. I poke around the shed, looking for something slim enough to fit into the door crack and bang against the latch.

There's a shovel. I figure I can force the edge of it between the door and the frame and use it as a lever or just to bang against the latch. I can't see enough through the door to know if the noise will bring someone running, or who it might be if it does. But it's better than not doing anything.

I tell Iris to stand to the side, grab hold of something solid and get ready to smash somebody with it if they come through the door looking like trouble. I manage to bang the shovel head up against the latch but can't hit it hard enough with my hand to break anything. I turn around to look for something to hammer on the handle. Iris is holding a large wrench. She gives it to me and I start pounding.

The noise is terrible.

But no one comes and the latch finally snaps. It was secured with a high-quality padlock and the steel bolt held, but the small screws that fastened its other end to the wood of the shed came loose. I hold onto the shovel and brandish it in front of me as I slowly push open the door and step outside.

No one's around. The pickup truck and the Land Rover are both gone. A few of the motorbikes are still there but I wouldn't know how to hotwire one if my life depended on it. Maybe it does.

I know we should get out of there quick, but a quick nose around in the office is too tempting. It's locked, of course, and more solidly than the shed was. One of the windows is cracked open, but latched. I can't reach into it, but Iris can. I tell her to keep out of sight, but keep an eye on the approaches to the place. Then I crawl inside.

There's a half-full bottle of Pernod, a couple of glasses and a big roll of duct tape in the top drawer of a file cabinet. The other three drawers are dirty, like they've had soil samples or rocks in them, but empty. There's nothing in the desk other than some pencils, blank paper, paperclips and a box of tissue. If Lucky Break does any business in this office, they take it with them whenever they leave. Why do they bother to lock the place?

I leave it unlocked when I walk out the door.

Iris had looked around while I was inside. She's found a path leading from behind the shed, into the woods. I'm worried about running into LeClerc or one of his guys on the road out to the highway, so we take the path.

In about ten minutes we come to the edge of a big muddy field surrounded by forest. There are people around but there's so much noise from what they're doing that they don't notice us. They're all Indonesians and are hard at work with pickaxes and buckets, digging holes and filling troughs with mud. There are six groups of two or three people each, laboring at small pits under makeshift canopies to fight off the sun. The noise comes from two gas-powered pumps that skim water off the bottom of the holes and shoot it in long brown arcs across the field into small ponds.

Iris and I walk to the nearest group of three people, a man and two women. They're completely caked in yellow-brown mud. Over the loud coughing of the pump I yell "hello" and ask what they're doing.

It isn't a big surprise. They're mining for gold. A foreign man gave them the pumps and showed them what to do. They haven't found any gold but he keeps coming back, bringing them food and money. He tells them that they can stop in another couple of weeks, but even if they don't find any gold, just keep working. They don't ask questions. If a crazy foreigner wants to pay them good money to dig holes in the ground, that's his business.

They aren't surprised to see us. They're too tired for anything as energetic as surprise. They have no idea when the other foreigners might come back. The Marinda river runs past the other side of the field. One of them offers to take us to the city. It's about four hours in a small boat.

We pay the guy with the boat. It isn't much.

CHAPTER **SIXTEEN**

Before we got on this boat I knew there were mosquitoes in Indonesia. I didn't realize how many. I'm not happy to provide dinner for the insect part of the ecosystem. I'm worried about Iris. She's smaller than me. I can hardly believe they won't drain her completely. She's sitting still though, dozy and silent, an uncomfortable smile lightly playing on her lips. I lurch around as much as possible in the small boat. I swat as many of the bastards as I can, groan and sputter, and for all my efforts I'm not bit any less.

About halfway to town the sun sets fast, like it always does in the tropics. The boy steering the motor launch hands me a kerosene lantern to light and put in the prow, and a large flashlight I'm only supposed to use when it looks like there might be something ahead to bump into. With nightfall the big swarms of mosquitoes go away. A bright highway of stars powders the sky in a line that follows the course of the river. It's almost peaceful.

We arrive at a small landing in the middle of town a little after eight that evening. I'm beginning to swell and itch. Iris, too, but she's annoyingly stoic. We walk to the hotel, where Emmy's been waiting. She isn't happy about how late we are.

The annoyed look on her face changes when she gets a good look at us. She fires questions at Iris in heavily accented Indonesian, shot through with slang. I get the impression it's deliberate, so that I won't understand. It sounds like an argument to me. Finally, Iris breaks away from it and turns to me.

"I want a shower. Emmy has clothes I can borrow. I am sorry, but can I use your room?"

She asks if I'd mind waiting downstairs for a half hour or so before coming up. I'm tired, dirty, itching like mad and I also want a shower. I do mind waiting but I feel guilty for having got Iris mixed up in something dangerous. It takes an effort to put any sincerity into it, but I smile and tell her to go ahead.

I order two double vodkas in the lobby bar. I toss the first one back and figure I'll make the second last at least a couple of minutes.

I'm almost finished, a little quicker than planned, when Emmy comes into the bar. She looks upset and yanks my sleeve. "Come now, problem room." I down the rest of my drink and follow her.

The room's been torn apart. My suitcase has been turned over, everything dumped and scattered out of it and the lining ripped. The papers on the desk are in order, but upside down; someone's gone through them. My laptop computer and camera are missing. Iris is in a chair in the corner, her chin cupped in her hands, taking it all in.

I sit on the edge of the bed across from her. Emmy sits down and puts an arm around me. Iris' eyes focus on mine.

"I think you made somebody angry."

"Nervous is more like it. I'm the one who's getting angry."

Emmy calls a friend in housekeeping. There aren't many secrets that can be kept from the staff in a hotel and maybe someone noticed something.

Iris stands and puts a hand on my shoulder. "Maybe I should go home."

"No, stay. Take your shower. You must be hungry. I'll buy dinner for the three of us."

She smiles and squeezes my shoulder. "Don't get any ideas."

"They'd only get me in trouble. Go, take a shower." Iris goes into the bathroom, closes and locks the door.

Emmy gets off the phone and takes a seat on my lap. "No *informasi*. They talk day boy tomorrow, but nobody see."

I lean to kiss her thanks on the cheek but she turns her lips to mine and our tongues tangle. I grow hard underneath her and the distraction is welcome. She pulls away from me grinning, reaches out and gives the bulge in my pants a playful tug. "Maybe Iris finish, take shower you and me."

"Later, dinner first, then we'll send Iris home and can come back up here." I pull her back onto the bed next to me.

She looks up at me and does her best to imitate Iris' smart aleck voice, "Okay, Boss Man."

"No, not you too." The shower stops and I try to think of anything I can to settle down before Iris comes out of the bathroom. Emmy keeps teasing me, reaching over and stroking my crotch, making me move her hand away, taking my hand and putting it up under her short skirt. When Iris comes out of the bathroom I'm tickling Emmy, who's trying to squirm away.

Iris looks like she's about to stamp her feet and start yelling. If she does, I'll probably laugh and that will not be the right thing to do.

Instead, she rolls her eyes and lets out an exasperated but resigned sounding sigh. "Aren't we going to dinner?"

I stand up, forgetting to be embarrassed. Iris leans against the door to the bathroom, dressed in one of Emmy's short skirts and very tight tops, looking good in a way that I haven't noticed before. She looks me up and down and frowns. "Maybe I should just go home."

"No, no, sorry. Let me take a quick shower and then we'll get out of here." I brush past her, making a point of turning my back when I do.

When I come out they're sitting on the bed watching MTV. They look at me, then at each other. Emmy tries on a Groucho for size and gets it about half right. It breaks them up laughing. It's a good natured, teasing sort of laughter, even if it is directed at me.

Us foreign guys can be pretty funny. Some of our needs and wants are fundamental and often embarrassingly obvious. We're also hairier, bigger, clumsier and louder than most Indonesian men and I suppose the whole package adds up to hilarity in certain circumstances. It bothers some expats. I kind of like it. If you're conscious of it you can use it, play with it to defuse awkward situations.

As we pass by the bar I see Hal and Gary hunkered down over drinks. I tell Iris and Emmy to go ahead, I'll join them soon. I sneak up on the two Aussies and tap Hal on the shoulder. His eyes widen when he sees me.

"G'day, mate. Isn't that what you fucking Aussies like to say?"

Gary turns around looking ready to fight, but reins himself in when he sees me.

"Wasn't expecting to see you here, mate." Hal raises his drink to me. I take a step back; thinking he might want to do something stupid with his glass, like hit me with it.

"I bet you weren't. Where'd your boss go?"

"He's around somewheres. I don't 'spect he'll be happy to see you."

"Probably not. You guys've made it clear you've got something to hide."

"What would that be, mate?"

"Let's not fuck around. I know the whole gold thing's a crock and frankly, until you guys started trying to hurt me I didn't give a shit about that. I was just doing my job and also trying to find Alex Truscott. Now it's personal. I'm gonna find out exactly what you're up to and what's happened to Truscott. You'd better be ready for it."

"Suit yourself, mate." Hal turns around on his barstool by way of dismissal. Gary's looking at me. He looks worried.

I'm trying to hide it, but my own worries are simmering, threatening to boil over. Iris and Emmy saw me go up to Hal and Gary. Iris must have filled Emmy in on what's going on. When I walk up to their table in the coffee shop, they look worried too. There's too much worry going around.

"Be careful—bad mans. I tell hotel security."

"It'll be okay Emmy. They're not gonna try anything here. Let's eat."

"I worry. You come my house tonight, okay?"

"Maybe, let's talk about that later. Now I'm hungry."

Iris, her face hidden behind a menu, doesn't say anything.

We eat, a lot, in silence. When we finish Iris gets up.

"I have to go home now. Do you want me to come back tomorrow?"

"What are we gonna do about the Land Rover? It's missing."

"I'll figure something out, don't worry. You should go home with Emmy. Don't stay here tonight."

"It oughta be okay. I really don't think they'll try anything here."

"Maybe no, maybe yes. It is safer at Emmy's *kampung*. People will see a white man coming and no one can sneak up on you."

"What makes you think they don't have any Indonesians working with them?"

"Up to you. Do you want me to pick you up in the morning? What time?"

"Meet me here at eight."

Emmy waits for me in the lobby while I walk Iris out to get a taxi. When I come back she takes both my hands in hers.

"We go my house. More safe. Small house, no air-con, maybe you no like."

We walk out onto the street and down a block before getting into a *bajaj*. A regular taxi would attract a lot of attention in Emmy's neighborhood. A *bajaj* also has the advantage that it can maneuver down tiny, narrow little alleys that are too big for a car. It makes it harder for anyone to follow us.

Emmy lives across the road from the entrance to River Village in a dense warren of tiny alleys and dilapidated apartment buildings. She directs the driver in a circuitous route, in case we're being tailed. We finally stop in front of a large, dirty whitewashed wall with a cheap plywood door that's illuminated by one fluorescent tube dangling over it, suspended from the top of the wall by a pair of exposed wires.

On the other side of the door a narrow concrete walkway wraps around a long, narrow two-story building. There's a clothesline from which laundry is hung, enclosing the walk like the walls of a hallway.

Music, a chaotic blend of *dangdut*, schmaltzy R&B, classical and disco, wafts out the open door of the building like the reek of something with too many confused ingredients burning on a stove. Emmy gently prods me through the door.

On the inside the building opens into what looks like a prison block. Four rows of metal doors, two downstairs and two upstairs, run along metal catwalks stretched from one end to the other. There's a trough in the concrete in the middle of the floor and water faucets connected by one long pipeline it. Up above, the ceiling is open to the sky. When it rains the water falls into the trough and rushes along a slight slope out the front door, under the street door and into the alley.

We walk along the ground floor, passing small rooms, some of which are open. A couple of people look up to watch us pass. One older woman comes to her door, says hello and listens as Emmy explains what I'm doing there. The woman peers over her reading glasses to get a better look at me, nods once and then scurries down the hall to knock on another door.

"Security." Emmy looks relieved and serious when she says it.

About two thirds of the way down the row we come to number twelve, Emmy's room. She unlocks a padlock from a hasp on the door and lets us in. She closes the door behind us and throws a dead-bolt. It's dark. I can make out a small window set high on the oppo-site wall, but that's about it. Emmy disappears into the dark and then switches on a dim lamp.

Her room is about ten feet square. In the far corner there's a shower stall without plumbing. A couple of buckets filled with water and a basket overflowing with hotel shampoo, conditioner, body lotion and soap are on its floor. A low table next to it holds more bathroom supplies. Next to the table is a small refrigerator and on top of that a one-burner gas stove. There's a small chest of drawers next to it, with a few plates, glasses, bowls and cups on top.

Emmy's bed, a thin mattress on the floor, is across the room, squeezed against the wall with a large chest of drawers at one end and a full length mirror illuminated at the edges with photos of fam-ily and friends at the other. Clothes hang from pegs in the wall next to it. A wooden crate serves as a bedside table. On it there's another lamp, a clock radio and a romance novel with a lurid cover. It's hot and stuffy until the rotating fan in the middle of the floor starts to move the air around, and then it's only hot.

She's right. I don't like it. I wouldn't want to live here. But a young Indonesian woman who wants to live by herself doesn't have much choice.

Emmy straightens after picking some clothes up off the floor. I'm still standing by the door, taking inventory.

"Small room, you no like. Want *cha*?"

"Sure, I'd like some tea. It's not so bad; at least it's your own."

"House family, two sister, mother, same bed."

She points at her bed and I sit on it. Emmy busies herself making tea, brings me a cup and sits down next to me to drink hers.

"You good heart, nice man, why trouble?"

"I don't know. I didn't think it was going to be trouble. It's my job. And I've got some personal reasons for it. What about you, your life? Don't you ever want something different, something new?"

"What I do? Poor Indonesia girl *harus* work, need money. Give money family, maybe little sister go university. Maybe someday me find good husband, no like Mr. Germany, but good man. Now, me okay, no problem."

We talk for a while. Emmy went to high school but had to quit when she was fifteen to go to work. She's paid about a dollar a day and meals working at the hotel, plus the occasional tip. It would almost be enough to eke by on if she wasn't also sending money home to help support her two younger sisters. So sometimes she goes with men for money. But only with men who treat her nice and who she thinks are at least okay looking. One night with a visiting foreigner can make her more than a month of working in the hotel. When she likes someone, she just takes money from him the first time.

"I no good prostitute. Fall love too easy." She drops her eyes to the floor when she says it. She looks sad and I want to comfort her.

But what am I supposed to say? No, no really, Emmy, don't say that, you're a great prostitute. I can't think of anything to say. I just put an arm around her.

And I'm beat. She wants to fuck but I'm too tired. It's all I can do to undress with her help. I don't usually fall asleep so fast. In the middle of the night she tries not to wake me up as she pulls me into her. There's no way to sleep through it. But I can't really wake up for it, either. Maybe she needs it. Maybe it makes her feel wanted. We have slow, groggy sex and I fall back to sleep still inside her.

Emmy set the alarm to get us up, so that I can meet Iris at eight. I get dressed and while she's down the hall in the bathroom I sneak a hundred thousand *rupiah* into her top dresser drawer. I think we're at the point that if she catches me doing it she'll be insulted, so I bury it deep, hoping that by the time she finds it, it'll simply be a welcome windfall.

CHAPTER **SEVENTEEN**

It's already hot and humid, blasts of exhaust and noise belching from commuters' two-stroke engined motorbikes and *bajaj* when I emerge from Emmy's place. She tried to convince me to get a ride from a friend of her's with a motorbike, but I want to clear my head with a walk.

In Indonesia, like most poor countries, there's so much street life that walking's one of the best ways to get to know the place; even if you do feel like you need a shower when you get where you're going.

This time of the morning the streets are lined with breakfast *warung*. I want coffee, but I want a good one and there just isn't any to be had. Most people who can afford to will drink Nescafé instant thickened with large amounts of sweetened condensed milk. Occasionally I'll drink it too, but I can't bring myself to think of it as coffee. I think of it as something else that I call "coffee drink." It isn't what I want.

Away from the tourist hotspots in Indonesia, a strolling foreigner is a rare sight. I begin to gather the usual pack of kids crying out "Hey meester." People on the benches at the *warung* reach out to me, inviting me to stop for something to eat or drink. I smile, nod, reply "*selamat pagi*," good morning, to everyone and keep moving like a local dignitary on parade.

I get to the hotel a little before eight. Iris is waiting in the lobby. She smiles and shakes her head when I come in.

"You walked? You Americans are crazy."

"Good to see you too. I need a shower and a change of clothes."

She waits in the coffee shop while I get someone from housekeeping to check out my room before I go up to it. It's still a mess, but at least there isn't anyone in it. I tip the shocked room boy ten thousand *rupiah* for the big cleanup that's going to have to come later. I'm back in the coffee shop in about fifteen minutes.

"You did stay at Emmy's. That was smart."

"Yeah. Maybe you shouldn't come with me today. It's getting dangerous and it's not your business. I feel terrible about having got you into that situation yesterday. I don't know what they planned to do with us, but I doubt they wanted to make friends."

"Why? What's going on?"

I tell her. She doesn't like it. "When I was in school in the U.S., people used to say horrible things about how corrupt and bad Indonesia is. I do not like it when they are right."

"Hey, remember, these bad guys are foreigners, *bule*."

She smiles at my use of the derogatory word for white people. "But they would not do this in a developed country. The police would stop them."

"Who knows? Maybe they would, maybe they wouldn't. Maybe the bribes would just be bigger. I'm gonna try and stop them, but it's my fight, not yours. I don't want you mixed up in it."

She thinks it over for a little while, picking at her plate of *nasi goring*.

"No, I'm going to help. Driving the shuttle is boring. These are bad men. It is my country. When it is finished you will help me get my job back, or help me find a better one."

She looks determined. I don't want to fight with her. For one thing, I'm not sure it's a fight I can win. I also might need her help. So I give in.

"Okay, but don't say I didn't warn you."

We take a taxi to the Motex compound. Iris goes to see how much trouble she's in with the motor pool for losing one of its cars. I head to my old office and wait around, shuffling papers in the heat. An hour later she picks me up in the same Land Rover as the day before. It's freshly washed, so bright in the sun that I have a hard time looking at it without my sunglasses.

"Where'd you get this?"

"Marco, the motor pool man, said it was parked in front when he got there this morning. He thought I left it."

"That's interesting. Someone's trying to cover our tracks."

"What?"

"They must've figured the company would think we'd returned the car. So if we're missing they wouldn't bother trying to figure out where we'd driven to before returning it."

"Maybe I shouldn't hang around with you."

"Told you so."

"Let's go."

"Where?"

"Santo's. Someone there will know something."

"How do you know Santo's?"

"Everybody knows Santo's."

The massage parlor is back in business in a large tent where the charred rubble's been cleared away. The old lady is hard at work with her cigarette, spatula and big burnt wok full of ashy fried noodles. There are a couple of foreign men at the picnic table, sipping a mid-morning beer. And Santo's there, in the pit, working on the under-carriage of an old Mercedes that looks like it's half made of rust.

Our shadows fall across him as we walk up. He pokes his head out from below to see who's there. Iris swaps a few sentences with him, then turns to me.

"You have to give him money."

"What for?"

"Information, he won't say anything for free."

I take out a twenty thousand *rupiah* note. Santo grins up at me, his teeth bright yellow in his oil-stained face, and holds up two fingers. I don't have two twenties; so I pull a fifty thousand out of my wallet, the one with President Suharto on one side and a Garuda Airlines 747 on the other, and fork it over. He nods at me and resumes talking with Iris.

When they finish I look at her and wait.

"He says there is no gold, everybody knows it."

"Even I know that, what else?"

"An Australian man and a man from France are paying a lot of money to villagers to dig holes, but they tell them to be quiet about what they are doing."

"Yeah, we found that out yesterday. I'm beginning to think I just wasted my money."

"He says he has heard there was an accident. A man, a foreigner, fell out of a helicopter into the forest."

"What man?"

"All he knows is that it was a foreigner and they are looking for the body."

"Where'd he hear that?"

"Those men over there were talking about it. They didn't know he understands some English."

"Okay then, I guess we'd better go talk to those guys."

I buy three bottles of beer from the old lady, then walk over to the picnic table to talk with the guys. Iris hangs back, making small talk with Santo.

I jiggle the bottles of beer at the two men. "I'm Ray Sharp. I'm working with Motex. Mind if I sit down?"

"If you're buying, no sweat."

I set the bottles down and size up my company. The man who spoke is American, or maybe Canadian. He's bland looking; brown hair, brown eyes, mid-brown complexion and brown clothes. He's too ordinary to peg. He might be a middle manager, a consultant, anything really. He looks tired.

The other guy grunts his assent and tilts his beer bottle in my direction when I sit down. He's thin, almost emaciated, with long hair the color of dusty tomatoes and stringy as limp vermicelli. His very sharp nose is burnt red to match the hair.

"You guys with Lucky Break?"

"Consultants," says Bland.

"Not for long," says Red.

"Oh yeah, problems?"

Red does most of the talking. "You mean like no gold? I guess they figured hiring us would make this scam look legit, but it's a waste of their money and our time."

"What kind of consulting do you guys do?"

"Environmental mostly, we're engineers."

"Lucky Break's planning to file an impact report?"

"No choice, even here. But I don't know why they're bothering with us. It's just the paperwork. No one reads it except maybe a few environmentalists. The government doesn't care so long as it's submitted with the right fees. They might as well just make it up."

"So what's the deal? Everyone knows it's a scam, what do they think they're doing?"

"No matter to those guys, they've already cashed in. I don't think they were trying to scam anyone here, just the stock markets, and that's already worked out fine."

I make a note to ask someone how Lucky Break ever managed to get listed in Sydney. Vancouver's no surprise; I've heard things. But I thought Australia was stricter than that. Maybe it isn't.

"So now they're trying to get out?"

"Looks like it."

"You guys hear anything about anything else?"

They look at each other. Bland looks away. Red leans toward me and lowers his voice. "Are you asking about somebody having an accident, like maybe falling out of a chopper?"

Maybe this is going to be worth the fifty thousand I gave Santo after all. "I've heard some talk. Do you guys know anything more about it?"

"Not much, just some talk."

"Any idea who it was?"

"One of their guys I think, maybe an analyst. A young guy. They didn't like him nosing around. They're still looking for the body."

"Where?"

"Hell if I know. Out there somewhere. It's jungle, could be anywhere."

"How do you just fall out of a helicopter?"

Bland looks at me, raises his eyebrows and finally speaks up, but low, so it's hard to hear. "That's the funny part, ain't it?"

"Not so funny maybe."

"You didn't hear any of this from us. We're out of here tomorrow."

I offer to buy them a couple more beers but they turn me down. They need to tie up some loose ends before they can get out. I walk back to Iris and we go to the car.

"What did they tell you?"

"This is uglier than I thought. Dangerous too. I think the guy I'm looking for is dead. It sounds like it might be him. And I think the guys who locked us in that shed are the ones who did it."

"What?"

"How?"

"I think they shoved him out of a helicopter. The body's in the jungle somewhere."

Iris looks at me and doesn't say anything. She gets into the car, starts it and turns on the radio. The Motex station is playing country-western, something keening and forlorn. I get in and put on my seat belt.

"Where to now, Boss Man?"

"Damned if I know. I've got to think about what to do next."

"Back to the compound?"

"Yeah, I guess. Let's go get some lunch and figure this out."

The dining hall at Motex is segregated by habit and taste buds. There're two cafeteria lines, one on the right as you enter for Western food and the other on the left for Indonesian. The right side is always loud and crowded with big oilmen piling their plates high with steak and potatoes. The left is quiet and orderly by comparison.

Iris looks surprised when I head for the left side. I'm the only non-Indonesian in line.

"Hey, Boss Man, why aren't you over there with all the other *bule*?"

"You're a smart ass. Isn't there some polite way of calling me a white guy?"

She smiles and slaps on her fake heavy accent. "You crazy white man, Boss Man, eat rice, eat chili."

The simple truth is that the Indonesian food is better, fresher, more carefully prepared. The oil guys'll eat pretty much anything so long as there's a lot of it, it's mostly beef and it goes well with ketchup. Local tastes are more discerning.

To the amusement of Iris and the other Indonesians around us I pile my plate with rice, vegetables, river fish, chicken and a lot of the spiciest of the fresh made chili condiment. We sit down at one of the few tables for two and fill our faces for a few minutes in silence before speaking.

"Boss Man."

"Iris, could you please just call me Ray? What's with this damn 'boss man' thing anyhow? I'm not your boss anymore."

She smiles and shrugs. "Okay, Ray, it is not my business, I should not say anything, but maybe you should stop this. It is dangerous. It isn't worth it."

"You're not very Indonesian. Aren't nice Indonesian girls supposed to be quiet and subservient and not have any opinions?"

"You can meet my older sister. But really, I worry. This is very bad. You told me you are doing this for your wife, so now you can tell her what you have found and you can be finished."

"For one thing, I'm not sure it was Alex who got shoved out of the helicopter. It's also my job. I'm supposed to write up as complete a report as I can and I don't have everything I need yet. If the Lucky Break guys murdered someone, I've got to be able to prove it and put it in the report.

"And there's something else. It'll probably sound stupid to you." She skewers me with a look saying, I can hardly wait to hear this. "I don't want these bastards to get away with it. Maybe there's some little old lady in Canada or Australia who bought stock in Lucky Break who's getting screwed by these guys. It's probably too late and why the hell is a little old lady buying stock in anything other than a blue chip anyhow, but maybe that's the way it is and maybe there's something I can do about it."

Iris looks at me like I've lost my mind. It's not the first time I've deserved a look like that. She moves her chair back a few inches from the table as if to avoid contamination while I lean forward and rant at her. I'm talking loud and fast, not at all like a polite Indonesian.

I tone it down. "Sorry. I didn't mean to blow up like that. I'm nervous and scared and tired. I can come up with a lot of reasons why I need to stick to this and a lot why I shouldn't. The fact is, it's mostly personal at this point.

"These guys had me beat up. They locked you and me in that shed and I don't know what they were planning to do with us but it wasn't good. One of those little old ladies isn't a little old lady at all, she's a friend of mine in Jakarta who can't afford to be cheated out of her money. The whole thing's made me mad, really mad, and I can't just let it drop. And I'm excited by it. Which is probably fucked up of me, but take it or leave it, that's the bottom line."

She edges her chair back closer to the table and puts a hand out as if to take hold of mine. "What will you do?"

"I'm not sure. Finish what I've started. You shouldn't be involved. I'll drive myself."

"Forget it. I am in this too and you need me. Your Indonesian is bad and I can talk to people who won't talk to you. What do we do next?"

"First, I've got to figure out who the hell to talk to. I don't think LeClerc or any of the Aussies are gonna tell me who they tossed out of a helicopter."

"Do you think it was the man you are looking for?"

"Maybe. From what I know of him, there's a lot of people who'd be happy to push him out of a helicopter."

"There is a small village in the forest close to where they took us. It is where the people live who are working in that field. We can go there. I can talk to people."

"How do we get there without the Lucky Break guys finding out?"

"We'll go early tomorrow morning. Bring bug spray."

CHAPTER **EIGHTEEN**

They don't make enough bug spray. The insects come at us in all shapes and sizes. I tuck my long pants into my socks, roll down my long sleeves and wrap myself in a thin cotton blanket. I sweat profusely the whole trip.

And none of it does me any good. The constant buzzing around my ears is maddening. The smaller beasts simply find ways to slip past my defenses. The larger ones skewer me right through the protective layers of fabric. I'm in a very foul mood when we pull the small motor launch up to some rocks about a half-mile upriver from the field in which the villagers were digging.

The teenage pilot of the boat wants his money when we get there. I give him half, hoping it will keep him in place until we return. We'd left Marinda a little after dawn and he is pleased at the prospect of snoozing through the hottest part of the day. Iris lights out on a small path through the woods and I follow.

The forest quickly folds in around us, shutting out most of the daylight. If it gets any darker we'll need flashlights. There isn't much underfoot other than a thin layer of slippery, dark gray-green moss. Nothing else can grow in the gloom. The trees are fat and tall, covered in lighter, glossy-green moss and long strands of creeper vines. There's an incessant chatter of insects, birds and probably some monkeys but I can't see any animals. The path is narrow, muddy at times; in places thin tree trunks and branches are laid across gullies, small streams and permanent puddles.

I'm startled at one point by a rustling in the bushes nearby but nothing jumps out. Iris stops suddenly and points ahead at what looks like a bright green stick. She stomps one of her feet and it slithers out of our way.

I'm terrified of snakes. I've never liked walking in the woods. It makes me nervous. Stick me in the most crime-ridden, dangerous urban neighborhood in the world and I'll blithely go about my business without much concern. Ten minutes alone in the woods, and I'm on the verge of panic. I'm just stupid that way.

We've been walking for about ten minutes when a slow, rolling *whomp whomp whomp* noise overhead comes at us from the front, passes over us and then recedes in the direction of the river. It sounds like a large helicopter blade rotating at slow speed before takeoff or the engine of a coal-fired train just before it picks up steam.

Iris and I pause to listen to it. I've never heard the sound before, but I know what it is from descriptions. It's a bird, a hornbill. As the creature beats its wings it causes an air sac to inflate and deflate making a noise that can be heard for a long distance. I strain my neck upwards to see through the jungle canopy, but it's too dense.

Another ten minutes further along the path the forest opens into a small, cultivated field. There's a vegetable patch, a patchwork of rice paddies, some corn, pineapples and a grove of small papaya trees weighted down with fruit. A scarecrow and a young boy watch over it. The scarecrow is dressed in a tattered batik sarong and a tie-dyed Grateful Dead t-shirt. The boy is wearing dirty white jockey shorts and flicking at a small puddle with a long stick. He doesn't notice us until we are within a few yards of him.

When he does look up he stares for a moment before turning

and running away, yelling something in a language other than Indonesian. We follow, walking in the direction he ran.

The path disappears into what looks like an impenetrable wall of foliage on the other side of the clearing, but we manage to find the narrow gap where it breaks through. Just a hundred feet or so back through the forest we come to the village.

We stop before we get to the first house, to give the people who live there a chance to look us over before we walk right in. It's the polite thing to do. The houses are simple rattan-mat and thatched-roof huts with wood support posts. I look for signs of anyone from Lucky Break, although I'm not sure what I'll do if I see them.

As always, the kids show up first, shy and tentative. Then once they achieve some kind of critical mass they make a beeline straight for me, shouting, "Hey meester!" I hadn't thought to bring any pens, pencils or candy, so I don't have anything with which to buy them off.

Before long a toothless, stooped old woman, her mouth bright red from chewing betel nut, shuffles out to greet us and shoosh the kids. She doesn't speak Indonesian but one of the older kids, a boy of maybe ten, translates for Iris.

Most of the younger people in the village have gone to find work in the city, or are at work in the mining field nearby. Some of them will be home for lunch in the middle of the day and we can talk with them then. The old woman invites us to her house for tea, and to wait in the shade.

She boils water in a large tin pot over an open fire in front of the door to her small hut. Her husband left many years before to find work, and never returned. Her daughter married a man in another village. Her son went to Jakarta to find work several years ago and has also never come back. She's the only person in the village who lives alone.

The old woman scratches out a meager living by making *jamu*. She forages in the woods for roots, fungus and herbs that she boils and bottles. When she was younger she'd wrap her bottles and packets of potions and powders into a sarong, hoist the bundle onto her back and travel to the city to sell them. She was beautiful then and made good money. Men like to buy their *jamu*, particularly the kind that's good for virility, from attractive women. Now that she's older she sells her medicines to younger women who take them to town.

The old woman makes us tea from viscous strands of what looks like dark brown clothes-dryer lint. She says it will help keep us cool and make our blood taste bad to mosquitoes. It's intensely bitter. If I was a mosquito and somebody's blood tasted like this, I wouldn't want to drink it either. It takes a lot of effort to avoid grimacing with every sip.

Like many poor village people, hospitality is a point of pride with her. She offers us betel nut to chew, which we decline, and some cold boiled peanuts that do help take the taste of the tea out of my mouth, but leave a lot of grit stuck in my teeth. About an hour creeps by before people begin to filter back into the village from the fields.

We recognize the woman who had helped us get the boat after we escaped from the shed. She looks startled when she sees us, and ducks quickly into her house. Iris asks our ten-year-old translator if he'll ask her if we can talk.

He comes back and says that if we wait for a little while he'll take us to meet her. She's afraid to have strangers in her house.

The old woman offers more tea. I'd stupidly forgotten my Indonesian manners and gagged down the entire first cup. That's considered a demand for more. I should have left some at the bottom so that my hostess could choose whether to offer more or be satisfied that I'd had enough.

I ask for water instead and she hands me a steaming cup from the pot. I scald my lips then set it down to wait for it to cool. By the time it's cool enough to drink, the boy comes to get us.

He leads the way behind the huts through a small grove of trees and down a short incline to some large rocks by a stream. Laundry is laid out on the rocks to dry, and a young woman dressed in a bathing sarong is soaping up in an eddy just offshore. We sit down in the shade and the woman we want to talk with steps out from behind some trees.

She looks up and down the river as if crossing a busy highway and approaches cautiously, ready to run away if anything at all spooks her. She squats on her calves in front of us in the way that Southeast Asians do so easily. I've tried it and can't do it. I just topple over. I'm envious.

She speaks softly in Indonesian. She and Iris tilt their heads close together. I can't hear what they're saying. The woman makes quick, nervous glances in my direction. I move away and sit on a rock.

About ten minutes later Iris comes over and asks if I have some money that she can give the woman. She hasn't asked for any, but she's taken a risk talking with us and Iris thinks we should give her something. I give her a ten thousand *rupiah* note.

At first the woman refuses the money, but Iris presses it on her, insisting that it isn't for her, but for her children. She accepts it and then shyly, with her eyes turned down at the ground, turns to me and says, "Thank you," in carefully enunciated English, before turning and walking swiftly back into the trees.

I look at Iris. "Well?"

"Big trouble. Everyone in the village is afraid. They heard about the man falling out of the helicopter and two village men were taken away in a truck a week ago. They have not come back."

"Why were the village men taken?"

"They were complaining that they weren't paid enough to dig in the dirt and that there wasn't anything there. They were asking a lot of questions and talking about going to Marinda."

"Who took them?"

"Two *bule*. I think the men from Australia."

"Did she say anything about the field, about the mines? Are they finding anything? Are they just supposed to keep digging forever?"

"She said the *bule* tell them only one more week of digging, then they will go away. The foreigners come to the field every day and warn them not to talk to anyone or they will have trouble. They also tell them to watch for strangers and to tell them if they see any."

"I guess the bad guys know we're here."

"Maybe not yet, but they will."

"She know anything more about the guy falling out of the chopper?"

"She heard that it was over the river, near the field. Some of the men from the village have been looking for the body, but they haven't found it."

"I guess we'd better get out of here while we can."

"I won't say no, Boss Man."

We avoid the village on the way back to the river and keep quiet on the path, carefully rounding bends so there'll be no surprises. The teenager is asleep in the boat. When we step aboard he wakes up instantly, with no more difficulty or surprise than if he'd just been resting his eyes.

There are about five hours of daylight left so I have the boat take it slow, zigzagging between the banks of the river. I don't really think there's much chance of coming across Alex's body, but it makes me feel like I'm doing something.

As we approach the mining site I have the driver shut off the motor and stick close to the far side of the river. I don't want anyone seeing us go past in case word has got out and they're watching.

It doesn't work.

Hal and the big goon who'd threatened me in River Village are tying a boat up to the small dock by the field when we drift past. For a moment I think they might be looking onshore rather than back at the river. The moment doesn't last any longer than that. The big guy spots us, yells something and points. Hal lifts a pair of binoculars from around his neck. I would wave and smile if I wasn't scared.

The two men clamber back into their boat and start it up with a cough that builds to a roar. Iris yells at the teenager to start our boat and get out of there as fast as he can, but it's a sick joke. Our little motor launch doesn't stand a chance.

He does get it started with one pull of the cord. The motor catches and quickly shifts from a dull putt-putt to a high-pitched whine that sounds something like a blender on the liquefy setting. But the speedboat is already exploding in our direction. We can't outrun it.

The only advantage we've got is that our boat is a lot smaller, lighter and has a much shallower draft. A bare trickle of a stream enters the river just ahead. If we can get to it ahead of the other boat, it's possible that they won't be able to follow.

A gunshot gets my attention. I look back. Hal's piloting the speedboat and the big guy's steadying a rifle. I yell at Iris and the kid to get as low as they can. Luckily the big guy's either a lousy shot or they're bouncing too much. If we stop or they slow down and their boat stops rocking, he'll be able to take proper aim.

We get to the mouth of the stream with them no more than a hundred feet behind. The sound of our motor takes on the frightening rattle of a blender straining to crush ice cubes as we crash over a small shoal of pebbles at the entrance to the stream. It's narrow and overgrown. Nipa fronds slash at us and slow the boat. The motor almost dies as its shaft comes up into the air, but then the stream deepens just enough that the rotor blades catch hold of a lifesaving few inches of water. The kid throttles forward to about puree and we motor steadily upstream.

The speedboat's close, but we're on the other side of a screen of tropical plants. Our pursuers pull up near shore but can't get any closer without running their boat aground. Their engine's roar dwindles to a hoarse, throaty chug. They keep firing shots in our direction. The big guy apparently has a good sense of sound-guided direction because several of his shots slice through the fronds and into the water closer to us than I'd like.

We round a slight curve in the stream and I gesture for the kid to throttle down to barely enough speed to keep us moving. Our motor still sounds as loud to me as the thumping of my heart, but I'm hoping it's low enough to blend with the background noise of the forest.

I have no idea if Hal and the big guy will come ashore to hunt. It doesn't make any sense to stick around and find out. The stream meanders and if there is any sort of relatively straight path through the jungle it's likely to cross our route in a number of places. We'll be an easy target.

As we continue upstream, the jungle gathers around us as dense as a thick coastal fog, and the air is even thicker than that. We all pour sweat. I'm too mindlessly frightened and insensate to even notice the bugs. It's noisy with birds. Caimans slide into the water at our approach. The boat bumps over something that I want to think is a log but the kid's convinced is a python. I know it's not rational but snakes terrify me even more than big guys with guns.

Iris and the kid whisper back and forth. She isn't talking to me. She'll hardly even look at me. I try thinking up a plan, but can't come up with anything other than to keep moving.

We putter upstream for about a half hour until it narrows even further, then disappears into a small cave in a low embankment. We tie the launch to a tree and Iris and I get up onto a small open patch of grass above where the stream went to ground.

I look around and don't see anything resembling a trail. I listen and can't hear anything human other than our own breathing. Chances are that Hal and the big guy are waiting us out, sitting in their boat, figuring we won't get anywhere and will have to come back out the way we went in.

I sit down to think. Iris sits next to me and puts a hand on one of mine. "What now, Ray?"

"I'm not sure. I'm thinking. Unless you or he knows some other way back to Marinda, we're going to have to go back to the river sometime. We can't just stay here."

"I'm scared. This isn't good."

"Me too. I'm sorry I got you into this."

She puts her head on my shoulder and I put my arm around her. The heat and stress have leached all the energy out of me. I'm not frightened enough to keep from dozing off.

CHAPTER **NINETEEN**

I wake up choking. Something is squeezing my chest so that I can't breathe. I try to flail my arms but they're pinned. My head is swollen, near to bursting. I can just open my eyes into narrow slits and it's hard to see through the red haze.

I'm fighting for breath, sucking in air like I need to get the last dregs of a really thick milk shake through a thin straw. But every time I inflate my lungs I have to deflate them before long and the squeezing gets worse. My ribs are being bent to the cracking point.

Something tight and moist is clamped onto the top of my head like a too-small hat on a hot and humid day. I start to go numb, begin to slip back into unconsciousness and it's a relief.

It might be seconds, minutes, hours or days later that I swim back into wakefulness. The pressure is gone, replaced by a dull ache in my chest and a terrible headache. It's dark and I can't see anything other than vague shapes. Someone's shaking me and whispering urgently.

"Ray, Ray, get up, Ray. What's going on? Where are we? Ray Ray, ya gotta get up, ya gotta help us, Ray."

The voice is familiar, the urgency isn't. It's Sylvia. She always sounds so cool and calm. It isn't like her to sound frantic.

I can barely hear her over a *whomp whomp whomp* coming from above us. Whatever I'm lying on is hard, metallic with little ridges like corrugated steel. Everything's vibrating in rhythm with the sound from overhead.

My eyes adjust to the dark but it doesn't matter, there isn't anything to see. Maybe we're in a room. There aren't any details. There's only a faint dark gray vertical rectangle a few feet to my left, but it looks no less solid than anything else around us.

"Ray, you've gotta get us out of here, Ray. Help me. Do something. Ray."

It isn't nice, but I take some small pleasure in Sylvia's panic. "Let me think dammit, let me think. I'll figure something out."

The sound above is steady, pulsing at about the same rate as the blood in my veins. The vibration's decreased, or I've gotten used to it.

"Ray, Ray, you've gotta do something, Ray, you've gotta." Sylvia wraps her arms around me and clings tight. Too tight. She squeezes and her arms grow longer, wrapping all around my torso several times. She squeezes harder and I can't breathe again. I can't get any words out to tell her to get off. My chest is caving in again.

I start rocking my body to dislodge her. We roll back and forth and tumble into the faint rectangle. It's a door and we dump out of it. We're falling through the air. Slow at first, then we pick up speed. It's so bright that now I can't see anything other than hot white light. I'm gasping, sucking air again, back where I started. The *whomp whomp whomp* is still loud, but receding as we fall away from it.

We flip over and over as we fall and I catch glimpses of green below us. The jungle is coming up fast. Sylvia is screaming my name and constricting me so that I can't scream back.

The green looms larger, closer, a beautiful deep shade that doesn't look all that bad as a place to land. But I'm being crushed worse than ever. My heart's humming, it's beating so fast, and moving up my chest as if it's being choked into my throat.

"Ray, Ray, Boss Man wake up, wake up." It's a softer voice, a nicer voice and as I hear it the pressure eases off my chest, my breathing slows. I open my eyes; slowly wobble my head to clear it and look up at the concerned face of Iris. She's looking down at me and shaking my shoulder. My whole body is slimy with sweat and I'm shivering. But then I wake up fast, alert.

There's still the *whomp whomp whomp*, but it's high above me. I look up and can just make out a flock of birds overhead in the dimly glowing light. They have great long red beaks and enormous bright white and yellow tail feathers, the wings are large and flat, maybe three feet long and beating in a steady, slow rhythm. There's a large swelling just under the wings that puffs in and out in time with the flapping. At least a dozen of them are passing overhead at a leisurely pace.

"You were asleep, dreaming. Maybe a bad dream."

"Yeah, I had malaria. Sometimes it's that. Sometimes it's just a dream. How long've we been here?"

"It's almost dark. What should we do?"

"I don't think we ought to stay here for the night. Maybe we should go back down the stream quietly and see if they're still there. If they aren't we might be able to make it down the river in the dark."

The kid doesn't like the idea of piloting the boat back downstream in the dark and then floating blind downriver to Marinda. But he hates the thought of spending the night in the jungle even worse. He figures we can do it if we take it easy. We paddle, rather than motor, down the stream. The channel is narrow but the water is slow and largely free of rocks or snags. Once we get to the river we'll have no choice but to use the motor, and at night in the forest sound carries. We'll have to risk it.

The only drama as we drift downstream is provided by the swarms of insects that swirl in a tornado around us the whole way. There's the occasional crashing sound of animals in the trees around us, but none so large or close by as to cause any concern. Once night falls we can't see a thing. We have a flashlight and a kerosene lantern but use them sparingly; we need to conserve them for the trip downriver.

We stop the boat just short of where the stream enters the river. I get out and move as quietly as I can through the foliage to where I can see whether or not anyone is watching for us. I don't see any-body, but there are places that they might be hiding. I go back to our boat.

"I don't see anything, but I think we ought to wait another hour or two before going out there."

"You're the boss, Boss Man."

"Ray, remember?"

"Right, just don't get us killed."

Iris whispers to the kid. He covers his head with a dirty rag and curls into a ball where he sits at the back of the boat. Iris moves around so that she can sit between my legs and lean back on me. I'm not sure what to do, if anything. I owe her at least some comfort after what she's been through. I drape my arms over her and we sit silently, listening, thinking, offering ourselves up as a buffet for the bugs.

It's oddly peaceful, almost pleasant. My mind wanders. I while away the time in a reverie of disjointed thought. I don't want to think about anything important if I can help it. Recollections of baseball games when I was a kid keep me occupied for a little while.

After that I start thinking about what in the hell I'm doing here, in this wretched little boat, hiding in the jungle from people who are trying to kill me. All I was supposed to do was find Alex and tell Sylvia where he is, and file a report on the gold find for the bank in Hong Kong. I'm pretty certain I know where Alex is, or at least what happened to him. I can tell Sylvia what I found out, let her cry on my shoulder if that's what it takes. I've almost got enough for my report. I don't have any real proof, no papers, no smoking gun. But it's probably enough to satisfy the client. I can go back to Marinda. Take the next flight back to Jakarta. Head back to Hong Kong and be done with it. That'd be the smart thing to do.

But then there's the whole other thing nagging me. I've stum-bled across a scam, a big one. There are innocent people getting screwed. Irina's one of them. There's been a murder. At least one. I know who the bad guys are. I ought to be doing something. But I'm no cop. What the hell am I supposed to do?

The police are probably in on it, or at least bought off, so it's not a good idea to take it to them. The army is certainly part of it, or at least making money off it. Is there anyone to take it to at Motex? The oil company's in bed with the bad guys and maybe they don't even know it. Or maybe they do and don't care. Oil companies aren't known for their scruples.

Lucky Break is getting ready to cut and run. They'll be gone in a week, or sooner. They've already made their killing in the market. I don't know what the stock is doing now. Maybe word's got out and it's already taken a dive. I have to make sure Irina sold her shares. I hope it's not already too late.

And I don't want LeClerc and his guys to get away with it. Not after what they've done to me, or tried to do to me and Iris. I'm not the kind of guy who wants to be a hero. But I watch out for myself and my friends, and sometimes that puts me on the right side of things.

I'm no smarter after mulling it all over, so I poke Iris in the ribs, tap the kid on a foot and tell them we need to get going.

We drag the boat as quietly as possible over the rocks at the mouth of the stream. Without the motor on we don't make a lot of noise. We pause for a little, listening carefully and looking out across the water. There's a light on the small pier. It might be the other boat. It isn't bright enough for anyone to see us at that distance.

The river's current is strong and fast in the middle. We'll hug the shore and avoid using the motor until the river turns and we have more trees and bank between us and the other boat. There's just the one paddle and our skiff is a little too wide to maneuver like a canoe, but the kid does the best he can. Iris and I try to help out with our hands in the water, but it isn't very effective and there are caimans around. Neither of us wants to lose a hand or some fingers to a hungry reptile.

The night's clear and the half-moon high. Once we're out of the trees, we have almost enough light to see where we're going. We can't risk using the flashlight or the lantern in sight of the dock across the river.

We edge along, close to shore, hitting a couple of logs and once getting stuck in some reeds. We're maybe a hundred yards downriver when the engine on the big speedboat roars to life. A bright spotlight flashes on and sweeps the water as the boat heads in our direction.

A large stand of Nipa palm hangs over the river just ahead of us. We maneuver our little boat into the thick of it, hoping for cover.

The speedboat picks up its pace, coming across the river not far above our hiding place. The searchlight thrusts ahead of it, threatening to pick us out. The three of us hunker further down into our boat, hoping to make ourselves invisible. The kid's wearing a dark green t-shirt. Iris and I are in light khaki; we'd heard that bugs like it less than dark colors. You couldn't prove it by me, and we're regretting it now.

I reach up and pull several large fronds down in front of us. The other boat approaches the shore, right around the mouth of the stream. The scorching light sears the fringe of the jungle.

The speedboat moves in as close as it can to the bank, throttles down low and starts cruising slowly in our direction, the spotlight cutting through the dark like a laser. We push and pull our small boat as far back into the fronds as we can, all three of us trying to hold big leaves down in front of us while at the same time keeping the boat from drifting back out into the river. I look around, trying to figure out where to go if they spot us, but it's no good. We're trapped.

"I'm sorry." I whisper to Iris. She holds my eyes with hers and nods.

The speedboat is going to pass no more than about twenty feet away. All we can do is hope that the foliage is dense enough, that the metal of our boat is dull enough, and that our clothes blend well enough into the background. I hold my breath when I feel the heat of the spotlight on me.

A picture of a cheeseburger idling stiff and dull under a heat lamp in a coffee shop passes through my head. I have to stifle a laugh. I'm hungry and growing punchy with nerves. Maybe I'm losing my mind.

I can't see the speedboat. I don't know if that's because I'm blinded by the searchlight or if it's hidden by the leaves that are hiding us. I take brief comfort thinking, If I can't see them, they can't see us, right? But then my brain follows that with, Says the blind man, and my heart skips a couple of beats. The speedboat isn't that big, but time has slowed. It's taking as long as a supertanker to pass.

Finally it does pass. We let the fronds part, but stay put, not moving, waiting to see if they're going to come back. We can hear the big engine chugging along for another ten minutes or so as it continues slowly down the river. Then the sound cranks up and we pull the fronds back down in case they're turning around for another look.

But instead, the rumble of the speedboat dies off as it moves away in the direction of Marinda. We wait until we can't hear it at all, then cautiously ease the nose of our launch out from behind the green screen.

The moon dimly lights the river, the line of trees on the far bank are scarcely visible. A sheet of stars drapes the sky. We sit still, listening carefully and looking for lights but can't see or hear anything more of the speedboat. After maybe ten more minutes we shove back into the current, paddling to keep the boat straight, afraid to start the engine.

We hug the bank where the current's gentle and cover is available. For another hour we let the river wash us downstream. By then we figure it's safe and the kid yanks the cord to get the motor going. He moves our skiff into the strong current in the center of the river and we make good time back to Marinda.

CHAPTER **TWENTY**

It's about two in the morning when the kid lets us off at the dock closest to the hotel. He disappears down the riverbank after I give him more money than we agreed on. He'd shot me a look that said we both knew it still wasn't enough. There isn't any sign of the speedboat; it must have docked somewhere else.

Iris and I walk up to the riverfront road and stand between a couple of darkened *warung*. "What now, Boss Man?"

She looks like she's hoping I won't come up with anything, and I don't. "I've got you into enough shit for one day. Go home. Sleep. Try and forget all this."

"What are you going to do?"

"I don't know. I'll think of something. Don't worry about it. Just go home."

She decides it's too late to go to her place, so I walk with her to find a *bajaj* to take her to Emmy's. She vanishes down the street in a cloud of thick black exhaust.

Going back to the hotel isn't a good idea. There's a neon glow coming from a side street. I follow the light. Maybe there'll be another hotel I can check into for a few hours.

Halfway down the block a blue and white sign reads, *"O.K. Panti pijat."* Massage parlors that are open this late and also offer karaoke are accustomed to customers spending the night. A bell rings when I push open the door.

The conditioned air is cool and refreshing. There's a water cooler and I'm on my third cup when a small man in a brown suit comes out through a door behind the reception desk. He speaks halting English with a Korean accent.

American and European companies contract with Korean companies to make shoes, clothing, small electrical components and a lot of other stuff. The Koreans often farm the business out overseas. It's a lot cheaper to hire Indonesians than it is to build factories in Korea. I'm not sure where massage parlors fit into that, but it's not unusual to find Korean-run ones in Indonesia, even in small cities.

I could do with a massage. I'm aching, stiff, all jacked up, something to help me relax is not at all a bad idea.

"One hour massage. Then can I sleep here?"

"Of course. Thirty thousand. Please to wait one minute. You happy, Miss Kim give very good massage."

The rich odor of baby powder and mineral oil wraps around me like a favorite old blanket. A faint note of sharp, sweet incense tickles me as I glide down the corridor. A large, thick Korean woman firmly holds my hand and pulls me along. From the curtained cubicles we're passing comes a *thwop, thwop, thwop* sound of gentle fists on flesh and the sweet music of grunts and groans.

I heard somewhere that everyone in Korea is named Kim, except for a few Parks. I hope Kim'll be gentle. I've had enough pain.

She shows me to an empty cubicle with a narrow massage table and a chair, tells me to take off my clothes and indicates that she'll be back. I don't know how naked she wants me, so I leave my shorts on. The room is spare, dimly lit, decorated with last year's 1995 Mitsubishi Forestry Products calendar and a framed picture of some mountains in Korea. There's a small cupboard on top of which are a bottle of mineral oil, a pink plastic container of talc, a jar of skin moisturizer and a gaudy floral print box of tissues. Country-western music tinkles into the room from a small crackly speaker high up on the wall. Tammy Wynette warbles "Stand By Your Man." An overhead fan churns the air making a light *pfft, pfft, pfft.*

Kim comes back with an armload of towels. She looks me up and down and smiles. She plucks at my shorts. "Take off." She motions for me to lie on a towel on the table. The towel gives off the scent of fresh warm oatmeal. It must be the laundry soap they use. I lie down and let my muscles go as slack as they can.

My face fits snug into the hole at the end of the table. It's bigger than the holes usually are; my head is trapped deep into it. But it's strangely comforting. I roll my eyes in their sockets and I can see the bottom of two table legs, a discarded tissue that looks like it might have been used to wipe off lipstick, and the green-flecked linoleum floor. I can hear the muffled country-western music, the *thwop, thwop, thwop* and the *pfft, pfft, pfft* and occasional crackles of Korean chatter from the other rooms. I'm lulled and dozy. Kim says, "Oil or powder?" I go for the oil.

It's cold and I tense briefly when she squirts it on my back. As she begins rubbing it in, it warms. I relax and drift away.

After a while Kim climbs onto my upper thighs, squatting over me on the table and putting considerable weight into kneading my muscles. I'm thinking of telling her to ease up, but as the heat from the friction of her hands seeps into me, I settle into it and add my own voice to the soft chorus of content.

She works her body down my legs and her hands down my back, occasionally pausing to squirt a little more oil. She digs her fingers into my butt, grinding it in slow deep circles into the table.

Her strong fingers and palms mash down the back of my thighs, onto the back of my knees, calves and finally down to my feet where her knuckles on my soles connect directly to other parts of my body. She takes hold of my toes, one by one, and cracks them, like you would crack your knuckles, with a swift motion.

Kim moves back up my body and squirts more oil on my legs and butt. Her fingers trail lightly up to the bottom of my ass. She brushes me there and gently snakes a greasy hand up underneath me.

She bends over, her lips headed for my right ear to ask in a whisper if I want anything else. I lift my face slightly from the hole in the table and catch a strong whiff of garlic and pickled cabbage on her breath. But with her hand on me I don't care. To anyone else watching, and probably to Kim, the moment must play like farce. But to me, in the state I'm growing into, it's ripe with intimacy and anticipation.

Three loud, sharp explosions snap me out of it. There's a thud, like a hammer hitting a piece of meat. Kim gasps, and before I can move, falls with all her weight onto me, pressing my head uncomfortably deep into the small hole in the massage table.

My eyes open wide and bounce wildly around the limited field of vision. One of Kim's hands is dangling off the table to the left; it's speckled with blood.

I try pushing my head back out of the hole and my body off the table, but my head is stuck. My hands can't find leverage anywhere. Her dead weight holds me in place.

It sounds like a war's breaking loose in the hallway. The machine guns don't make a noise like "chatter" at all. They're too loud, too harsh, more like the screaming of enraged pre-schoolers than the pitter-patter of conversation. There's shouting but I can't make out any words. There's the splatter of bare feet on linoleum running in all directions.

A boom erupts just outside my cubicle. It claps my ears and deafens me. A body falls into my vision, the shoulder and upper arm tangled into the curtain that closed off the doorway. Rolling my eyes up as far as they'll go, I can just make out a gun, still grasped by an unmoving hand. Part of the arm is barely in reach of my right hand. I tug on the sleeve, trying to get the gun.

My hearing starts to come back. There's still the soft country-western music. Somehow the *pfft, pfft, pfft* of the fan has grown louder and blended with an engorged *whomp, whomp, whomp* of blood pulsing through my heart, swelling through my veins and arteries and breaking in waves against my temples. There's a faint *splishing* from the left where Kim's blood drips to the floor. I can hear feeble groans that aren't so very different from the ones I was hearing just a few moments ago. In the distance are sirens.

I hear footsteps and they're coming my way, slow, cautious. The scrape of metal rings on metal bars moves toward me, down the hall as the curtains in front of the cubicles are flung open. Twice, just after that sound, I hear shots. Someone's coming. They're getting rid of survivors.

As the footsteps approach, I frantically yank at the arm, trying to pull the gun to me. The footsteps are getting closer as I wrest the gun from the rubbery, cooling hand that holds it. I wrap my palm around the grip, put a finger on the trigger and wait.

I don't know who the hell I'm going to be able to shoot with it anyhow. If someone walks right up to the end of the massage table I'll be able to see their shoes. What good does that do me? If it's brown wing tips, shoot them in the foot?

There's a screech of cars outside, a crash that might be a door caving in, unintelligible shouts, the high harsh fuzztone of walkie talkies. The footsteps that were coming down the hall stop, then run past my cubicle. There're more shouts, a crackle of shots; a *thunk*, *splat* and *ching* of bullets hitting something soft, maybe a piece of wood and something else hard like metal. Then more shouts. And then it's quiet while the air swirls with the crisp mineral reek of gunpowder.

I'm still waiting, the gun's grip tight in my hand, the barrel pointed at the door. A sharp voice barks out, *"Polis."* Then the cops wait for a response. There's a few groans from down the hall, but no words I can understand.

I'm trying to figure out if I ought to shout something when I hear footsteps stop outside my cubicle. I can't see anything. Should I start shooting? Wave the gun around? Drop it? The decision is taken out of my hands, literally, when a baton cracks down on my wrist, forcing me to drop the gun.

I hold my hands up, spreading my fingers to indicate surrender. A voice calls out something that sounds like "lieutenant."

There's shuffling and muttering and then a pair of highly polished, black military-style shoes appear a few feet in front of me.

"Apa ini?"

I gather I'm the "this" the voice is asking about.

I'd better make friends. Before anyone else can speak up, I answer for them. "*Saya bule bodoh lain.*" Once they get over a moment of shock, it cracks them all up. And why wouldn't it? They're standing there looking at a naked guy trapped underneath a fat, dead Korean woman and he's telling them that he's just another stupid white man. Who wouldn't laugh at that? I'd be laughing myself if I wasn't the butt of the joke.

When the laughter dies down, a voice, the lieutenant's presumably, cracks out a command. Kim's body is lifted off me and my body creaks and moans as it makes the big effort to sit up. The lieutenant issues another command and a young cop steps past me to the pile of towels on the chair, then hands me a small face towel.

Three other cops are also crowded into the room. They all break out laughing again. The lieutenant begins to, but catches himself and barks at the young cop, who then gets me a full-sized towel. The lieutenant snaps again and it sends everyone other than him and me scurrying out of the room.

He looks young for the job, maybe in his early thirties, tall for an Indonesian. And he's rugged, movie-star handsome. He picks up the remaining towels on the chair and moves them to the end of the massage table so he can sit down across from me.

His eyes, which are a little lighter than usual for someone with his complexion, fix me in a stare. The look on his face is neutral. He hasn't decided what to make of me or what to do with me.

He asks if I speak Indonesian. I tell him I prefer to speak in English. I don't want to risk his misunderstanding anything I say and my Indonesian isn't all that good. He speaks carefully, slow, but in surprisingly good English for a cop.

"I am Detective Lieutenant Arsiyanto. Who are you? What are you doing here?"

I look over at the body of Miss Kim, lying on the floor where it fell when the cops shoved it off me. Arsiyanto catches the look.

"Do not concern yourself with her. Her body must stay until the forensic team will finish."

This isn't the place and time I'd choose to answer anybody's questions, but I don't have much choice.

"I'm Ray Sharp. I'm a corporate investigator from Hong Kong. I'm here doing a job that involves Motex. I wanted a massage."

"It is rather late for a massage, isn't it, Mr. Sharp?"

"I was up late, couldn't sleep, thought it would relax me. Guess I was wrong."

"Yes, I think it was not a very relaxing massage, Mr. Sharp. You have been spending time in the forest. Is that necessary for your investigation?"

"The forest? What makes you think that, Lieutenant?"

"You have provided sustenance for many insects, Mr. Sharp. They are not so hungry here in the city."

He's right. Anyone would have to be blind to miss all the small, red, swollen spots on my body. But I don't know if it's a good idea to let him know what I've been up to. Cops in Indonesia are horribly underpaid. It's hard to blame them when they're corrupt. I don't know whose side he's on. I don't want to lie, in case he catches me at it, but there's only so much of the truth I want to give him.

"My investigation has to do with the gold discovery that was made on Motex's land. I've spent some time out in the field where they're mining."

"I have heard something about this, Mr. Sharp. There are many suspicions. We have been asked to help look for a young man who had the misfortune to fall from a helicopter. Perhaps you can tell me more, Mr. Sharp."

"I'd like to, Lieutenant. But so far I don't know any more about that than you do."

"What do you know about the incident here tonight, Mr. Sharp?"

"Why? Do you think it's got something to do with Motex and the gold?"

"I did not say that, Mr. Sharp. Why would you think so? Perhaps you do know something I do not know."

Maybe it did have something to do with me. Maybe word got back to Hal and the big guy that I was here and they barged in and shot up the place looking for me. Maybe I'm just being paranoid. After all, Santo's was burned down. Maybe there's some sort of massage parlor war going on.

"I doubt it, Lieutenant. I'm pretty sure you know as much as I do. But unless I get the say so from my boss and our clients, I can't discuss my investigation with you."

"Okay, Mr. Sharp. Let us put that aside for now. Please tell me what you can, everything you can, about what happened here after you arrived tonight."

I tell him, but it doesn't help him much and he's not happy.

"If there were any other people here who were alive when we came, Mr. Sharp, they have all run away. Are you certain that you don't recall anything more than that? You saw nothing?"

"Stick your head in the hole in this table, Lieutenant, and tell me what you can see. That's what I saw, nothing more."

"What can you tell me about this woman?" He gestures toward the fast cooling body of Miss Kim.

"Not much. She gives—gave—a great massage. They told me her name was Kim."

"The women who work here must be licensed by the police, Mr. Sharp. They are all called Kim. There is a Chinese massage parlor on the next street. There, they are all named Lee."

"I should have gone to that one instead. You have any ideas why this place got shot up?"

He cracks a smile; a warm, slightly wry, verging on friendly one. "There are many possible reasons. But I think I shall not discuss my investigation with you if my boss does not tell me to do so, Mr. Sharp."

I smile back. "Fair enough, Lieutenant. But I have told you everything I know about what happened here. Can I go now?"

"You may put on your clothes now, Mr. Sharp. Then please, go to the reception and wait. There will be forms and the other investigators may wish to ask you more questions."

CHAPTER **TWENTY-ONE**

I t's nine in the morning before the cops cut me loose with a warning to keep in touch. I'd bought a bowl of instant noodles from a vendor who passed by the front door, and managed to doze a little on the sofa in the waiting room, but I'm still a wreck. It's probably safe to go back to my hotel room, at least long enough for a shower and a change of clothes. I tip a bellboy to go into the room first. I tell him to look in the closets and under the bed. The boogey man's not there.

The message light's blinking on the phone. There're two from Emmy the night before, wondering where I am. There's one that morning from Iris. She wants to meet at my old Motex office around noon.

Iris is sitting at the desk when I get there. She's drinking tea and talking with her ex-colleagues. They all grow quiet and give me funny looks when I walk in.

"Hey, Boss Man, we were just talking about you."

"Oh, anything I want to know about?"

"No, but now they think you're some kind of great detective."

"Just what I need." I caution them all to keep quiet about what I'm doing, but I know they won't. Before long every Indonesian in the company will know about it, although it's a toss-up as to whether or not word will get around to the foreigners.

I take the whole group to the commissary for lunch. After that, Iris walks with me back to the office.

"Ray, do you think you can get me my job back?"

"It's not that great a job—you can do better, you're smart."

"Maybe in Jakarta, maybe in America; there isn't anything better here."

"I've got to go back to Jakarta tomorrow. You want me to ask around and see if there's anything for you there?"

"I don't know. I don't know what my family would do."

"If you get a better job you can send them money."

"I know, but..."

"No buts about it, you're too smart to stick around here. You'll end up marrying some dull local guy, have a bunch of babies and that'll be that."

"Well, you can ask. Maybe there will be something good."

"I will. But now I've got to figure out what to do about this Lucky Break thing. I could just forget about it. That would be the smart thing to do."

"Yes, but I don't think you will."

"Why not?"

"You like this. You like playing detective. You were bored when you worked for Motex."

"You're right. But I keep telling myself it's stupid. How'd you get so smart?"

"I no smart, meester, only poor Indonesia girl."

"Just can it with the phony accent will ya? But what do I do next?"

"They have not found the body?"

"I don't think so, not yet."

"How do you know it is the man you are looking for?"

"I can't think of who else it would be. Nobody liked him. He knew too much. From what I've heard almost anyone who ever met him would have been happy to shove him out of a helicopter."

"Maybe it was not him."

"Maybe not, but if it's not, then where is he?"

"Maybe he is hiding."

"Maybe. The question is, from who? If he's in on it then why would he be hiding from them? But then who else would have tossed him out of one of Lucky Break's helicopters? But if he is in on it, why would they want to kill him?"

"Too many maybes. Maybe you are not so great a detective."

"Maybe not, but I'm gonna figure this out."

"Okay, what do we do now?"

"We don't do anything. I'm not going to let you take any more risks over this. For the time being just get back to your work. If I need anything more from you I'll let you know."

She starts to argue with me, but it's obvious to the both of us that her heart's not in it.

I close myself into the office and call Emmy to ask her to get my stuff out of my room in the hotel and change me to another room under a different name. I don't know if that'll do any good, but it's better than nothing. Then I busy myself working on my report.

I haven't checked in for a while, so I call Bill Warner, my boss in Hong Kong.

"Ray, what the hell're you doing? I'm getting calls. Except from you of course."

"What sort of calls?"

"From Motex. I'm told you're being a nuisance, you're getting in the way of the Lucky Break guys."

"Who called, Bill? It might be important."

"Suryanto, from Motex security."

"That's very interesting. I must be doing something right then. I'm flushing the bad guys out of hiding. The whole thing's a scam."

"What whole thing?"

"There's no gold. It's a fraud, mostly a stock fraud. There's been at least one person killed that I know of, probably a couple more. It looks like Lucky Break's about to pull up stakes and get away."

"Have you got proof?"

"Not exactly, not yet. But don't let our clients sink any money into this. Stall 'em if you have to."

"I can do that, but sooner or later they're gonna want proof."

"They won't need it. It'll break in the press before too long. That'll be enough to scare them off."

"Is that going to be your doing?"

"Yeah, mostly. I need to tie a few things up, nail down some facts. I'll let you know before it breaks so you can warn the client."

"Okay, stay out of trouble."

"I'm already in trouble."

"Need any help? I can send Lei Yue."

Wen Lei Yue's my friend and colleague. She'd been shot a couple of months before when working with me on a case in Cambodia.

"How's she doing?"

"It takes a while to get over getting shot. She's tough though, on the mend. Fighting mad, if the truth be known. Anxious to get back in the world and beat the bad guys."

"That's not surprising."

"Really though, Ray, I can send her down there to help you out."

"Driving you a bit nuts, is she?"

"Yeah, a bit."

"Nah. Things are coming to a head. By the time she got down here and up to speed, it might already be over with. Don't worry about it."

"You have a bad habit of getting in trouble, Ray. I do worry about it."

"Hell, Bill, for an ex-spook you worry too much." Warner used to be a C.I.A. operative before he quit to start his own corporate investigations firm.

"Truth, justice and the American way was more abstract. And it wasn't running on my dime. Take care of yourself."

I'm about to say something about how I didn't know he cared, but he hangs up before I get the chance.

Suryanto is the head of external security for Motex in Marinda. He works with the local police and the army. I don't know him, other than by sight and sound.

You can hear him coming from miles away. He drives a huge, supercharged, candy-apple-red Toyota pickup truck that rides ludi-

crously high above the ground. To get down from it he's perfected a
jaunty little leap. He tries not to let anyone see him climb back in.
He could use a ladder. That doesn't fit with the image he wants. He
likes needlessly revving the engine and never looks at anyone except
through a pair of highway-patrol-style, mirrored Ray Bans. So far as
I know, he's about average on the local corruption scale. There are a
few things, I think, he won't do for money.

His office is across the road and I heard him pull up to it a little while ago. I decide to pay him a visit. I can hear someone shouting when I'm halfway across the street. It stops as soon as I open the
door. When I walk into the small bungalow Suryanto's standing at
the front desk leaning over the receptionist. He looks up and
smooths the look of annoyance on his face into a tight smile. I suppose he's hoping I didn't notice the effort it took.

"Mr. Sharp, I have heard that you have returned in another
employment."

"Mr. Suryanto, can we talk in your office?"

"Of course, please."

He sweeps open the swinging door in the counter and gestures
me toward the back.

His office is freezing. He's another true believer in the healthful
properties of air-conditioning. The largest window unit I've ever
seen blows gale force Arctic winds into the room. It's impossible to
see out the windows; they're covered with condensation on the outside and what looks like a thin layer of frost on the inside. Suryanto
sits behind his desk. I sit in front of it in a wooden armchair that
must have been deliberately engineered for discomfort. He notices
me shivering.

"I enjoy the fresh, clean air, Mr. Sharp."

"Cut the crap, Suryanto. What've you got to do with Lucky
Break?"

"You Americans are so direct. How do you say, rude. I understand that you are now detective. That can be dangerous game."

"What do you know about a man falling out of a helicopter?"

"A terrible accident, I understand. They look body, but tigers,
animals, maybe no body." He shrugs.

"Do you know who it was?"

"I not know. *Bule,* I think."

"He was pushed."

"Maybe you tell police."

"They're in on it, so are you. You like your job here, you like your big noisy red truck? You could lose all that if the company finds out you're mixed up in this."

"You no frighten me, Mr. Sharp. Maybe you be frighten? Be careful, Mr. Sharp. Too easy have accident here. I work now. You go."

He picks up the phone on his desk and rapid fires something in a nasty tone to the receptionist. I get up to leave. As I walk past the front desk the woman catches my eye and holds a hand out to me. I put mine out and she slips a folded piece of paper into it.

I don't open it until I get back to my office. It's the name of a hotel in Jakarta, the Jayapura, and a room number, 710, nothing more. What the hell does this mean? Does Suryanto want me to go there? Is it a clumsy trap? Is it a clue? His receptionist probably hates him, almost everybody does. Maybe she's trying to tell me something to get back at him. A great detective would know. I don't.

I'm still puzzling over it when I hear the roar of Suryanto's truck, the crash of his gears and the screech of his tires. I get to the window in time to see him flip a fast u-turn, narrowly missing a maintenance cart, and tear away in the direction of the main road.

CHAPTER **TWENTY-TWO**

The company shuttle drops me at the hotel. Suryanto's truck is parked prominently in front. I grease the doorman's palm with five grand and ask him to get Emmy to meet me around the back, by the service entrance. I don't want any of the Lucky Break guys to see me come into the hotel.

Emmy's gotten me a suite, with as commanding a view of the town as it's possible to have, and a bathroom as big as my old hotel room.

"Emmy this is great, but my company won't approve the price."

"Same same, no worry. Now you Mr. Smith, okay?"

"No problem, that's great. Thanks."

I tell her that I want to take a shower. We can meet in the restaurant upstairs for dinner in about an hour. She says she's finished work for the day and would rather just wait for me.

My hair's foaming with shampoo and my eyes are closed when the shower curtain pulls open. For a moment I panic, thinking they've found out where I am. But then I feel someone smooth and friendly rub against me.

"You need relax. I help shower."

She reaches around me for the soap and I rinse my hair as she lathers my back. She turns me around to lather the front as well and before long the soap falls from her hand as we slip and slide all over each other. It's a little bit of work, trying to balance, but it does relieve a lot of stress.

We get dressed for dinner. Emmy says she wants to take me somewhere different, so we leave the hotel by the service elevator and the back entrance and take the long way around to the riverfront. We stop at a large *warung.* Twinkling Christmas tree lights and long fluorescent tubes outline garish paintings on a canvas of huge bug-eyed fish and crustaceans. Red plastic tables and chairs line the sidewalk in front of it.

I sit down and drink a beer while Emmy goes to look over the menu. Dinner's swimming and burbling in tanks behind the canvas. She works out our meal with the cook and comes back smiling with an orange Fanta for herself.

"Best food here. Cheap. Chinese man good cooking."

I put my hand on top of hers. "Thanks for ordering. I am very relaxed now."

She smiles and squeezes my hand. I move my chair closer to hers and we lean comfortably against each other, not talking, while we drink and savor the faintly sour breeze off the river.

There is, of course, way too much to eat. If we could consume everything brought to the table, Emmy would feel like she'd fallen down on the job, that she hadn't ordered enough. I do my best to eat as much as I can, but make sure to leave some on my plate.

First come fresh *krupuk,* almost too hot to pick up with our fingers, and a couple of sauces to dip them in. Then a *lalap,* a salad of lightly boiled and raw vegetables with a bowl of blisteringly spicy chili sauce to dip them into. Then steaming bowls of *sayur asam,* a vegetable stew astringent with tamarind. Then large plates of rice surrounded with pieces of fried chicken, peanuts mixed with anchovies and chilies, potatoes with a light curry sauce, small shrimp quick fried with green beans that are known as "stink beans" because they make your sweat smell bad, and long green beans cooked with slivers of fried tofu. On top of the rice we each get two enormous, grilled fresh-water river shrimp. They're the size of small lobsters, charred on the outside and slathered with a tart green lime and bright red chili sauce. They burst with a loud snap when we bite into them.

I wash as much of it down with beer as I can. It's hot and humid like always, and when the sweat soaking my shirt becomes obvious, the waitress points one of the electric fans directly at me. I undo a couple of buttons and sit back, cooling. I'm sated, bloated, happy to have eaten it all and relieved to be done.

But then they bring out the fish. A huge, whole, steamed river fish smothered in green onions and thinly sliced pieces of ginger, redolent with lime juice, fresh coriander and Chinese rice wine. The cook himself has brought it out, gently and proudly setting it down before me. Emmy beams, her eyes sparkling, and with a fork and spoon hacks off a large chunk to put on my plate. With chopsticks she digs out one of its bulging cheeks, the juiciest, most flavorful morsel. It's usually offered to an honored guest. She holds it to my mouth, feeding me.

I doubt there's anywhere I can put it, but I know I have to try. So I take the bite and it's delicious, the best part of the whole meal. Emmy and the cook grin crazily and laugh. I can only eat so much though, and they're disappointed with how little it is.

The whole meal for the two of us, including several beers and orange Fantas, comes to a bit over fifteen thousand *rupiah*, around seven and a half U.S. dollars. I try to pay, but Emmy won't let me. It's her treat, a matter of pride that she can. As I slump in food induced lethargy in my plastic chair, I wonder why anyone would live anywhere else than Indonesia.

I still feel like I can't move when Emmy wants to go dancing. She teases me into lumbering out of my chair. I wobble to my feet and it takes a few moments to gain a solid footing. Hoping to speed along digestion, I insist that we walk first. We hold hands and stroll quietly and slowly along the waterfront.

At night along the water's edge the odors of the jungle and the town intermingle. A dank stench of organic decay rises from the jungle flotsam that's drifted downstream and caught up on shore. A sharp reek of rot wafts from the jetsam that's been tossed from town into the water. But that's just a small part of an overall symphony of smells that includes the sweet notes of orchids and clove cigarettes, incense, brewing coffee and frying garlic, and the faint wisp of perfume that clings like a thin fog to Emmy's lightly perspiring skin.

Dangdut lows softly from radios and boom boxes in the numerous *warung* we walk past. Soft voices greet us, just enough dim light guides us along the walkway. There's life all around, a lot of it, but it wraps around us gently, delicately rather than intruding on us. There're times when everything in this country is romantic, seductive.

And that's dangerous. Every foreigner I know is always falling in love with something, or someone, and later on, feeling jilted. One moment you love the place and it can do no wrong. The next you hate it for betraying you. Whole days pass where both emotions flicker on and off in your head and leave you reeling in confusion.

Tonight is one of those love-fest moments. I'm not in love with Emmy but she's included in the upwelling of emotion that's going on inside me. Maybe I'm just tired, worn out, defenseless. I keep my mouth shut for fear of saying something stupid. I know what she wants. She wants a foreigner, a kind one with some money, to fall in love with her and take her away from her life. She wants a good, easy life with a nice man and some babies. I hope she finds it. I'm not him.

We walk for about a half hour then go back to the hotel. Suryanto's truck is gone. As we approach the front door, a shiny black, new Toyota sedan pulls up and the big thug with the little voice gets out. He smiles at me in a way that is neither comforting nor friendly as he walks around the car to open the rear passenger-side door. Emmy and I pause to see who he's picking up.

Tony LeClerc and Hal walk out, their heads knitted together in conversation. They stop when they see me. LeClerc motions Hal into the car and then steps over to me.

"Monsieur Sharp, you are not yet returned to Jakarta."

"Nope, not yet. You're still here too."

"To finish my business, but I think you have no more business here."

"My business is both here and in Jakarta."

"Perhaps then we will meet again." He gets into the car. The big guy, who's been standing by the door, slams it shut and then knocks into me with a brick-solid shoulder when he walks past to get to the driver's side. I'm beginning to really hate polite conversations that mean something else.

Emmy and I go inside and downstairs to the disco where we join Tommy. He's sitting in a booth with two girls. Emmy makes a point of putting herself between them and me, parking a hand possessively on my shoulder. I've noticed the two of them before; they apparently work as a team. I sit and nurse my vodka, slumping further and further into my seat while I watch the four of them take turns dancing with each other.

It's not all that late when Emmy and I sneak to the service elevator and take it up to Mr. Smith's suite. Once I lie down I'm too tired to move. Emmy doesn't mind, she can move enough for the both of us.

The next morning, I'm packing, Emmy's pouting. "I have to go, Emmy, but I'll be back. I'll call and let you know when."

I try to give her money but she won't take it. I press it on her, telling her that I want to buy her a gift but I don't have the time, so she should go shopping for something nice. She accepts it then. It's all part of the pretense that she's not a hooker and I'm not a john. And maybe she isn't, and maybe I'm not. Who can say? I'm not a mind reader, but I'm pretty sure she doesn't think I'm paying her for sex. I'm not sure what I think.

CHAPTER **TWENTY-THREE**

Back in Jakarta I call Ben and ask him to meet me for lunch. I call Sylvia and leave a message for her to meet me at B.A.T.S. after work. I try calling Irina but can't find her and I try Annie's wireless phone but it isn't turned on.

Ben wants to meet at the American Club. I can't figure out what he likes about the place. Sure, the food's cheap, but it should be, it's lousy. I don't care if I get real American potato chips with my thin, greasy burger or not. The café overlooks the Olympic-sized swimming pool. Children of embassy employees, oil execs and financial services expats splash noisily, watched over by anxious young village-girl nannies. The expat-moms sit in their klatches under umbrellas, gossiping and swilling day-glo colored cocktails. The café has a big screen TV that shows programs and sporting events I wouldn't even watch back in the States. Maybe I'd show up to watch the World Series once a year. I do miss baseball.

When I get there Ben's transfixed by a college football game. A half-drunk watery Budweiser's in front of him along with a bowl of fresh roasted, hot, salty peanuts, which are the only thing I like about the place. I take a handful of the peanuts and sit down.

"Who's winning?"

"Some state or another. Don't ask me which one."

"Why do you bother?"

"I dunno, gotta do something to feel like I'm still a Yank."

"You're not drinking Bud are you?"

"It's the American Club, it's part of the deal."

"Not for me, I'll stick to Bintang."

"Suit yourself. How's the detecting biz?"

"I'm pretty sure Sylvia's Alex is dead. Shoved out of a helicopter."

"Nasty way to go."

"Nasty guy from what I hear."

"Still."

"Yeah. I have some idea who did it, but I don't know what to do with that."

"Tell it to the cops."

"Yeah, right. Up there, they're probably in on it."

"Let it drop then. You've got enough to get Sylvia off your back don't you? What about the due diligence?"

"I've almost got enough for that too; not totally nailed down with proof, but getting there. I feel like I need to see this thing through."

"Don't tell me you're back on your white horse. You've always suffered from that. Who's the girl?"

"Huh?"

"You know, the love interest? Every time you get into trouble there's a girl involved."

"Hey, you're one to talk, Mr. Do Gooder Environmentalist Guy. How's Juli?"

"She's good. Worried about you. She's seen that Russian babe of yours a couple of times."

"Irina? I guess she's the love interest. Some broker got her into Lucky Break shares."

"Not too many, I hope. I saw in the *Journal* this morning that the stock tanked. They suspended trading."

"Shit, when was that?"

"Yesterday, in both Vancouver and Sydney."

"I told her to sell a few days ago. I hope she did."

"Lotta shares?"

"Yeah, too many. I think she sank most of her money into it."

"I hate it when people do that. Hasn't she ever heard of not putting all her eggs in one basket? Or hadn't your conversations got that mundane yet?"

"What, like your's and Juli's? What's she think of Irina, anyhow?"

"Thinks she's a good kid; fucked up, but a good kid. Sort of like you. She figures you're a good match."

"She's not such a kid. Irina's packed a lot into her years."

"Whatever she is, Juli likes her. Just treat her good and you'll keep Juli happy too."

I pick up the menu and try to look serious. "What's good today?"

"You kidding? I'm having the usual."

Ben always has spaghetti with meat sauce and a near frozen salad of iceberg lettuce and cabbage. It's barely edible. I have *nasi goring*.

"You can get that shit anywhere. Why have it here?"

"Because I can get it anywhere. At least they know what they're doing."

"Your stomach."

We eat lunch, drink a few more beers and make small talk. There's not a lot I can do about anything this afternoon, so I go back to the house, read for a little while, then take a nap before going to meet Sylvia.

She's usually late, but not by this much. After two hours it's a sure thing she isn't coming. I nurse an overpriced drink and watch the place fill up with the after-work crowd. I fend off a few models looking for someone to buy them an expensive dinner they won't eat. Finally, I walk up to a pretty-boy functionary from the Brazilian embassy. He's leaning two-thirds of the way into the impressive cleavage of an Australian PR woman who works for the local branch of a pulp and paper firm. He used to be one of Sylvia's boy toys.

"Sorry to bother you, but I'm supposed to meet Sylvia Franks here." She'd kept her own last name. "She hasn't shown up and I'm wondering if you've seen her."

He looks me over, trying to figure out if there's any trouble in this for him. His body tenses and leans away from me when he speaks, but I don't think he's lying.

"No, I have not seen her for the week."

Over his shoulder I see Sylvia's friend Maria walk in on the arm of another pretty boy, a tweedy and pale one from a British investment bank. I wait for her to settle at the bar and order a drink before I head over.

"Hey Maria, how are ya?"

"Ray." She doesn't bother to introduce the boy. She looks at me blankly.

"I'm supposed to meet Sylvia but she's a couple hours late."

"Is that late for Sylvia? Haven't seen her, but that's not unusual is it?"

"An hour maybe. Two's a bit much, even for her. I saw her a week ago, but then I was out of town."

"Didn't you talk to her to set up this meeting?"

"No, just left a message, but I've got some information she wants."

"Well, I don't know where she is. I guess it's been about a week since I saw her too. You're looking for Alex?"

"Yeah and I've got some news."

"Anything I ought to know?"

"I'd rather tell her first. If you hear from her, let her know I'm looking for her, will you?"

She nods and turns back to her companion.

I return to drinking and waiting. Over the next hour I ask a couple more friends of Sylvia if they've seen her, but no one has. That's strange. She's just too much of a social butterfly to stay out of the scene for more than a day or two if she's in town, and no one's heard anything about her taking a trip.

Maria and the boy toy are still at the bar. She's thrown back a few drinks and is laughing too much and talking too loud. I barge in again.

"Maria, sorry to bother you again, but I've asked a few people if they've seen Sylvia. No one has. You have any idea where she's been staying? It's important."

"I told you I haven't seen her."

Maybe not, but there's something about the way she says it that makes me think she knows more than she's letting on.

"Come on, Maria, it really is important. I promise I won't let her know where I found out."

"I don't know if she'd want me to give you that information, Ray."

"Look, Maria, I don't want to be melodramatic, but her guy Alex was into some very bad stuff. It's possible she's in trouble. I want to make sure she's okay."

"Was?"

"Is, whatever."

"She's been at the Jayapura."

"Room 710?"

"How'd you know that? What's going on?"

"Never mind. Thanks, I'll let you know if anything's going on."

I walk away before she can ask any more questions, go outside and get a taxi to the Jayapura.

It's an odd choice for Sylvia. The Jayapura is well kept, but it's one of the older hotels in town. It's popular for large functions, like weddings, where middle class Indonesian families feel compelled to go into debt on an event but have to keep it within limits. The government owns a big chunk of it and the less glamorous ministries—mining and minerals, agriculture, education—throw their parties and meetings there. The hotel's guests mostly come from around Southeast Asia, either on business or package tours. Whenever we used to have to attend something in one of its three large ballrooms, Sylvia complained. Like most expats she prefers the modern, glitzy, international brand name, five-star hotels.

I take an elevator to the seventh floor. There's a "Do Not Disturb" sign hung on the knob of 710. I knock anyway. No one answers, which doesn't surprise me. I walk to the end of the hall where there's a small desk and a glum floor attendant who's outfitted in the native garb of one or another of the country's seventeen-thousand islands.

Labor's cheap in Indonesia, cheaper than most things. So companies hire a lot more people than they would if it was more expensive. Most hotel floors have their own full-time attendant. In the fancier places they call them a concierge. What they are is underpaid and bored, sitting around all shift long, hoping that there aren't any real problems to deal with and that there might be an opportunity for a tip. They've got passkeys.

Before I get to the desk I take a twenty thousand *rupiah* bill out of my wallet and fold it discreetly into my right hand so that it's visible to someone looking for it. When I speak to him the floor attendant's eyes aren't on mine, his gaze is fixed on my fingers.

I move my hand up to my face so that he'll look at me. *"Istri,"* I say, while rolling my eyes to indicate that there's some problem with my wife. *"Wanita gila."* He catches my drift. My wife's a crazy woman. We're both guys and we can relate.

I ask if he'll let me into the room. He says "yes" to my right hand. After he opens the door I give him the handshake he's been waiting for.

The room's a mess. The mattress has been overturned, there're clothes tossed everywhere and three emptied suitcases with their linings torn out. In the bathroom a toiletry bag has been ripped open and bottles, jars and tubes of all sorts are littered on the counter and floor. The sink is filled with water the color of blood, a stained towel hanging half out of it. The last thing I want to do is worry about Sylvia. It's looking like I've got to.

The floor attendant hadn't even looked into the room when he opened it. I take a peek down the hall. He's back at his station, twiddling his thumbs, hoping someone else will need something worth paying for. I bolt the door from the inside and start going over the room. I have no idea what I'm looking for. I hope I'll know what it is if I find it.

There are some monogrammed men's shirts on the floor with Sylvia's clothes. Unless she's been collecting guys with the same initials, they're Alex's. There're a lot of shoes. That's no clue. I'm surprised there aren't even more.

Nothing speaks to me, much less shouts. It doesn't even whisper. I'm on the verge of giving up when I remember something I used to do when I was a kid. There's a pad of hotel note paper by the phone. I hold the first sheet up to the light and see scratch marks. There's a pencil, so I rub the side of its point across the paper until I can make out what's been written on the page that was torn out before it.

"Ancol Wed 12 tents." It doesn't look like Sylvia's writing, but I think I know what it means. Ancol is a huge park along the Jakarta waterfront. I hope "Wed" is Wednesday, and that "12" is at night. There's a place in the park where there are a lot of small, concrete "tents." It's a well known trysting spot for lovers with nowhere else to go. If I'm right, someone's going to meet someone later tonight. I don't know where the blood in the sink fits in, but if I show up at the meeting I might get a little closer to finding out.

I make sure that the door locks behind me and that the "Do Not Disturb" sign is still in place. I've got a few hours before the meeting and I've got to figure out what to do about it. It might be dangerous. Should I bring someone to back me up? Who? My mind is racing, but mostly in circles. I go back to the house to change and get something to eat before heading to Ancol.

CHAPTER **TWENTY-FOUR**

I rina's there. I'd told her she could come over whenever she wanted and told Wazir to let her in. I'm happy to see her but I don't know if her being there is going to complicate things or not. We spend a long time kissing hello.

"Sorry I am here at your house, but you say it is okay. Is no problem?"

"No, no problem. I'm glad you're here. Have you sold your stock yet?"

"No, I still cannot talk with my friend. I will call again tomorrow."

I sit down next to her and take her hand. "Irina, it might be too late. The stock started going down, fast. They stopped trading in it."

She moves back a little from me, still clutching my hand, a little tighter than before. "What does that mean, Ray?"

"I'm not sure yet, but it isn't good. If the stock starts trading again you have to do anything you can to sell it right away, no matter what the price."

"Is my money gone, Ray?"

"I don't know, maybe. I hate to say it—probably. How much is it?"

"It is my savings, Ray. I send money to Russia, to my family, but it is all the money I keep myself. What can I do?"

I was afraid of that. Irina's shrewd when it comes to making money, conservative about saving it, but like too many people she's apparently not so smart about investing it.

"I don't know what you can do. I'll find out what I can. Even if you lose your money now, if these guys get caught they might have money stashed away that can be used to pay back the people they cheated, at least something, maybe."

"Now I have no money?"

"Irina, I don't know. I'll make some calls and see what I can find out. If you need money I can give you some."

"No, Ray. Before, I am poor. If I am poor again, I am okay. I will make more money and save again."

I don't like the ways I'm thinking that she'll do that. I'm about to start arguing with her when she covers my mouth with hers and kisses me long and hard. We break and she's right up against my face, nose to nose.

"No more talk about money, Ray. No more. I will take care of problem. I am waiting here for you. Happy to see you."

I start to say something and she closes my mouth with another kiss. She's an adult, it's her life. Tomorrow, when people are in their offices, I'll make some calls and see if I can find out anything to help her. Tonight, there're other things I've got to do. When we stop kissing, I change the subject.

"I had lunch with Ben today. He says you and Juli have become friends."

"Yes, I like her very much. She is a good, smart woman. But I think maybe he is a sad man. Maybe sometime there will be trouble with them."

That's not anything I want to talk about. I try not to speculate about my friends' relationships. I have enough trouble with my own.

"Maybe. You had dinner yet? I can see what Wazir's got."

"Already cooking."

"Great. I'm gonna take a shower and change. I've got to go back out again soon."

"I come with you?"

"It's nothing fun. It might even be dangerous. I don't want to get you in any trouble. Probably better if you don't come along."

"Tell me later. Go take shower."

I'm hoping Irina might join me in the shower, it might settle my nerves. But I don't ask and she doesn't.

Wazir's been cooking all day, ever since I called this morning and told him I'd be back. He's prepared a feast fit for a mid-sized dinner party. He's disappointed when I eat lightly, but I don't want to risk a food stupor at Ancol. While we eat I fill Irina in on the latest developments and tell her about the meeting later that night. If there is a meeting.

She insists on coming with me. She used to work at the nightclub in Ancol and she knows all the security men there. She wants us to go early. She wants to get one of her pals to keep an eye on me. It sounds like a good idea.

I don't know if I'm going to be lurking in the shadows, running around, confronting someone or what. I dress in dark, loose clothes and running shoes, and take a walking stick. Irina says she'll wait for me in the nightclub, so she puts on something slinky, sparkly, low cut and black. It makes me want to do the sensible thing and stay home to take my sweet time inching it off her. But I don't. We make an odd looking couple on the street hailing a cab.

Ancol is a sprawling complex. There are amusement park rides, an aquarium, an arts and crafts marketplace, several outdoor stages and indoor theaters, a golf course, sports fields, restaurants, campground, beaches, a nightclub/disco/massage parlor and the Hotel Horison that locals jokingly refer to as the "Horizontal." The park is popular with families during the day and dating couples—or single men looking for dates—at night.

We're dropped off at the nightclub entrance. Irina's called ahead to let the doorman know we're coming and he greets her with a big, very familiar hug. He looks at me over her shoulder and grins nervously. I smile and stick out a hand for him to shake.

Irina needs to talk with the head of security alone. While she does, one of the *mamasans* takes me under her wing for a tour. *Ibu* Mary is probably in her mid-forties and doesn't look much like a mother to me. She was clearly once a great beauty, but years of working in dark, smoky nightclubs and a long parade of too many men, too much booze, chain-smoking and most likely some bad breaks that I don't want to guess at, have whittled a sallow, prematurely-aged woman out of her. A white sequined dress drapes on her no differently than it would on a hanger in her closet. She folds my arm into hers and leads me into the club.

It's cavernous. Booths with deep sofas and low tables form a semi-circle around a gleaming hardwood dance floor. A disc jockey spins records on a large stage set with a drum kit, microphones and guitars. Waitresses in short, very tight Chinese style dresses scurry in and out of the curtained booths carrying bottles of booze, dishes of nuts and fruit platters. Several other *mamasans* ply their trade, leading short trains of hostesses to the customers for inspection. The hostesses are mostly Asian—Indonesian, Thai and Filipina—but there's a smattering of Western women as well, almost all blondes.

Just behind the stage is the fish bowl. It's large and brightly lit. Customers stand in the shadows on one side of the glass and window-shop the forty or fifty hostesses sitting on the other. The women are chatting, grooming, some play cards, some are watching a TV in the corner. They all have numbers pinned to their dresses. Irina used to sit in there. She says it wasn't so bad, but it doesn't look like much fun to me.

The *mamasan* asks if I see anyone I like. I tell her I'm there with Irina, maybe some other time. She takes me back to the front entrance where Irina's laughing with a couple of security men and another *mamasan*.

Irina throws an arm around me. "Good club, you like? Many beautiful girls. Come back later, we meet beautiful girl."

I wrap my arm around her. "It's tempting. I've gotta do this thing at midnight first. You find anyone to come along?"

"Yes, this is Wayan. He is a very good man in fight, strong." She punches a short but sturdy looking dark-skinned man on the shoulder. He laughs and sticks out a hand that's at least three sizes larger than it ought to be for his height. I slap mine into it and get the feeling he could twist it off at the wrist as easily as opening a slightly stuck jar. But it's just something I sense. He's being gentle, not doing anything to demonstrate his strength. His English is terrible, worse than my Indonesian.

"We go. Mans no see Wayan, no problem."

It's eleven-thirty. We need to get into position.

The concrete "tents" are clustered along a beach near the arts and crafts shops. There are bushes and trees that screen them from the road, so there are plenty of places to hide. We run a flirtatious gauntlet to get there.

At night the roadways that cut through Ancol are lined with prostitutes. Several hundred of them on big nights, never less than fifty or sixty. They come in all shapes, sizes and ages, and at the darker end of the park, a variety of sexes too. Most men cruise by in cars; gesturing to the women they want to come up for a closer inspection. When a deal is struck the woman gets into the car and the couple drive off to a nearby short-time hotel, or a shadowed place to park, or sometimes they use the small cluster of tents. It's cheap and popular.

It's rare for a couple of men, at least dressed like men, to be walking rather than driving in that part of the park at night. We cause a stir. We're approached by a pair of teenaged identical twins and by an elderly woman who removes her false teeth and makes sucking noises. I'm not tempted and I'll be happier if we can keep a lower profile.

As we get closer to the tents I hold a finger up to my lips and gesture at the women around us. Wayan takes a couple of them aside, whispers something to them, and passes them some money. After that they leave us alone. I thank him and get out my wallet to pay him back, but he waves me off.

It's about a quarter to twelve when we settle into some bushes that give us both the cover and the view that we need. I tell Wayan that I might go to meet whoever shows up, but that he should stay hidden unless it looks like there's going to be trouble. We crouch silently, waiting and watching.

A few minutes after midnight a man carrying a thin briefcase pads along the edge of the water up to the tents. He leans against one of the concrete domes and lights a cigarette. The match flares and it's Alex. I recognize him from the picture. No one shoved him out of a helicopter after all. This might complicate things. He was less trouble when he was dead. Now I've got to talk to him.

I'm about to break cover when I catch movement in the periphery of my left eye. Someone big but quiet is closing in from the trees behind Alex. Whoever it is keeps low and in the shadows. I stop, hoping to get a good look at him but he keeps dodging behind the low tent domes. I'm torn between warning Alex and waiting to see what happens. I've just about decided to shout when the big guy with the little voice, who'd beaten on me in River Village, rises to his feet behind the unaware, no-longer dead fiancé with the cigarette.

Before I manage to yell anything he takes a gun he's holding by the barrel and brings it down hard just behind Alex's right ear. Alex crumples without a sound, like someone's kicked his legs out from under him. The big guy grabs the briefcase and melts quickly back into the trees.

I look at Wayan, point to myself and to the crumpled heap that's on the sand next to the tent, then point at him and in the direction the big guy has gone. He catches my drift and takes off fast.

No one's seen the assault, or if they have they aren't paying attention. Walking past the tents I hear whispers, moans and groans, panting, but no one sticks a head out to see what's going on.

When I get to Alex, different kinds of moans and groans are coming from him. He rolls over onto his back and blinks his eyes up at me. I gently lift his head to view the damage. There's a little blood and he'll have a very sore lump, but it doesn't look like he needs a trip to the emergency room.

"Uh, um, wha happened?"

"You'll be okay, Alex, you got hit in the head with a gun butt."

"Uh, fuck, Jesus." He starts feeling the area around him. "My briefcase, what happened to my briefcase?"

"The guy who hit you got it. I've got someone following him."

"What, how, who are you? How do you know my name?"

"I'm Ray, Sylvia's husband. She asked me to find you."

"What's it to you?"

"I don't want to get into it. Good to see you're alive. I thought you'd been pushed out of a chopper."

"That was some other guy."

"Yeah, apparently. Let's get you out of here. I'd like to buy you a drink and ask some questions." He sits up and starts gingerly poking at the back of his head.

"Maybe I don't wanna talk."

I'm trying to work out how to respond to that when Wayan comes back. He's carrying the briefcase. His knuckles on top of the handle look scraped and a little bloody. Alex makes a grab for it. I shake a "no" at Wayan, who steps out of reach.

"You want your briefcase back, you're gonna talk to me."

"It's mine, you don't have any right to keep it. Tell him to give it to me."

"Nope. I'll trade it for some answers."

"You don't know what you're fucking with here."

"I think I've got a pretty good idea. Why don't I buy you that drink and we'll talk it over."

He grumbles but gets up, dusts himself off and follows Wayan and I back to the nightclub. I park the briefcase at the coat check and keep the tag. I ask Wayan to let Irina know where I am, then have a *mamasan* lead Alex and I to one of the curtained booths. She motions a waitress over who takes our drink orders. The *mamasan* asks if there are any particular girls we want to see. I ask her to let us have some privacy for a few minutes. I'll ring the buzzer that's hidden under the table if we want anything.

Alex drains his brandy as soon as the waitress comes back with it, and asks for another. I consider cautioning him to take it easy in case he's got a concussion. But I don't, because I don't really give a damn. He sits back on the sofa, laces his fingers on his lap and looks at me.

"Okay, so it's your party. Whaddaya want?"

"Who'd you think you were meeting?"

"None a your business."

"I'll find out soon as I pry open your case. You might as well tell me and save the lock."

"Fuck you."

"Look guy, I'm not trying to give you any grief. I think you're in over your head enough already. I just want to know what's going on. I'd like to know where Sylvia is, and maybe, just maybe I can be some help."

"Sylvia? What's up with Sylvia? Where'd that foolish bitch get herself off to now?"

"I thought you were her fiancé?"

"Yeah, right. Is that what she told you? Maybe I told her that. I can't remember. I can't exactly take bargirls to social events can I? Sylvia looks good for her age, she's smart, she can even be charming sometimes. She gives great head, but you'd know that wouldn't you? Why the hell would I want to marry her?"

"You know, if I didn't think she deserved you I'd just throw you to the wolves. But now she's missing, too. What's in the case?"

"Papers."

"Look pal, I'm tired, you're beat up, let's not make this take all night. I didn't think it was Lucky Break's missing gold."

"Might as well be. It's the real assay showing they don't have any."

"There've gotta be some regulators and lawyers who'd love to get their hands on that."

"No shit. LeClerc wants it back."

"What were you supposed to get for it? Other than a lump on the head that is."

He reaches back and touches the spot. It makes him grimace and it brings a smile to my face.

"What's the deal with Sylvia?"

I figure hearing it might sober him up for talking.

"She's missing. No one's seen her for at least a few days. I went to her room at the Jayapura. When's the last time you saw her there, by the way? It's been torn up and there's a bloody towel in the sink. Somebody made a note of your meeting on the pad by the bed. It didn't look like her writing. That's how I got onto it."

He slumps into his seat. "Blood? Missing? Shit, I didn't mean for her to get tangled up in this like that. I really didn't."

"She is though. So am I. So are you. Lay it all out for me, maybe I can help."

"How the hell can you help?"

"That's what I'm trying to figure out. I'm an outsider. I've got some connections. If I know everything there might be something I can do. At least maybe I can find Sylvia."

"How do I know I can trust you?"

"You don't. But at this point, what's it matter? It was the big ape from Lucky Break that clobbered you and took your briefcase. I don't think you've got a lot of friends left around here."

He chews that over for a bit, orders another drink and is halfway through it before he makes up his mind.

"All right, so what do you need to know?"

"Just tell me the story, how you got involved, what you were doing, who you were doing it with, what Sylvia knows, anything you can think of. I'll ask you questions if I need to."

He's tired and still a little woozy from taking his lump, and he's fast filling up with booze. He spills it.

"What the fuck am I supposed to know about gold? I come from an oil family. So I'm here to learn some of the business and these guys from Lucky Break want to make a presentation. No one in the office wants to bother, but I'm the new guy so I get picked to meet with 'em.

"So I fly up to Marinda and see the French guy, LeClerc, and a couple of Australian dudes. They're in the hotel there with some lab stuff and a bunch of rocks and a lot of dust and some nuggets and it looks like gold to me. What the fuck do I know? One of the Australian guys is their geologist and he tells me all about it and pulls out some charts and a lot of numbers and it all sounds pretty good. I figure they know more about what they're talking about than I do. They take me out to some shithole muddy field and there's a lot of people digging and more rocks and dust locked up in a trailer and it all looks good to me.

"I don't know these guys but they're okay. Their company's list-ed in Sydney and Vancouver and those are real stock exchanges, real enough anyhow. So I believed 'em and wrote up a report about it.

"I bought some shares for myself, suggested that some of our clients buy some. It seemed straight to me. I told Sylvia about it. Told her she ought to buy some shares. Soon as my report came out, it was all going to be public knowledge. They were gonna have a press conference. I guess back home it might be a little dicey, me buying up shares before that, but here, shit, people do that kind of stuff all the time. It's no big deal."

"It is when you're also working for them. Even here. Why'd they give you one of their corporate cards? What'd you do for them?"

"Where'd you find that? You've got my wallet too? Fuck you—give me my stuff back."

"Tough shit. Report it lost. Why'd they give it to you?"

"None of your fucking business."

"Okay fine, it's not that important and I can guess anyway. They wanted a tame analyst, so anything they could do to own you kept you in line. How'd it all go south?"

"I had to go back up to Marinda to talk with some guys at Motex. I ran into the geologist, Gary, from Lucky Break, and some guy they'd hired to work with him. We had a few drinks. The geologist left and his assistant and I had a couple more.

"Once Gary left, the assistant, his name was Walt, a young Canadian guy from some other mining company, started grumbling about the company and how he wasn't getting enough out of the deal. I asked him what the problem was and it all came out.

"They'd done it the old-fashioned way, like in Westerns. Load some shotgun shells with real gold, blast 'em into the ground somewhere, cut some bent geologist in on the stock deal and bingo, you've got a gold rush. Shit, had I ever been suckered.

"The next day I drove out to the trailer near the mining field to talk to LeClerc. He told me to sell my stock, keep my mouth shut and everything'd be okay. He went out to talk to someone and I looked at his desk.

"There was an assay report on it, a real one that said there wasn't any gold. Someone at Motex had commissioned it. I don't know what LeClerc was doing with it. I took it, shuffled some papers around on the desk hoping he wouldn't notice. When he came back I told him he could count on me and I got the hell out of there.

"I didn't know what to do. I went back to the hotel. That night I heard people talking about someone falling out of a helicopter. I'm pretty sure it was Walt and he that didn't fall. I got scared and disappeared quick as I could. I called Sylvia and told her to sell her stock, that I was in trouble and I didn't know when I'd be able to see her again. She started asking a bunch of questions and I hung up. We'd been staying together at the Jayapura and I didn't go back. I've been staying in a cheap hotel in Chinatown, trying to figure out what to do next."

"What were you trying to do? You had the assay, were you selling it back to them or what?"

"I figured if I just gave it back to them they'd leave me alone."

"Bullshit. Why all the secrecy then? You were trying to sell it back to them."

"So what. They'd made a killing on their stock thanks to me. I wrote the report. I deserve something extra for that."

"Sure you do, but there might be some difference of opinion about what it is you deserve."

"Fuck you. I'm not doing anything anyone else wouldn't do."

"Let's not get into that. What do you think's the deal with Sylvia?"

"I dunno. You're so smart, you tell me."

"I saw her with LeClerc a while back. Maybe they've got her somewhere. You know where LeClerc stays in Jakarta?"

"I think he usually stays in a bungalow at the Borobudur."

"Which one?"

"I don't remember the number. It's the furthest one on the left on the other side of the pool."

"Great, now get the hell out of here. As a matter of fact, why don't you head back to mommy and daddy in Texas."

"I think I'll stick around for some more drinks. There's some mighty fine women in here."

Other than handsome, I don't know what anyone sees in this guy. I guess that connections and too much family money will get even the worst people pretty far.

"Suit yourself, but not on my dime. Get out of here and get your own table."

"What about my briefcase?"

"I'm holding on to it. I might need it to get Sylvia back."

"You can't. It's mine."

"I can and too bad. You're done making money from this deal. Go home. Maybe you can save your own neck. I'm sure if you stick around somebody's gonna be happy to toss your sorry ass out of a helicopter."

He starts to speak but I shoo him away and turn my attention to my drink. After he leaves the *mamasan* comes back wanting to know if I want company. I ask her to find Irina.

Irina shows up about two minutes later with a very tall, striking blonde sporting the kind of figure I've mostly seen in cartoons. Irina's friend's name is Marta and they sit down on either side of me, both of them hooking hands high up on the inside of my legs.

"My friend, she is very beautiful, yes?"

Marta's nuzzling my neck and there's no denying that she's very beautiful.

"Uh, yeah."

"We can bring her with us to your house."

"That would be great, but I can't tonight."

Irina pouts. "No? What is problem tonight?"

"I've got to go to the Borobudur. I have to look for someone. There might be trouble."

"I go with you?"

"No, it might be dangerous."

We argue for a little while. Irina's friend keeps nuzzling my neck and kneading my thigh and I come close to deciding this other thing can wait until tomorrow.

Finally the little angel perched on my left shoulder and the little devil on the right work out a compromise. I pay to take Marta out of the club for the rest of the night and send her and Irina back to my house in a taxi. I tell them I'll be home as soon as possible. I get the briefcase from the coat check and take a cab to the Borobudur.

CHAPTER **TWENTY-FIVE**

The Borobudur is an enormous hotel near the national Mosque and Cathedral. It was one of the first five-star hotels built in Jakarta and is known for its sprawling, lushly planted grounds surrounding one of the biggest swimming pools in the country. Its cottages are set back into the garden and far enough apart from each other to provide their occupants with a lot of privacy. Guests pay through the nose for all that. In a country where someone is edging into the middle class if they make two hundred dollars a month, the bungalows at the Borobudur run for a whole lot more than that for a night. The only room in the hotel that's more expensive than the cottage Tony LeClerc's in is the Presidential Suite that takes up the entire top floor of the main building.

LeClerc might want his privacy, but I don't think it's such a good idea for me. I call him from a house phone in the lobby. It's late. If I haven't woken him up, he's trying to make it sound like I did.

"*Qui?*"

"You can speak English, LeClerc, I don't mind."

"Who is this? I have no wish to be disturbed."

"It's that meddlesome guy, Ray Sharp."

"It is late and you are not a smart man, Monsieur Sharp."

"You're probably right, but I've got something you want."

"What could that be?"

"Something Alex Truscott was trying to sell back to you."

"Where are you, monsieur?"

"In the lobby."

"Permit me a minute or two to dress, then come to my bungalow."

"I don't think so. Give me a minute or two to order a drink then meet me in the lobby bar. I like it where there're people."

"You are too nervous, monsieur."

"That might be, but I'm not crazy. Come alone, I don't want to do business with your ape."

"Ape?"

"Never mind. I'll be in the bar for one drink; I've already had enough tonight. Show up or don't. I'm sure someone's gonna want what I've got."

I hang up, check the briefcase with the concierge and take a well-stuffed armchair at a table facing the garden entrance to the lobby. I've almost finished my drink when LeClerc walks in.

He's alone and disheveled. I have gotten him out of bed and I take a little pleasure in it. He sits down across from me and waves away the waitress when she comes over. I hold up my near empty glass, smile and rattle the lonely cubes at her. LeClerc looks me over and scowls.

"Where is my assay? What do you imagine I will pay you for it? I have already paid too much for it the first time."

"I was wondering where you got it. Was it Suryanto who snuck it out of a file cabinet for you?"

"It is of no concern to you, Mr. Sharp. Hand it over and we shall part company."

"Where's Sylvia, LeClerc? That's my concern."

He turns up his palms and smiles. "Women. It is so hard to know them, to know where they go."

"It's not so hard if you're the one who took them. Don't play coy. Where is she?"

"I think maybe she is visiting the forest. It is very beautiful in this country."

"You're just a crooked businessman, LeClerc. Stop trying to play this like you're a mob kingpin."

"You return to me my assay and I will tell you where to find her. My man will take you to her."

"No he won't, he'll bring her to me and then you'll get the paperwork."

"But, monsieur, you have no choice." He nods just over my left shoulder and I turn my head.

The big guy's tippy-toed up behind me. He's wearing a loose, plaid sports jacket and his hand's in a pocket that's pointing at me.

"What, you gonna have your ape shoot me in the hotel lobby? I don't think so. Even you don't have the kind of money to smooth that over."

The big guy moves closer and taps me, hard, in the temple with his pocket. It hurts. He does have something more than his fingers in there. He leans down to my ear. His squeaky voice tickles like a buzzing mosquito. "I'm looking forward to playing with you, dipshit."

LeClerc moves to sit next to me. "It is not necessary for William to shoot you. If you insist upon not cooperating, I will provide him with Sylvia to, what did he say, play with."

I come close to smiling and saying something witty. But getting rid of Sylvia isn't worth feeling that crappy about myself.

So instead I paste on a big, fake smile and put a lot of phony enthusiasm into my voice. "Okay boys, where're we going?"

First the big guy has to pat me down. He isn't very thorough and misses the claim check for the briefcase. It's in a small pocket, hidden in the seam of my pants, under my belt.

"Monsieur, where do you keep my papers? Perhaps you have nothing to trade."

"They're safe. You'll get 'em when I get Sylvia and when I'm safe."

"Already, monsieur, you are not safe. But I am, as you say, a businessman. When no longer you can hurt me, I have no interest in you, or in Sylvia."

"I get Sylvia, you get your assay. It's simple as that."

That time of night it doesn't take long to get to the airport. A twin-engine Indonesian-made plane bearing an army unit's insignia is lit up on the tarmac just outside the private VIP terminal. The big guy's got a tight grip on my left elbow and his pocket keeps poking me in the back as we walk to the plane. At least it isn't a helicopter.

We start taxiing even before the door is fully closed, take off steep and head west above the coast. I pretend to sleep for the two hours it takes us to get to Marinda. I want some time to think, to figure out what, if anything, I can do to get out of this jam.

I must've drifted off. I wake up with a start with the first bounce of a rough landing. The plane rolls to a stop at the end of the runway and doesn't even turn around to taxi to the terminal. The pilot comes out of the cockpit, opens the door, lets down the stairs and I'm quickly herded into a pickup truck, sandwiched in the front seat between LeClerc, who's behind the wheel, and the big guy whose name is apparently William.

We rattle out a back road from the airport, through a short stretch of forest, then onto the highway.

"We going to Santo's for a beer?"

William digs an elbow hard into my ribs. "Shut up."

I shut up. We pass Santo's and turn in where I knew we would, at the dirt road leading to Lucky Break's trailer office. We stop in front of it. The big guy doesn't need to be discreet any longer, so he pulls the same small gun I'd seen before from his pocket and pokes at my nose with its barrel.

"I hope to fuck you give me some trouble, wise-ass."

"It's your party."

William backs out of the truck cab and motions for me to get out. LeClerc's gone ahead and unlocked the door to the office. I walk just fine, wherever I'm told, when there's a gun pointed in my direction. The big guy must have some hostility to get out of his system though. He keeps shoving me to the ground, having me get up, walk a little way toward the office, then down I go again. I guess it's his idea of fun.

LeClerc's standing in the doorway looking impatient. "William, there will be time for that later. Bring him in here. Put him on the sofa."

When I'm seated, LeClerc takes the gun and holds it while the big guy straps my wrists behind my back and my ankles together with duct tape. He yanks off a length to wrap around my mouth but the boss stops him. "He will need to speak. Leave it."

William punches me hard in the gut. While I'm doubled over trying to get my breath back LeClerc hands him the gun and leaves the room. I've scarcely managed to get myself back upright when he returns with a struggling bundle of woman.

Sylvia's poured into a tight red dress that must've looked great on her before she'd been wearing it for several days. She does have a flair for style. Even the streaks of dried blood on the towel wrapped around her head match what she's wearing. She stops squirming when she sees me.

"It's about time you showed up to get me away from these idiots." She hasn't noticed my wrists and ankles. I nod and smile.

"Good to see you, Sylvia. You make a very nice looking hostage."

"Fuck you, Ray. Just get me the hell out of here."

LeClerc pushes her down onto the sofa, gets the gun back from the big guy and watches, smirking, while William takes the tape to Sylvia. I'm hoping he won't forget to tape her mouth shut, but he does.

Her dress rides up, exposing the merest wisp of a matching red thong underneath. She wiggles around trying to push the dress back down with her bound hands. The big guy moves back and admires his handiwork and Sylvia's lingerie.

"What the fuck are you looking at, asshole?" She swivels her head at me. "Some rescuer you turned out to be."

I ignore her. The big guy doesn't. He slaps her face hard then reaches down and gives a rough squeeze to her crotch, bringing his face up close to hers. "Shut the fuck up, lady, if you want me to treat you nice."

She recoils as far as she can on the sofa, drops her chin and starts whimpering.

There's not a lot I can do. I start to pipe up, to ask LeClerc to rein in his gorilla, but as soon as I open my mouth, I get punched in it, hard. That shuts me up fast. When the shock of it wears off I feel around with my tongue to see if I've lost any teeth. At least William's rubbing his knuckles. There's some slight consolation in that.

LeClerc emits a villainous sounding chuckle. "Now, monsieur, you have what you want. Where is it, what I want?"

"The big guy searched me. Maybe I've got it up my ass. He didn't look there. Whaddaya think? Like I said, it's safe, when we're safe you can have it."

LeClerc looks at the big guy, barely tilts his head in my direction and in an instant I'm thinking, Me and my big mouth. A fist buries itself into my stomach but I don't even have time to double over in agony before William sets me straight with an uppercut to the chin. He's good, too good. After the first few punches—or is it a few dozen, I lose count after about the third—I'm hoping he'll knock me out. I met a boxer once who claimed he liked getting hit, it woke him up, helped him focus. This isn't like that.

I try rolling off the sofa and curling up tight, but he's too fast and it isn't part of his plan. He keeps me right where he wants me with his fists. I try closing my eyes but that's even worse.

An old girlfriend of mine used to meditate. She'd tell me about her out of body experiences. She'd try to get me to go to classes with her. I wish I'd taken her seriously and learned something. Then again, this would have been enough to bring even the furthest-out yogi back to ground.

I don't know how long it lasts. A year, ten years, it's that much hurt rolled up into however long it takes. He stops finally and I fall to the floor, sobbing and heaving. I'd like to throw up, but if I do all my insides will come pouring out. I'm sure they've been jarred loose. Sylvia's screaming, or is it just a shrill drone vibrating along the thin nerves in my head? It sounds like someone without talent or training is scraping at a violin, an electric one, hooked up to a tall bank of amplifiers.

I lie there wishing the big guy had killed me. He's standing over me and he knows I'm finished.

There's no way of knowing how long it takes, and at first I didn't think it was going to be possible, but I'm slowly getting my wind back. Maybe if I can take shallow breaths it won't hurt so much to breathe. It doesn't help. Breathing hurts, no matter how I do it. Not breathing isn't an option.

I'm a whole lot more conscious than I want to be. I try to keep still but my body won't cooperate. I'm spasming with sobs and hiccups and involuntary jerks every time I take a breath. If I can only pretend I'm out cold, that might buy me some time, but I'm way beyond being able to pretend anything.

LeClerc's shoes approach my face. They're handmade out of some sort of endangered animal. They must have cost a lot of money, more than anyone in their right mind would pay for shoes. The word "sucker" comes to mind. I guess that means I'm recovering. I don't know if it's going to do me any good.

"I think, monsieur, William, he does not like you. Where is my assay?"

I roll over and look up at him. He almost looks gentle, concerned. I want to tell him what he wants to hear. I really do. I'll tell him anything to keep from getting beat up some more. But I can't. My voice isn't working.

Sylvia's crying, weeping even. She's never done that for me before. It's sweet. I start to smile but it hurts too much.

LeClerc moves away. "William."

I can sense the big guy somewhere down near my feet and I know I've got to say something fast, anything, to avoid more beating.

Clearing my throat almost makes me faint with pain, but I do it, making whatever sound I can.

"One moment, William. I think maybe Monsieur Sharp is trying to speak. It is true, monsieur?"

I nod my head yes and that hurts too.

Finally I'm able to gasp out some words. "Pants, waist, pocket under belt."

The big guy bends down and roughly yanks out my belt. The pocket's not hard to find once someone knows where to look. William digs out the stub and hands it to LeClerc. The Frenchman turns his back to us to make a phone call. When he hangs up, he wags a finger at me.

"You, monsieur, will have many regrets if this is not my assay." He tells William to take Sylvia and I to the shed, to lock us in but keep us taped up. I got out of that shed once before and he knows it. He isn't going to make it easy this time.

The big guy pulls the roll of duct tape over his hand and onto his wrist like a bracelet, pulls out a knife and cuts the tape binding my feet. He drags me upright, but as soon as he lets go I fall onto the sofa. He picks me up again, rough, and with one hand holds onto me and drags me to the door and down the steps. LeClerc unbinds Sylvia's feet, points the gun at her and tells her to follow.

A few minutes later our ankles are wrapped again and we're locked into the shed. I hear a bolt being thrown on the outside of the door. They must've replaced the lock I'd broken, probably with a better one. I'm propped against an overturned wheelbarrow. Sylvia's across from me, tossed onto a pile of metal netting. Her dress has ridden up again and a beam of early morning light cuts through a hole in the tin roof, lighting up her crotch like a spotlight at a strip club. She's shaking, her eyes glazed, slowly bobbing her head back and forth. I think she might be in shock.

My head still throbs but the pain's subsiding. I've got to say something to jerk Sylvia out of her stupor. I need her alert if we're gonna figure a way out. I regain my wit, if you want to call it that. My sense of humor, especially when it's directed at anything she thinks of as sex, has always irritated her. Maybe I can use it to rile her up.

I stare straight at the tiny red strip of cloth covering her crotch. "Nice bikini wax."

She looks at me like I've slapped her. Good, that's what I was hoping for. "What? Are you fucking insane? Shut the fuck up and get us out of here."

"You always did have a nasty way with words. I found your boyfriend. He's a real shit, you two deserve each other."

"Alex, he's—"

"All right? Is that what you were gonna ask? Last I saw he was healthy. A lot of people don't like him though, so he might not stay that way for long. It's his fooling around with these guys that got us into this." She takes a deep breath and appears to calm down.

"How do you feel? Are you better?"

"Gee, I didn't think you cared."

"I don't, you asshole, but you've got to do something to get us out of here. They aren't going to just let us go."

"Can you move?"

"I can wiggle around."

"See if you can wiggle this way. I'll try to meet you halfway. Your hands are taped in front, maybe you can loosen mine."

"I'm going to ruin this dress."

"And it's a hot one too."

I admire her technique for a moment or two as she rolls off the netting and snakes her way across the dirt floor toward me. Then I fall over to my side and start toward her. I still hurt, but not so bad that I'm willing to give up and let them kill me. They've missed their chance—a few minutes earlier I would have welcomed it.

We meet in the middle and Sylvia starts clawing at the tape around my wrists. She's got long fingernails that slip occasionally and dig into my skin. I grit my teeth and keep my mouth clamped tight. I don't want to distract her. Her hands aren't in the best position to get the job done and it takes a while. I hope it isn't taking too long.

She finally gets the tape and a couple of layers of skin off me. Between that and the blood rushing back into my fingertips it hurts like hell. But it's the first pain I've enjoyed in a while. It's the kind of pain that boxer told me about. I rub usefulness back into my hands and wrists and then unwrap my ankles.

"Okay Ray, now hurry up and untie me."

I carefully remove her tape. I've got an idea and I'll need the tape to make it work.

"Great, Ray, now let's get the hell out of here."

"We can't, yet. We won't get far. There's nothing out here. They'll hear us breaking out of this place, if we can even do it, and they've got the gun."

"So, what're we going to do?"

"I've got a plan." I explain it to her. She doesn't like it.

"That sort of crap only works in bad movies. Are you stupid, or what? You're gonna get us killed."

"You have a better plan?"

She doesn't answer right away. Her brow furrows. I can see that she's thinking.

"Fuck you. I don't want to die."

"Does that mean you'll do it?"

"What the hell choice have I got?"

Sylvia gets up and goes back to the metal netting. She makes herself as comfortable as she can and then I place the tape loosely back around her ankles and wrists, making sure she can slip out of it quickly.

I find the shovel I'd used to break out the first time and hide it within my reach. I sit back down against the wheelbarrow and drape the tape over my ankles, hoping it looks like they're still bound. I keep my hands behind my back, where they'd been taped together.

I settle into place, and then look across at Sylvia. "Pull your dress back up and spread your legs as much as you can with your ankles tied."

"Jesus Christ, Ray, don't you ever think about anything else?"

"You've got to get the big guy's attention. Maybe it's like a bull and a red cape. He was hot on your panties back in the office. He's got to have his back to me for this to work."

"Okay, have your fucking thrill."

"It's not a thrill anymore, Sylvia. I'm over it. Let's just get out of this and then never see each other again, okay?"

"You got that right, asshole."

Screaming is one of Sylvia's talents that I've never had any use for until now. Once we're in position, her screams slice through the air and stab into my ears, mincing my still delicate gray matter. They reverberate in my head until I'm not sure I'll be able to function. But I've got to try.

The bolt is thrown and the door to the shed shoves open. William, holding the pistol out in front of him, cautiously enters. He looks me over and I play possum, like I'm still out of it. It's not all acting. Once he's satisfied that I'm not going anywhere, he turns his attention to the still screaming Sylvia.

"Shut the fuck up, lady. What's your problem?"

"A snake, a big snake. I saw it go behind me somewhere."

He keeps the gun on her and carefully steps behind the piled netting to take a look.

"There's nothin' there, lady. All your yelling must've scared it off."

He comes back to stand in front of her and then squats down to talk at her level and to better appreciate the view. He keeps his gun pointed at her and with the other hand reaches out to stroke the thin strip of red fabric between her legs. Sylvia's got his attention. She squeezes her eyes shut but doesn't squirm away.

I move. Slowly. The big guy's stroking her panties and Sylvia's making noises to cover any sound I might make. I pick up my weapon, stand and edge my way toward the big guy. I raise the shovel and am about to bring it back down hard when he turns and sees me. He's fast with the gun, but not fast enough. I catch him against the side of his head with the curved back of the scoop and he goes down with just a short, soft "duh." He falls on top of the gun.

"Sure took your sweet time, asshole."

"Put a sock in it, Sylvia. It wouldn't have done either of us any good if he'd shot me. Now help me get the gun."

It takes both of us to roll him over. I give Sylvia the gun and tell her to keep it pointed at him while I truss him up with some rope I spotted in a corner. I wad up some of the tape and stuff it in his mouth, strapping it in place with the rest of the tape wound tightly around his jaw and behind his head.

I take the gun back from her. There's no trusting her with it. I tell her to keep quiet and we slip out of the shed into the late morning light and heat. I figure LeClerc's still in the office and I don't know if he has another gun or not.

I stay low to the ground as I approach a window, then risk sticking my head up for a peep. LeClerc's prone on the sofa with his eyes closed. Even the bad guys have to rest sometimes.

There's only three stairs up to the door of the trailer. They're thin metal and they buckle and ring out with my footsteps.

"William, what was the problem with that woman?" LeClerc thinks it's the big guy coming back to report on all the racket.

I get to the door fast, open it and swivel inside, the gun held at my waist, pointed at the sofa. The Frenchman opens his eyes, makes a sound of surprise and tries to roll to the floor. I stop him with a wave of the gun.

"Uh huh. Stay put."

Sylvia comes in behind me and takes a seat on the edge of the desk. She crosses her legs and looks surprisingly cool. I swear if she had a compact she'd start fixing her makeup. The red dress is a mess, but you wouldn't know it from her body language. But her voice gives the lie to all that. It's got a hard edge of hysteria poking out of it.

"Shoot him, Ray. Kill the Frog."

I move into the middle of the room, away from the door, to where I can see both of them.

"Think that's a good idea, LeClerc? Lucky for you I'm the one with the gun."

"Come on, Ray, just shoot him or something. Let's get out of here. Someone else might show up and then we'll be fucked."

LeClerc starts to move off the sofa.

"I will shoot you if you don't stay where you are." He settles back down.

"Come on, Ray, what the fuck are you waiting for? Stop screwing around. Let's get out of here! We've gotta get out of here."

It's been a rough few days for her and she sounds like she's losing it. I feel a twinge of sympathy for her.

But it hasn't been any easier for me and I'm not patient with her in any case. I'm sick of both her and LeClerc. That isn't doing much for my sensitivity. The twinge goes away without me even having to scratch it.

"Jesus, Sylvia, maybe I oughta shoot you instead. Shut up, will ya? I'm thinking."

She begins to open her mouth to say something and I wag the gun in her direction. She looks shocked, furious, then determined, all in the space of a few seconds. But she sets her lips tight and keeps quiet. I smile and turn back to the Frenchman.

"I don't know what to do with you, LeClerc. I could give you to the police or the army, but I don't know who's in this with you or not. There's the little matter of the guy who got shoved out of the helicopter, but my guess is that you had William do the dirty work. There's probably no way to tie you to it. You're finished anyhow. I'll get Alex Truscott to write out the whole scam and there'll be people in Canada and Australia looking to put you away for a very long time."

LeClerc snorts and graces me with one of his sneers. "Please, monsieur, do not be the fool. Monsieur Truscott? He will say nothing. He has no desire to destroy himself."

He's probably right. My thinking is still muddy and it's hard to figure out my next step. Sylvia's stood up and is swaying back and forth, looking impatient.

"Ray, I've got to pee."

"Fine, you're an adult, I think, go pee. I'm sure there's a toilet somewhere, and if there isn't, we're in the middle of the woods. Find a bush."

She harumphs and walks out the door. It sounds like she's going behind the trailer.

"What do you do now, monsieur?"

"I'll tie you up and turn you over to someone at Motex. There's people there who'd probably like to get their hands on you."

I move to the shelves behind the desk where there's another roll of duct tape. I toss it to LeClerc. "Tape your ankles together. Do a good job of it—I'm still the one with the gun."

He wraps the tape around his ankles while I watch him carefully. When he's done I have him turn around and put his hands behind his back. I'm moving toward him to tape his wrists when I hear the pickup truck start. I shove him down onto the sofa, put a knee in his back and the gun to his head. I can crane my neck and see out the window.

The Toyota truck spins around on the gravel, its tires get a grip and Sylvia shoots down the dirt road. She must've found the keys on the desk.

"Shit."

LeClerc chuckles under my knee. I can feel his back shaking. I'm glad he finds it funny. It makes me all the happier to knock him on the right temple with the gun butt.

That just makes him mad and squirmy. It makes me mad, too. Mad enough to hit him again, harder, no matter what that might do. It puts him out like a light.

That makes tying him up easier. I get the tape and bind him tightly around his wrists. I check and then redo the work he's done on his ankles. I push him to the floor then look around the room to make sure there isn't anything he can use to get himself free. I empty his pockets, figuring if he somehow does get free he won't have any money on him. That might slow him down.

I find two bottles of water, holster the gun under my belt at the small of my back, and then set out on the long, hot walk back to civilization, or what passes for it around here.

CHAPTER **TWENTY-SIX**

It takes over an hour to get to the highway, which is an awfully grand word to describe a small country road. It takes another hour before anyone comes along who's willing to stop for a beat-up looking foreigner. It's an old, rickety pickup truck driven by a young, strong man. There's no room in the cab so I climb into the back where I'm bounced and jarred and slammed into hunks of scrap metal and rusty but still sharp logging tools. Somehow I avoid getting cut up.

I also avoid getting blown up. The driver's chewing betel nut and simultaneously chain-smoking clove cigarettes with one hand on the steering wheel. He's got the other arm, the one he occasionally uses to remove the butt from his mouth, loosely gripping a couple of large glass bottles that slosh with gasoline. I sit as far back in the truck bed as I can get.

He offers to take me into the city after stopping at Santo's, but he wants some fried noodles, a beer and a massage first. There's a grease-spattered phone next to the old lady's wok and for the price of about a dozen bowls of noodles she lets me use it. Iris says she'll pick me up. I nurse a beer and wait. It takes her a half hour to show up.

It takes me a few tries to boost myself up into the passenger seat. She looks at me without saying anything until we're a couple of minutes down the road.

"Hey, Boss Man, I thought you were in Jakarta."

"I was. It's a long story and I think I'm too tired to tell it now."

"You look terrible. You okay?"

"I'm beat." Why'd I say that? I wish to hell I was too far gone to notice the pun, but I'm not. Everything wells up in me and I start laughing, hard and loud and long and it's the most excruciating sound I've ever made. I can't stop and the whole time it feels like it's going to kill me. It feels like something sharp is clawing its way out of my chest, but I can't stop laughing. I hadn't noticed how much I hurt until now; adrenalin must have been holding it at bay. Iris pulls the Land Rover to the side of the road, shuts off the motor and gapes at me.

When I'm finished I slump forward, held up by the seatbelt, gasping for air, tears streaming down my face. Iris reaches over and undoes the belt. She pulls my head over onto her shoulder. She hands me a tissue and holds my hand.

"Ray, Boss Man, what is it? What's wrong?"

It takes me a couple more minutes before I can speak, then I tell her the story.

She doesn't like it. Why would she?

"This is bad. You should stop it now."

"I can't."

"Why?"

"Because I'm mad, really mad. I can't just let it go. I can't just let them get away."

"They have already got away."

"Not quite, and I want to make sure they get caught."

"You are a crazy man. Maybe get yourself killed."

She sounds peeved, like she's dealing with a naughty child. She shoves my head away from her. I buckle myself back in and we take off down the road. "Where do you want to go now? The hotel?"

"I do need some rest. I also need some help. Is there anyone around here honest enough to help me? An honest cop, a soldier, somebody?"

"Maybe I know someone. I will ask."

Iris parks a couple of blocks away from the hotel. I slump in the seat while she goes to get Emmy to check Mr. Jones, this time, into another anonymous room. She comes back to the Rover, and then drops me at the back entrance. She says she'll be back in the evening after getting off work. In the meantime she'll call her friend who's a cop. Maybe he'll be interested, maybe not.

Emmy gets me up to the room and offers to stay. I just want sleep. I tell her to come back later, after work.

I don't know if I've slept or not. I can't keep my eyes open but my brain's churning, boiling over with thoughts. Dreaming and thinking blend together so that I can't tell where one stops and the other begins. My aches and pains won't let me get comfortable. I'm still tired, but I give up and decide to take a bath.

Near frozen water would probably do me the most good but I can't stand the thought of it. I fill the tub with the hottest water I can. It's brutal as I ease into it, but just what I want once I'm immersed and lying still. I soak until the water cools then take a long, hot shower to get clean.

The only clothes I've got are filthy. I call downstairs and have the operator pass me around the hotel until I find Emmy. I tell her my sizes and ask if she can find me a pair of pants and a shirt. She brings them to the room about twenty minutes later. I don't ask where she got them.

I tell her a little of what's happened. I describe Sylvia, and Emmy calls the front desk to see if anyone fitting the description has checked in. "Mrs. Smith" checked into room 511 earlier in the day. I decide to pay her a visit.

She doesn't use the peephole when opening the door. "Alex, thank god you've…" is as much as she blurts out before she sees it's me.

I push in past her. "Sorry Syl, not Alex." She always hated it when I called her Syl.

I sit down on a chair next to a small table. There's an ice bucket, a couple of glasses and a bottle of vodka. I pour myself a large shot, neat, and throw it straight back. It burns. Everything hurts or burns at the moment, but the shot helps clear my head. I look at Sylvia and decide to have one more before I say anything. I drain the second shot at a leisurely but steady pace. It does the trick going down, but then a sudden dizziness reminds me I haven't eaten in a while.

"Ray, I'm glad to see you're all right. You got away."

"Could've used a ride. It was lousy hitchhiking out there."

"I'm sorry, Ray, really." She actually looks like she means it. "I just panicked and got out of there. You shouldn't have pointed the gun at me. What'd you do to LeClerc?"

"Never mind that. Where'd you find Alex? Why are you expecting him?"

"I called his mobile phone. He answered."

"Where is he?"

"I don't know, but he said he'd be here soon and not to leave the room."

"I don't think we want to be here when he gets here."

"Why not, what's he going to do to me?"

"I don't know, but my guess is you won't like it. He's too mixed up in this business, and by now he's probably feeling cornered. There's no telling what he's planning. Let's go wait for him in the bar. There are people there."

"But he told me to wait here."

"You know Sylvia, I'm tempted to let you do that. But I've come this far, been beaten up, kidnapped and just plain messed with too much to not see this thing through. You're coming to the bar whether it's on your own or I have to carry you."

Emmy's still in my room. I call and ask her to meet me at Sylvia's with a couple of security guards. They escort us to the bar downstairs. I give the guards a fistful of LeClerc's cash to change into plainclothes, sit nearby and keep an eye on things. I sit on a padded bench at a table against the wall. Sylvia sits down in a deep chair across from me. Emmy moves in and sits down close to me. Sylvia rakes her over with her eyes and snorts.

"Your latest conquest, Ray?"

"Emmy, meet Sylvia. I hope she will soon be my ex-wife."

"*Istri?* Maybe not good be here. See you later?"

Emmy doesn't need to be here. "Okay. Iris is meeting me here for dinner. Why don't you two eat something and I'll find you in the coffee shop, or later in the disco."

She smiles, gives me a peck on the cheek, collects a dirty look from Sylvia and scampers away.

"So, Iris, too, is it? I guess you need two 'cause they're small."

I've been trying to sustain a little sympathy for Sylvia. What she's been through would be enough to make most people freak out. But she isn't making it easy. I take a deep breath before answering her.

"Let's just have a nice, quiet drink and wait for your boyfriend."

I want another vodka but it's a bad idea. I don't know what's going on or what Alex is up to. I'm already exhausted and a little hazy. I ask for coffee. Sylvia orders something pink with an umbrella poking out of it and half a fruit basket on toothpicks bathing in it. She makes a face when she tastes it.

"They make these better at the Borobudur."

"Of course they do, that's why I stick with the basics when I'm in the boonies." I raise my coffee to her and try to filter out the grit with my lips when I take a sip. I'm nibbling on my second bowl of mixed nuts. I'm feeling better by the minute.

Emmy's guard pals are sitting at the table next to ours. They're both good Muslims and I spring for all the fruit juice they want. We're all on our second round when Alex comes through the lobby with Suryanto in tow. He's almost at the elevator when I yell at him.

"Hey Alex, she's not there."

He looks around. Suryanto turns, a hand on top of the pistol in his holster, and raises his sunglasses for a better view.

"Over here in the bar. She's with me."

The two men start toward the bar, Suryanto's hand still fondling the butt of his gun. I reach behind me and get the gun I took off the big guy. I make sure the safety's off and hold it under the table, pointing it at them as they approach.

Sylvia gets up to greet Alex. She throws her arms out to hug him, but he pushes her away.

She gets a look like a hurt puppy, its tail fallen between its legs, about to start whimpering. She sits down next to me and grabs my arm. Luckily it's the left arm; the right one is holding the gun steady under the table.

I nod my head at them. "Sit down boys, let's jabber." Maybe it's the vodka I had in Sylvia's room, maybe the beating, or the gun in my hand, but I'm punchy and bad dialog is what spills out of me.

Suryanto looks at Alex for a clue. Alex motions to a chair and sits down in the other one, giving me a funny look. "What's got into you?"

I notice Suryanto trying to ease his gun out of its holster. I tap the underside of the table with mine and shake my head slowly up and down. "Chill," I direct my eyes down at the tabletop. "Bang, you're dead."

He stoops to peer under the table and comes up with a frown. He folds his fingers into his lap and sits quietly. "Thatta boy.

"So Alex, why do you need a fake cop babysitting you to come and see your betrothed?"

"She called, said she was in trouble. I didn't know what to expect, thought we might need some help."

"I'm not buying it."

"Suit yourself, I was worried about her."

"You've never worried about anyone other than yourself. Try again."

"You know these guys play rough. I don't want anyone to get hurt."

"Yeah, and your pal here is one of 'em. How does that fit in?"

"What do you mean? Mr. Suryanto is the head of security at Motex, you know that."

"And you're an impartial stock analyst and I'm just some polite corporate investigator who doesn't do things like point guns at people." I'm trying to figure out why Alex is here. The last I saw of him I would have bet dollars to donuts he'd be on his way back to mom and dad in Texas by now. There's gotta be something else going on, something he wants or thinks he can get.

I'm about to start trying to wheedle it out of him when Sylvia breaks in. She's been stewing in her juices next to me since Alex spurned her.

"What's this about, Alex? How dare you shove me? I thought I meant something to you. What about us?"

She's sincere and I can't figure it out. Is it her pride? Is it that she's a woman scorned? I think she really loves him. I don't know Alex well, maybe there's more to him than I think. But I don't think so. As for Sylvia, maybe I never really knew her, or I've been wrong about her, or something?

Whatever it is, I can't let it distract me now, not when I've got a gun pointed at someone.

Alex has one of those nasty little superior laughs. He directs it at her. "Us? Don't be stupid Sylvia, you were never even that great a lay. You're fine so long as you keep your mouth shut. Just close it and stay out of this."

"Alex, how could…"

I look from one to the other, incredulous. Now I really have no idea what he's doing here, what he wants, what he thinks he's going to get out of it. There are a lot of questions I want to ask, but I've got to get things calmed down first. I wish I knew how to do it.

Suryanto mistakes all the emotional chaos for an opportunity to get the drop on me. He starts going for his gun again. I lean forward and crack him on the kneecap with my pistol. "I've just about had it with you, buster."

I tell Alex to take the security cop's gun out of his holster, using two fingers, and put it on the table in front of me. He does. Suryanto slumps in his chair like he's been deflated. I take the gun and put it on top of the bench behind me.

Sylvia's blubbering now. I can't tell if she's actually crying, or just huffy with some sort of righteous indignation. "Alex, you said you loved me, you said we'd get married, remember? You said I was going to be the Queen of Houston. You…"

Alex shakes his head like he's dealing with a not very bright child who ought to know better. "Jeeezus you stupid, silly bitch, would you just shut up. Marry you? I must've been totally wasted if I ever said anything like that. You were just good arm candy for fancy parties. Marry you? You're outta your fucking mind."

Sylvia freezes in place and softly shakes, as if someone's pointed a remote control at her and pushed the pause button. I look from him to her and back to him again. I'm aghast. Even Sylvia doesn't deserve this from the arrogant little prick. I'm beginning to feel defensive toward her. But I figure the best thing I can do for everybody is to ignore it and finish up what we're doing here as quick as I can. That's a mistake.

Alex is opening his mouth to say something, maybe even something useful for a change, when she shoots him. I noticed her hand snaking behind my back, but I didn't think about it. She comes out blasting with Suryanto's gun. The first shot drills the Texas oil prince dead center in the chest.

She keeps pulling the trigger but he isn't there to shoot anymore. He's tilting back in his chair and the first round startles him over and onto the floor. If she really wants to be sure, she'll stand up and plug him again, but Sylvia sits there, dead still, the gun pointing straight out, her eyes squeezed shut, until she's slammed the next five bullets into the teak paneling of the bar.

If Suryanto didn't carry such a wimpy gun, Alex might have survived. I'd been surprised when he forked it over that it was a .22 caliber target pistol. I guess he doesn't have good enough connections to the army or the real police to get anything bigger. A larger caliber bullet, a .38 or a .45 or a nine-millimeter, might have just missed the nasty, young, stock analyst's heart on a clean pass through his chest. It would have been touch and go, but he might have made it. The less powerful .22 slug must have hit something in there, something it couldn't break through, and then rattled around like a die in a cup, scrambling his insides. He doesn't have any time for last words, just one last dumb, surprised look, a gasp and a brief exhalation.

While Sylvia's still shooting, Suryanto dives to the side, gets his footing and tries to run out. The two hotel security guys grab him and are holding him down on the floor, keeping themselves covered as well. I reach out to grab the gun from Sylvia but it's empty anyway by the time I get it from her. She lets it drop into my hand and then she topples over, across my lap, sobbing.

The small lobby bar begins filling with people. The bartender comes out from hiding, checks to make sure the guy on the floor is dead, and then goes back to his station to serve the swelling crowd of customers who are suddenly very thirsty.

I sit there, Sylvia wetting my lap with her tears. I have no idea what to do.

One of the security guys comes over to see if I'm okay, the other's holding on to Suryanto. The hotel manager bustles in and insists on clearing a space around Alex's body. He's called the cops and he knows it will mean more grief for him if it looks like he hasn't been trying to control the situation.

Emmy and Iris wriggle through the throng and sit down next to me. Emmy holds my hand and strokes my arm. Iris asks questions.

"What happened, Boss Man?"

I point at the heaving head of hair in my lap. "She shot him."

"Who?"

"Her fiancé, the guy who wasn't pushed out of the helicopter."

"He wasn't?"

"No, he was shot. That was some other guy."

"What did Suryanto do?"

"It was his gun."

"He gave it to her?"

"No, I took it from him, she took it from me. It's confusing."

"Do not talk. I will call my friend with the police."

Emmy's taken my gun and hidden it somewhere by the time Iris' friend arrives. It's Lieutenant Arsiyanto. He sits down across from me, in the chair that Suryanto had been in. He doesn't look happy.

"It is a problem for me, Mr. Sharp, when the same person is at the scene of more than one shooting."

"Aren't there any other cops in this town, Lieutenant?"

"Not many who speak English, Mr. Sharp. I have the unfortunate pleasure of being called whenever a foreigner is involved in trouble here."

"You're Iris' friend?"

"Yes, we are both alumni of Cal State Riverside in California. She tells me that you were her boss at Motex, the one who fired her. I am confused as to why she thinks of you as a friend, but she does."

I shrug my shoulders. "I doubt that it's my special charm, Lieutenant."

"I would not know. Please tell me what happened here tonight. You are not face down on a massage table, I expect that you have seen something more than the last time we met."

I tell him enough to get myself off the hook, at least for a little while. I still don't want to go into detail about Lucky Break and my investigation. I avoid telling him that I'd tied up LeClerc and the big guy and left them at their mine site. By now, they'd either got loose, or they'll keep. Either way I don't care.

He senses I'm hiding something. But after talking with the bartender and some of the other people who'd been in the bar, he's got to admit that I've told him everything he needs to know about tonight's events.

In the end he hauls Sylvia, kicking and screaming, and a steaming mad Suryanto, off to jail. He cuts me loose after making me promise to show up in his office tomorrow morning.

By midnight I'm done. Iris comes with me to my room for a drink because she doesn't think I should be alone. We open the door on Emmy and Tommy. They're sitting on the bed watching MTV and picking at the remnants of a large room service order. They're there to cheer me up. Emmy jumps up, throws her arms around me and plants a long wet kiss on my mouth.

Eventually she comes up for air. "No worry, we pay money room service, buy vodka, you drink." Tommy passes her the unopened bottle and she holds it up to me.

I kick off my shoes, prop a couple of pillows against the headboard, sit back on them with my legs out in front of me, crack open the bottle and take a long, hot swallow. I raise the bottle and wave it at the three of them. I intend to get drunk, very drunk.

"Thanks. You're all welcome to hang out. Don't mind me if I just sit here and get fucked up."

Emmy moves up close to me. Iris and Tommy sit at the end of the bed and turn their attention to the TV.

By the time I'm halfway through the bottle I feel like I'm back in high school. It's all strangely innocent and comforting. The lights are down low. Emmy's loosened my clothes to give her hands access to my body. I lie there enjoying it and occasionally doing a little exploring of my own to encourage her. Iris and Tommy are lying on the floor with a couple of extra pillows, dozy in front of the fireplace-like glow of pop videos. I drift in and out of sleep, finally floating away entirely.

I wake up just as the early morning sun is angling into the room. Emmy's draped over me, asleep. The TV's showing a test pattern. Tommy's curled into a ball, asleep on the cushioned chair. Iris is gone. I get up to pee then come back to knit myself into the tangle of Emmy's arms and legs.

CHAPTER **TWENTY-SEVEN**

The phone rings a little after nine. It's Arsiyanto making sure I'm going to show up at the cop shop. My guess is that he's going to lean on me to tell him more. There might be no way around it. I call Iris and ask her to meet me there at eleven in case I need help with translating, and in the hope that a friendly face might help.

I hang up the phone and am crushed back into the mattress by Emmy. She's all over me. I'm too groggy to do much other than lie there and succumb to the sensations. I don't know what Tommy's doing. My eyes are closed and for all I know he's gotten into the act too. It feels so good that I don't much care who's doing what.

Afterwards Tommy leaves and Emmy and I take a shower. In the light, all the bruises on my body startle her. I wasn't too happy when I saw them in the mirror either. I have to reassure her that they're nothing she's done. She soaps me up carefully. I soap her too. Somehow I get excited again.

I'm surprised that I feel as good as I do. My muscles ache in the places where they've been pummeled and my skin is a collage of unnatural colors, but the really bad pain is gone. A surprisingly slight hangover is the worst of it.

The room's a mess and before we leave I slip a few *rupiah* notes under the pillow for the housekeeper. For all I know that might be Emmy.

I also sneak some bills into Emmy's purse. She wants more from me than money. But I don't have anything other than friendship and cash for her. I'm hoping the money will help keep things at a distance.

Police headquarters is on the waterfront, just a few blocks away. It's one of the only modern, fully air-conditioned buildings in town. It was built a little over a year ago with money from Motex. For that, and other reasons, the company's got a lot of clout with the local cops.

The receptionist at the front desk takes my name. She makes a call, and then with great deference ushers me into a large conference room hung with beautiful Sumatran textiles, and offers me coffee. It's half of what I really need—a fistful of aspirin would make the morning right, but I don't ask.

She comes back with the coffee and Iris. The coffee's very strong —very bitter and hot enough to singe my lips. It jolts my system. I might not need the painkillers.

"Good dreams, Boss Man?"

"What time did you leave?"

"You were busy. Maybe two o' clock."

"Thanks for everything yesterday. I'm really sorry you're getting dragged into all this."

"It's interesting, more interesting than anything else I'm doing."

"Maybe a little too interesting."

"How was Emmy this morning?"

"Tired. I think a little worried about me. I'm a little worried about her. She likes me more than she should. I like her too, but it's not going any further than that."

"Why do you tell me this?"

"You're her friend. Her English isn't that good. My Indonesian isn't that good. I'm afraid I might hurt her feelings if I say anything to her about it."

"You're right, you might. I'll try to tell her you are what some girls call a 'butterfly.'"

"Huh? Doesn't *kupu kupu malam* mean 'butterfly of the night'? Isn't that a prostitute?"

Iris raises her eyebrows in a full Groucho.

I change the subject. "How well do you know Lieutenant Arsiyanto?"

She's about to answer when he strides in. He looked a bit beleagured the two times I'd seen him before. This morning he's cool and neat looking in crisply ironed khakis with an expensive but simple batik shirt. I stand up to shake his hand.

"Thanks for your help last night. It was a terrible thing that happened. I hope I can be some help."

He nods in response, unimpressed. He drops my hand and reaches for Iris'. It isn't so much a handshake as a caress. He says something to her but his voice is very soft and low and he speaks rapidly. I don't catch what he says, but it makes Iris laugh.

We sit and the lieutenant stares at me for a little while over the rim of his coffee cup. Finally he speaks up.

"Your wife, Mr. Sharp, is comfortable but unhappy. She is in a lot of trouble."

"We're separated. I'm hoping she'll soon be my ex-wife."

"Yes, of course, you told me that last night. Do you know why she killed Mr. Truscott?"

"Didn't we cover all this ground last night?"

"We will go over it again, Mr. Sharp. I have not yet decided what to do with you."

"Okay. She thought he loved her, thought they were going to be married. He didn't and they weren't. Truscott said something insulting and I think she just snapped. She'd been kidnapped, tied up, abused. She just went amok, and shot him. I doubt she even knew what she was doing."

"It was *Pak* Suryanto's gun?"

"Yes, I took it from him and put it behind me on the bench. She reached behind me and grabbed it."

"But I do not understand. How did you take the gun from *Pak* Suryanto?"

I don't know how to answer that. Somehow I'd avoided bringing up the fact that I had a gun also. That would lead to where I got it and that would lead to the whole story. And I still don't know if I can trust him with the whole story. He's friendly enough, but if he knows I have a gun of my own, even if I've taken it off another bad guy, he's got me wherever he wants me. I lean over to whisper to Iris.

"What should I say? How much can we trust this guy?"

She answers me at full volume, giving me no choice.

"He will know if you don't say the truth. He is a very smart policeman. I think he is a good man and there will be no trouble."

Arsiyanto looks patient enough, waiting for me to answer his question. I straighten up and spill it, the whole story, start to finish, at least up to now. He listens well and interrupts only a couple of times to ask questions. He doesn't take any notes. When I finish I get up and go to the sideboard where there's a pitcher of water and some glasses. I pour myself a glass and gulp it down.

While I'm up, the Lieutenant's consulting with Iris. Their heads are almost touching across the table and they're talking low and fast. I can't make out what they're talking about, but it's not hard to guess. I drink another glass of water before Arsiyanto motions me back to my seat.

"Mr. Sharp, Iris says that you are a good man and are not lying. What you have told me can make a lot of trouble. Maybe I cannot talk with my boss about this. Maybe I cannot talk with anybody. If you help me, I will help you. Okay?"

I stick out my hand to shake again. "Deal. What do we do?"

"Where is your gun now?"

"I don't know. A friend took it from me before the police arrived and hid it. I can get it."

"Can you get it now, please?"

"I think so, why?"

"Go, get it, come back in one hour. We will go to get Mr. LeClerc. Maybe there will be trouble."

Iris and I leave to find Emmy. She's at work. The gun's in a safe deposit box behind the front desk. She's hesitant to give it to me.

"Why want gun? What you do?"

"Don't worry, I'm going with Iris' friend, Arsiyanto."

Emmy grabs Iris by the arm and pulls her away around a corner. When they come back Iris makes a show of nodding at her purse. She has the gun. Emmy doesn't say anything, just pecks me on the cheek and punches me in the arm before turning and walking away.

"She likes you, Boss Man. Wants you to be careful. Even if you are butterfly." We walk back to police headquarters.

We page Arsiyanto from the front desk, then wait out front until he pulls up in front in his jeep. Iris hands me the gun in front of him. We drop her off at the front gate of the compound on our way to the Lucky Break site.

LeClerc and the big guy aren't there. Enough local people come around that someone probably found them and let them loose. We search the office and the shed, but anything incriminating is long gone. We decide to go to the village to see if anyone there knows anything. We set out through the forest, skirting the edge of the fake goldmine field. We're about halfway to the village, doing our best to stay in the shade on a path that meanders in and out of the tree line, when Arsiyanto sees something, or someone, lying at the edge of an open pit a few hundred feet into the field. We walk over. As we approach, a terrible, sour stench hammers at our noses. He's smelled it before and knows what it is. It's my first time.

The cop holds up a hand and stops when we're about fifty feet away. It's a body, bloated and blackened by the sun. It's swollen and the clothes it's wearing are stretched to the bursting point. We look over the scene from afar. I'm not sure what we're looking for but we approach carefully.

Arsiyanto and I walk lightly up to the wreckage of what used to be William, LeClerc's big ape. The body's lying face down, one hand clenched to its head the other reaching out as if to grab for something to cling to.

I stand back a little and upwind. The policeman squats down and looks the corpse over carefully. After a while he gets up and finds a couple of planks that have been used in one of the mines. He hands me one and asks me to help him turn the body.

Luckily there's not much in my stomach to bother keeping

down. The foul odor pours off the body in a wave that almost knocks me over. The face is set into a gruesome last scream. The mouth's wide open and the teeth are askew and broken, as if William had gritted them against some pain too terrible to endure until they'd shattered from the pressure.

I turn away and fight back dry heaves that feel like they're trying to turn me inside out. Arsiyanto squats again to examine the body. From where I stand I can't see any sign of what killed the big guy.

After a while the cop gets up. He looks around at the ground. He looks nervous.

"What is it, Lieutenant?"

"*Ular berbisa.*"

"*Ular*" means snake and I don't need to know what the other word means. If I ever come across a snake that wants to bite me, it won't need to—I'll just die of fright. I look around, trying not to panic. Unconsciously I start gritting my teeth, and then I think of William and make an effort to unclench my jaw.

I look up, hoping a breath of fresh air will find its way down to me from above. A wake of buzzards circles hungrily overhead. I imagine them impatiently scowling down at us, cursing us, hoping we'll soon get out of the way of their lunch.

I choke back more dry heaves. I try thinking about what we can do with the body, but a line from a Clint Eastwood movie, *The Outlaw Josey Wales*, keeps coming to mind. "Why?" the actor snarls when a group of well-meaning pioneers want to bury some dead bad guys. "Buzzards gotta eat, same as worms."

I'm standing around feeling sick, my head pounding, when Arsiyanto puts a hand on my shoulder. He points to a stack of boards and rocks next to a nearby pit and suggests we pile them on top of the body until somebody can come get it. There's going to have to be an autopsy, especially since it's a foreigner.

I walk heavily through the low brush and the mud, making as much noise and vibration as I can to scare away the snakes that I'm now certain are all around us. We cover the big guy's corpse with planks and hold them down with rocks. The buzzards still wheel around above us, but they're in for a rude shock when they swoop in to dine.

Arsiyanto and I stomp our way back to the path, skirting well-around small clumps of brush and other places that snakes might hide. We pause when we get under the trees.

"What kind of snake was it?"

"I think a viper. Very dangerous, very painful. Small snake, but it can kill you fast."

Now I'm really nervous. I've seen big snakes in the wilds before, not many, but a few. They're usually slow and hard to miss. They scare me. Even snakes in a cage scare me. But if I can see them, I figure I've got a fighting chance to get out of their way. A little snake's something else.

"How small? What's it look like?"

Arsiyanto holds his hands about a foot apart, then two feet apart. Then he points at the grass underfoot and the trees all around us. "Green."

The rest of the way to the village I whistle and sing and clap my hands and, after looking down, crash my feet onto the ground heavily with each step. I've got a friend who swears that snakes really hate the tune "Hello Dolly," so that's what I sing and whistle. The cop looks at me like he thinks I'm nuts, but he doesn't look at ease either.

LeClerc's been to the village and he hasn't made any friends. They'd have fed and helped him for the asking, but like most crooks he doesn't expect anybody to act any better than he does. I'd taken his money and was on my way to turn him in, his gorilla had died horribly and he must've been panicking. So he did what he knew best, he held them up.

He'd grabbed a machete, hacked a goat to prove he was serious, then held the blade to the throat of the old medicine lady until everyone in the village collected all the money they had and brought it to him. There's just no accounting for some people. The guy's swindled millions of dollars out of shareholders and here he is plundering a poor rural community for no more than a few hundred thousand *rupiah*. He's obviously scared, and that makes him stupid and dangerous.

Having stuffed his pockets with wads of tired, crumpled banknotes, LeClerc swung his weapon around at one of the only young men in the village, marched him down to the river and into the best boat tied up at the little dock. The last anyone had seen of him, the skiff was puttering around a bend in the direction of Marinda. LeClerc was leaning comfortably against a fishing net, holding up an umbrella with one hand and the machete with the other.

CHAPTER **TWENTY-EIGHT**

The Frenchman's had more than enough time to get away before we can walk to Arsiyanto's jeep and drive back. The cop's wireless phone doesn't work in the forest and when we get to his car he hesitates before calling anything in on his police radio. Neither of us know who else to trust and too many of the wrong people might hear his police band. There's a phone in the Lucky Break trailer, but the line's dead.

We bounce out of the woods, onto the highway and down the road to Santo's. The old lady squawks, but Arsiyanto commandeers her phone for "police business" without paying. He calls the direct line of a friend of his; a sergeant who he claims wouldn't take a bribe if his family's life depended on it. He tells the sergeant to take some other cops and watch the river for LeClerc, to hold onto him if they get him.

There's an accident blocking the highway into town. A timber truck's rolled over. At that point the jungle's too dense along the road for us to detour through, so we wait while a bulldozer trundles slowly up from the Motex compound to move the wreckage to the side. It takes almost an hour.

Arsiyanto's friend flags us down at a police post just as we come back into Marinda. He looks uncomfortable when he sees me. If he's an honest cop that makes sense. He's embarrassed. At any intersection at the edge of almost every city in the country, where a road leads out of town, there's a small rough wood guardhouse and a stoplight. They're there to supplement the meager salaries of policemen.

Inside the shack there's a switch that can change the light instantly from green to red. When a car that looks like it might be carrying some spare cash comes by, it always runs the red light. When it does that, a second cop, standing on the other side of the intersection, flags it down.

The driver can insist on going to the police station, and from there to the courthouse to either fight the ticket or pay it through official channels. But that takes a lot of time. It's quicker, and cheaper, to simply pay the fine, in cash, on the spot.

Policemen in Indonesia are paid barely enough to feed, clothe and shelter their families. If they have big families, it's not enough. I've never begrudged them their little tricks. Motex's cars avoid the unofficial toll thanks to the company's generous monthly contribution to the local police benevolence fund.

The two young patrolmen manning the post look annoyed. What they're doing isn't a secret, but like a lot of things that everyone is aware of in the country, it's only ignored so long as it's discreet. Sooner or later there's gonna be one of the periodic crackdowns that pays lip service to combating corruption. If their officers have seen them at it, they'll make good scapegoats. With a sergeant around, and now a lieutenant, traffic flows through the intersection uninterrupted by anything other than the set mechanical rhythm of the stoplight. Every few minutes we're there costs a couple of poor families five or ten thousand *rupiah*.

I get out at first, but Arsiyanto waves me back into the jeep. He wants to talk with his friend alone. He's not happy when he comes back.

"*Sudah*, already, he is gone. He took an army airplane, maybe to Jakarta, maybe another place."

"Shit. Is there anything we can do?"

"I can call a friend who is a policeman in Jakarta, but..."

"Yeah, I guess not."

We drive back to police headquarters where I ask if I can see Sylvia.

Arsiyanto has to pull some strings. I've been waiting in the conference room for forty-five minutes when two no-nonsense police matrons bring her in. She's dressed in a baggy, rough, white burlap smock and a pair of bright pink plastic flip-flops. Her hands are cuffed in front of her and she keeps lifting them to her face, trying to brush the hair out of her bloodshot eyes. Her face is smudged with soot or dust or both.

I used to think I loved her. That isn't even close to the case anymore, but I hate seeing her like this.

The policewomen nudge her into a chair across from me, and then retreat to the far end of the room to watch us. Sylvia's not happy.

"Who do these fucking people think they are—they can't fucking keep me here. Get me the hell out of here, Ray."

"I don't think I can, Sylvia. I'll call the embassy and some of the legal guys I know at Motex and see what anyone can do. But I think you're really screwed."

"He was an asshole, Ray, a real little shit. I never should have listened to him."

"Yeah, that's true. What'd you ever see in him in the first place?"

"He was good to me. We had fun. I never had much to do when I was here with you, Ray. I'm sorry, but it's true. We were here for your work, not for anything to do with me. He took me to the best places, the best parties. He introduced me to people as his fiancé. He dressed so nice. And he liked it when I dressed nice. I don't know, Ray. He was young and handsome and I'm not getting any younger. I don't want to grow old here. I can't get old here, Ray."

"Now he's dead, Sylvia. You killed him. I'll do what I can to help, but I don't know how much help I can be."

"I can't stay here, Ray. I can't stay in jail in this place. I'll go crazy." She starts sniffling, her head crunches onto the table and she starts sobbing. I don't want to, but I feel sorry for her.

I reach across the table to stroke her head but one of the matrons takes a step forward and waves me back. There's a box of tissues near the water pitcher. I get her a few tissues and a glass of water and set them down within reach of her cuffed hands.

When she stops crying she looks up. She manages to dab at her eyes with the tissues and hold the glass up to take a drink.

"What can I get you, Sylvia? Is there anything you need?"

"I need you to get me out of here, Ray. I really do. They can send me to jail back home if they want. I just can't stay here."

"I'll make some calls. I can't make any promises."

"It should've been him. I wish it'd been him pushed out of that helicopter."

"Well, that would've saved you killing him, all right."

The matrons move to get her. They hoist her by the armpits and she starts to walk out between them, clutching the tissues in her hands.

"I'll see what I can do, Sylvia. Try and keep it together."

She looks back at me, miserable and angry and hurt. I'm finally rid of her. It'll be easy to get a divorce with her on trial for murder. And I should be glad. But all the cheer's been drained out of it.

After she's gone I ask to see Arsiyanto again. I thank him and promise that if I find out anything more he might be able to use, he'll hear from me. I hand him five crisp hundred U.S. dollar notes that I'd got from LeClerc's wallet. I ask him to make sure Sylvia's as comfortable as possible. He figures it's a bribe, but doesn't know what I want for that much money. Around here it's enough to have somebody killed.

"No, I cannot take money. I am not *korupsi*."

"I know, I know, it's not for you. But if someone in jail has money, they can get better food, medical attention if they need it, things like that. I just want—if you can, give it to Sylvia, or keep it for her."

"But now you will divorce."

"Yeah, I know, but it's cheaper than alimony."

He has no idea what I'm talking about. I'm not so sure what that means either. It sounds good though. He doesn't need to know that it's not my money. "Look, Lieutenant, please, I know it's a little crazy, but please."

He shrugs; puts the five bills in his shirt pocket and we shake hands. I find a taxi to take me out to Motex.

On the way, we're stopped at the traffic light. But as soon as the cops recognize me they grin sheepishly and wave the driver on. I stop him anyway, get out of the car and walk up to the cop who stands fidgeting next to the light pole. I like being generous with LeClerc's cash. I've palmed a twenty thousand *rupiah* note. I hold out my hand to shake and point up at the red light with the other one. He smiles, we shake and I get back in the cab feeling like I've done a couple of good deeds for the day.

Iris is sitting in what used to be my office, waiting for me.

"Is it all over now?"

"Is what all over, Iris?"

"All this, all the trouble."

"Maybe. I think. I'm not sure."

"What about me?"

"Iris, I'm tired. I'm sorry, you'll have to be more specific."

"What am I going to do?"

"About what?"

"My job. I told you, I don't want to be a driver anymore. I need something else."

"I might have an idea. Let's have dinner later and I'll tell you about it. In the meantime I've got some other stuff to do."

She gets out of the office and I get on the phone. My contact at the embassy in Jakarta says he'll poke around and see if he can come up with anything to help Sylvia. They'll send someone to see her in a day or two.

There's an attorney I still know at Motex. He says he'll make some calls, try and find a good criminal lawyer. He doesn't hold out much hope. The big rush of foreign investment into the country, mostly from the U.S., has made the government nervous about looking too much like it's playing favorites. A hard-hitting prosecution of a foreigner might play very well in the local press.

I don't know who else to call for Sylvia. She hasn't been in touch with her family for years. She's got a married sister who lives somewhere in New York, or maybe New Jersey, whose name I don't know. I'll do what I can to help her get a lawyer, but that'll be the most I can do.

Bill Warner's glad to hear from me, glad I'm all right, but he wants to know more than I can tell him.

"Bill, it's not that I don't want to tell you, it's that I don't know it all. Alex Truscott's dead. They haven't found the body of the geologist who got pushed out of the helicopter. LeClerc's in the wind. Any minute now Motex and the Indonesian government are going to start back peddling like crazy, pretending they never had anything to do with Lucky Break. When we hang up I'm giving it to the press. The story will break in tomorrow's papers. That's it, done, there's nothing more I can do. I'll write it all up and fax it to you."

There's a long pause. I can hear him trying to control his breathing. "Okay, Ray, but don't give it to the press yet. Hold off a day. I want our client to get it all from me, not from the newspaper."

I agree to that. What else can I do? It's my job.

Maybe I don't know everything, but there aren't any loose ends, at least regarding what I'd set out to do. The client's going to find out what they need. I found Alex. I'm rid of Sylvia. Lucky Break's been put out of business and LeClerc's on the run.

But he's getting away with millions, maybe hundreds of millions of dollars he's swindled out of investors. He's getting away with Irina's life savings. If he doesn't get away, maybe she'll get some of it back. Maybe I'll get her back.

I ask Iris to come into my office.

"You still want to have dinner?"

"Yes, you already say."

"In Jakarta?"

"What?"

"I have to go to Jakarta. There's some people there I want you to meet. Come with me."

"Why? I... what about my job?"

"I have an idea. I might be able to get you a job, a better job than here. In Jakarta. You interested?"

"Yes, but..."

"No buts. Go home and pack some clothes, enough for two or three days. Meet me at the airport in two hours." That'll give me just enough time to type up a report and fax it to Warner.

"Okay, Boss Man."

I call Ben Phillips and ask if he and Juli want to have dinner that night. I call Irina and ask her to come too. She's mad at me. I didn't come home the other night and it made her look bad with her friend Marta. She had to give Marta three hundred thousand *rupiah*. Nightclub hostesses don't come cheap.

I tell her I'm sorry and explain why I hadn't shown up. Her anger turns to concern. She insists that I not pay her back the money she gave to her friend. Before we hang up I ask her if she can get Wayan, her security guard friend to go to the Lucky Break office in Jakarta and see if LeClerc is there. If he is, I want the guard to keep him there.

Iris and I get the last two seats on the afternoon flight to Jakarta. She wants to know what I'm planning, but I won't tell her. I try sleeping but can't. I don't want to talk anymore so I pretend that I am.

CHAPTER **TWENTY-NINE**

My house is between the airport and the restaurant where we're meeting Ben and Juli. I tell Iris she's welcome to stay in the guest room, or I'll check her into a hotel if she wants. She decides to stay. Irina shows up just after we do. She makes a big scene of hugging and kissing me. She doesn't know who Iris is and maybe it's a way of marking her territory. Does this mean things are okay between us again? I'll have to ask later. For now I hug and kiss back, enjoying it at face value. When we break so that she can talk, she tells me that Wayan will call her portable phone when he gets to the Lucky Break office.

Irina goes to change and when she leaves the room Iris puts her hands on her hips, a traditional Indonesian posture of anger, and at the same time throws a Groucho at me. It's an impressive sight. "How many girls, Boss Man? You will not add me to your *koleksi*. I lock the door tonight."

"Me too."

She laughs. Irina's coming out from the bedroom. "What is funny?"

I shrug my shoulders and point at Iris. "She'll tell you if she wants."

Irina breaks into a torrent of *Bahasa Prokem*, an Indonesian street slang that I can't follow. Iris is taken aback at first, then a big smile lights up her face. She cuts in with a few wary sentences of her own. She doesn't speak it as well as Irina does.

Irina sits down on the sofa and pats the seat next to her. When I walk away they don't notice, they're too busy chattering. I putter around, changing into fresh clothes, checking the mail, paying bills, replenishing my cash from the lock box, making sure Wazir's been paid and catching up on all the other tasks I've been neglecting over the past few weeks.

By the time I get back to the two women they're laughing like old chums.

"I hate to break up this love fest, but we've got to meet Ben and Juli." They bust up laughing even more and can hardly stand up to follow me out the door. I don't want to know what's so funny. I spend a lot of time lately being laughed at. That's okay. I just don't want to hear about it at the moment.

I find Nasir at his usual station and offer him forty thousand *rupiah* to drive us for the night. He's happy to take it, business has been slow.

We meet Ben and Juli at a French restaurant on a thickly tree-lined residential street in Menteng, not far from the president's house. There's surprisingly little visible security in the area. The restaurant, run in the front room of their home by a pot-bellied, handlebar-mustachioed, jovial Frenchman of indeterminate age and his eternally youthful Balinese wife, has terrible and overpriced food. But Ben likes it. He insists on going there about every third or fourth time we go out.

It's always a long evening. The trick is to toss back the first few glasses of vinegary wine. If you're fast enough you can slip it past your taste buds before they notice. At least it's strong. After a few glasses nothing, mercifully, has much flavor.

When we get there, Juli's already on her third glass of wine. Ben's looking over the menu. It hardly matters, everything tastes equally bad. I always order the pepper steak. It's Indonesia, the Spice Islands, at least the peppercorns are fresh.

Juli and Irina greet each other like long lost pals. Ben hugs me hello. Iris hangs back, not sure what she's doing there. I gently pull her up to the table and introduce her. Irina leans over and whispers something to Iris, then leans over and whispers to Juli. The three of them sit down, Juli in the middle.

I sit next to Ben, pour myself a glass of the almost black wine from a cracked carafe, throw it straight down my throat and turn to my friend. "When're you gonna get over this place?"

"Ah come on, you don't want good food all the time do you? Besides, where else can you get this sort of atmosphere?"

I know what's coming and I'm resigned to it. "I'm just a little sick of being assaulted by Frenchmen. I'm not so sure that an accordion and a hypnotized chicken are any better than fists and a gun. At least I didn't have to pay those other guys to beat me up."

"Oh stop your whining, drink some wine, and order your pepper steak. Why'd you call this little get together anyhow?"

I look over and see Iris and Juli, their heads bent together, deep in conversation. "I think my deed's been done. Iris needs a job, Juli could use an assistant. It's a good fit."

"Okay, so we can relax and get drunk then."

"Not too drunk for me. Irina's waiting for a call. I've got some unfinished business with an even nastier French guy than the one who runs this place. If he's around, I've got to go see him."

"Thought you were done with that. I read about Sylvia in the *Post*. What's the story? I never liked her, but is she gonna be okay?"

"Sylvia's never gonna be okay. Now she's gonna be worse than ever. They'll probably make an example out of her."

"Shit, I wouldn't wish that on anybody."

"I guess not, but even that fuckwit Truscott didn't deserve being killed."

"Ugly stuff."

"That's for sure. Speaking of which, let's order."

The evening takes its expected turn for the worse just about the time I've begun pushing my main course around the plate hoping it might look like I've eaten some of it. The Frenchman, by now roaring drunk, staggers out of the kitchen wielding an accordion. He sways between the tables bellowing out what little he knows of Edith Piaf songs, alternately losing control of the instrument's bellows and the lyrics.

Irina looks like she's in pain. She leans over to me and whispers. "Do you enjoy this? Maybe you are a crazy man."

"No, it's Ben. It's okay the first time if you're drunk enough. Better drink fast though, it gets worse."

She casts me a helpless look then leans over to whisper to Iris, who looks around the table and the room while Irina's got her ear. When she's heard enough she looks at me and nods her head as if to say, "Now I understand, it's just some strange *bule* thing."

I nod my agreement.

Sweating profusely, having massacred three or four songs, the Frenchman finally tires of his assault and stumbles back toward the kitchen. Irina and Iris look relieved. Juli and I sit impassively sucking on our wine glasses, knowing what's next. And Ben looks happy as a kid anticipating his Christmas presents.

The big Frenchman is back in short order with a live chicken. He scrapes a chair into the center of the room, making a noise like fingernails on a blackboard, and slumps into it, holding the chicken on his lap. He announces that he is now going to hypnotize the clucking bird. He starts lightly stroking it on its beak, over and over, cooing softly to it, humming, until it goes limp in his hands. "Voila!" he exclaims, holding the limp clucker up for everyone to see. "Le poulet, eet eez heepnoteeze!" Then he starts singing again.

I guess it's good and funny when you're good and drunk and in the right mood. I'm not.

Unfortunately Wayan doesn't call until the show is over. But he has good news. He's found LeClerc at the small office Lucky Break rents in Jakarta. The lights are on and he's busy inside. Near as the security guard can tell, he's alone. I get up to go. Iris looks up, and then also starts to get up. I wave her back into her seat.

"You can't come. Stay here, talk Juli into giving you a job. I'll meet you back at my place later. You too Irina."

Ben puts a hand on my arm. "Christ, Ray, just stay out of it. Call the cops or something."

"Whose cops?"

Juli puts her arms around the shoulders of Irina and Iris. It looks awkward, like an airplane in a steep bank, one wing reaching up and around the tall Russian, the other stretched down around the short Indonesian. "Be careful Ray, I'll make sure they get to your place. Remember, I get the story when you're done. Thanks for the introduction by the way."

I smile, thank everybody, throw some money on the table to cover a big part of the bill and go out to the street to find Nasir. He's engaged with some other drivers in idle chat, a bowl of noodle soup, and a clove cigarette. He's the only one who bothers taking his smoke out of his mouth to slurp the noodles. I can't figure out how the others eat and smoke at the same time. I hate to interrupt.

It's about ten minutes to the large, modern, dull steel and black glass building where both Motex and Lucky Break have their offices. The government owns the building, but Motex has a ninety-nine year lease on the whole thing. The company rents out everything below the twelfth floor. Lucky Break's got a small suite of rooms on the fourth floor that they got cheap because four is an unlucky number in Chinese, Korean and Japanese. Most of the other prospective tenants are companies from those countries.

Wayan meets me in the lobby and we take the stairs. I don't have a gun. I gave it up to Arsiyanto in Marinda. Wayan doesn't have one either.

LeClerc does. When we slip into the office, quietly we think, the Frenchman turns around from the shredding machine and points it at us. It looks big. I've become far too familiar with guns lately. I'm beginning to learn to relax around them. I don't know if that's a good thing.

Wayan edges away from me so we're not easy to cover at the same time. But we aren't close enough to LeClerc to rush him, even if one of us doesn't mind getting shot. He'd have plenty of time to shoot both of us.

"Again, monsieur, you arrive to make trouble for me."

"Yeah, well, everybody needs a hobby."

"Do not make light of your situation, monsieur. I am holding the gun and I will be happy to shoot you."

"What're you gonna tell the cops if you do? This isn't Marinda. I won't be so easy to get rid of."

"You are of no consequence, monsieur, and there are no more papers." He reaches behind him and pulls the basket out from under the shredding machine. He dumps confetti all over the floor. I was in New York once when the Yankees had one of their innumerable championship parades down Broadway. This isn't festive like that.

"The janitors must love you."

"*Ca va,* monsieur. No more assay, only what you say and what I say."

"You should've been a poet, LeClerc. You'd be a lot poorer, but at least you'd be honest."

Wayan's edging further to the periphery of LeClerc's sight, trying to get closer to him. I do what I can to keep the Frenchman's attention on me. I begin to move the other way and to reach for a large glass ashtray on a small table.

"Do not move, monsieur. If you do not, there will be no purpose to my shooting you. If you do, I do not wish revenge, but if it is necessary I may enjoy it."

"You really need a little mustache, LeClerc. One of those twisted pointy ones. It would suit you."

"Always joking, monsieur. You have spent too much time in the cinemas, perhaps."

I'm trying to think of something witty and nasty to say about the French love of Jerry Lewis, when Wayan rushes him. It's a valiant effort but a bad move. LeClerc calmly turns at the first sound and pulls the trigger.

It feels too much like slow-motion as I grab up the ashtray and rear back to throw it. LeClerc turns in my direction with the gun. I'm sure I'm about to be shot. But sometimes adrenalin speeds up your body, while slowing down your brain. It's a good combination, except when it makes you do something stupid.

I've always had a strong arm. The ashtray's heavy and slams into the Frenchman's forehead just before he pulls the trigger. His gun hand jerks up, sending a bullet into the ceiling. I dive for his legs as he staggers, blood coursing down over his eyes, and tackle him. His hand crashes into the edge of a desk and the gun flies out of it, thumping onto the floor a few feet away.

I scramble over him, planting a knee hard into his chest, trying to knock the air out of him. I hear a crack, feel something give. I've broken a rib or more. LeClerc shrieks, then goes limp under me.

I get to the gun, then get to my feet and stand over him. I bend over, holding the gun to his forehead, my finger twitchy on the trigger. He's out, breathing shallowly with a little wheeze at the end of each breath.

Wayan is bellowing where he fell. If the curses that are coming from him on the floor are any indication, he isn't mortally wounded. I walk to the other side of him so that I can still keep an eye on LeClerc while checking him out.

He's been shot clean through the upper thigh and it'll hurt like hell once the shock wears off. The bullet's missed the artery and the hole will patch up nicely. I look around for something to use as a bandage. There's a beautiful *ikat* blanket on the wall above the sofa. It's good work, possibly an antique, undoubtedly valuable and it works just fine to stop the bleeding.

LeClerc still hasn't come around. I check on him again. His breathing is even more shallow, irregular and wet. His forehead's still bleeding, but it's slowed down. His chest looks caved in. He doesn't look like he's going to make it, but I'm not a doctor.

There's no noise in the building other than the low hum of the air-conditioning. I listen carefully for indications that someone else heard the ruckus, but there aren't any.

Wayan refuses to let me call an ambulance. He has a friend who'll take care of it, but he won't let me take him there. His friend will get very nervous if a *bule* shows up at his door. He's in no shape to go alone. The phone in the office is still connected so I call Irina and ask her to come and take care of him.

He's conscious enough to tell me that he has a friend who's a cop. Not exactly an honest one, but one who will be pissed off enough about LeClerc shooting a pal of his that he'll gladly arrest the Frenchman. And make it stick. He manages to make the call before his voice becomes too thick with pain to talk anymore.

I poke around while waiting for Irina and Wayan's cop pal, but there's nothing to find. I run my fingers through the shredded paper on the floor. I read once that the students who took over the U.S. embassy in Tehran pieced together a lot of shredded top-secret documents. It took them a couple of years and by the time they put them all together they were obsolete. This was a newer shredder than the one in Iran.

CHAPTER **THIRTY**

The next morning Warner doesn't sound happy on the other end of the phone. "What happened to LeClerc?"

"He's in the hospital. I cracked a rib when I kneed him and it punctured a lung."

"Is he going to make it?"

"Don't know. If it was me, I'd want to be medevaced out to Singapore or somewhere with better hospitals. He's not going anywhere though, even if he does pull through. He's under arrest."

"Is that going to come to anything? You know Indonesia."

"Yeah, I know, but it might this time. They're trying to attract investment to the country. They need to make it look like a safe place to put your money. Plus, if they put a foreigner on trial, some ambitious prosecutor's gonna get all swelled up with nationalistic pride."

"Make an example out of him?"

"Yeah, sure, he'd be good for it."

"Like your wife?"

"Yeah, like Sylvia. So where do we stand, Bill? What'd you tell the client? You need anything more from me on this?"

"I've told the client what they need to know. You're done with it. Take a week off. Take two."

"You want me to write it up again and fax it to you?"

"Nope. It'll keep. I want you to go sit on a beach in Bali or something. I want you fresh when you get back here, ready to work. I think I'm gonna have something for you in a couple of weeks."

"What?"

"You'll find out when you get back." He hangs up before I can ask anything more.

I don't much like the beach, but Bali sounds good. I know a valley about halfway up the west side. There's a small hotel; just a dozen cheap, clean rooms strung along a rice terrace a couple hundred feet above the valley floor.

Irina's drinking coffee in the kitchen with Iris. She wants to go with me for a week, not two. I call the place and book two weeks anyhow.

We make it onto the noon flight. At the airport in Bali we rent a Volkswagen Thing. Bali must be where they all retired to because I haven't seen any anywhere else since the mid-seventies.

We get pulled over by the cops at the big crossroads just north of the turnoff for Denpasar. I walk over to them smiling. They look a little confused when I give them regards from their fellow traffic cops in Marinda. They send me on my way with a grin and a wave after I slip them each ten thousand.

It's a perfect week. Most mornings I'm up before dawn, sitting on the porch of our room, watching the rice *padi* take on dim shape, then definition in shades of gray, then color as the sun rises behind the hill at my back. Irina and I take long hikes, doing a tightrope walk along the curving mud embankments of the narrow rice terraces. We stop for breakfast or lunch in small villages deep back in the hills, places that seldom get any tourists but welcome us as if we're expected guests.

At night we listen to the percussion of the insects, the soft lowing of the water buffalo tethered under bamboo roofs in the fields, the tinkling of a village *gamelan* group rehearsing for an upcoming festival. We make love and Irina falls in love with me again—I hope, I think. And I hope and think the past is fading from our memories and we can be happy together again.

And the night before she leaves to go back to Jakarta, back to the nightclubs and bars, back to fucking men for a living, back to what she says she must do, what she wants to do—back to what I can't, and won't ask her not to do—she turns to me in the dark, and in the dull wash of moonlight I can see tears streaking her face.

"Ray, I am thinking about Sasha."

And I don't say anything because I'm afraid of what she's thinking, afraid of what I might start thinking if I let myself, afraid of the ghost that's been living between us.

"I am thinking Sasha wants me to be happy, Ray. Wants you happy too."

And I get a little teary eyed myself. And I hold her tight. And I want to keep holding her and not let go.

But the next morning she packs and I drive her to the airport.

By the end of that second week I need a city. I require some noise, some crowds, some pollution. It doesn't take that long for all that relaxation to get on my nerves. I've got three days in Jakarta before heading back to Hong Kong. I make a bunch of calls to catch up. It's been a busy couple of weeks.

LeClerc survived, barely. But enough that he'd been moved out of the hospital and into Jakarta's main jail. The drumbeat to lock him away and toss out the key is well underway in the local papers. Australia and Canada are both claiming him, but Indonesia's in no mood to extradite.

Juli wrote the story. The international press picked it up and ran with it for a couple of days until the latest celebrity divorce knocked it off the front pages. There's not enough of Lucky Break left that anyone who got cheated is going to get anything back. LeClerc's got his money stashed somewhere, but so far at least, no one knows how to get at it.

Iris got the job with Juli. She's so busy she barely has time to talk. But she does have a message from Emmy, who says hello, she's doing fine, a Dutch geologist wants to marry her. He wants her to move to Rotterdam. It's what she's been hoping for, but it sure happened fast. I hope it works out.

I can't get ahold of Annie. On my third try, Billy answers her mobile phone and asks me for money for her. She robbed the wrong German banker who was staying at the Mandarin Hotel. She's already been sentenced to eighteen months. Billy gives me the name and address of the prison they've stuck her in. I find out that every prisoner has an account. If I make regular contributions to the prison's general fund, I can make sure she'll get the money. I'm going to have to open some sort of general prison fund. Sylvia needs money too and I can't quite bring myself to cut her off. She's been transferred to Jakarta for trial. I try to see her but don't have the time to bribe enough people before I leave town. The embassy found her a lawyer. He thinks he might be able to get her twenty years and that with enough money to spread around she might be able to get out in five, or at least be transferred to serve out the rest of her sentence in a U.S. prison. I give him the thousand-dollar bill I've still got from Alex's wallet. He says he'll make sure Sylvia gets it. I hope he's honest.

I can't find Irina anywhere. She doesn't answer her phone. No one's seen her. The day before I'm leaving I go by the small hotel where she's lived for several years. She's checked out. There's no forwarding address. She's left an envelope, addressed to me. I'm afraid of what's inside.

A taxi drops me off at the shore end of *Sunda Kelapa*. It's the old harbor in Jakarta. Walking toward the Java Sea along the jetty, there are trucks and forklifts and cranes and modern ships on my right. On my left, it's the fifteenth century. The freighters lining the docks are made of teak and mahogany. They're held together with wood pegs rather than screws or nails or welded seams. Some of them have small motors to get them in and out of harbor, but once at sea they hoist their sails, just as they've been doing for the past five hundred years.

It's one of my favorite places in Indonesia, in the world. I like to come here to think about things, to contemplate life, the past and the future. I walk about halfway down the mile long jetty, then sit on one of the large, brass stumps that the ships tie up to.

I hold the letter to my forehead like a carnival psychic guessing its contents. That doesn't work. Tearing it along the seam, pulling out the folded piece of paper, unfolding it, does.

"Ray. I have gone home, to Russia. I must go home. There is a man, very rich man, he wants to marry me. Now, I have no money and cannot do what I want to do. For my family, my future, I must have money. Please, remember, I come from a very poor country. I will always remember you. Maybe one day I will see you again. I do not know. Please, do not try find me. Maybe someday I will find you. I want you always to have happy life. With me, it is not possible now. Please do not hate me. Love, always, Irina."

I fold the letter up and put it back in the envelope. I stand and look at the filthy, oily water between the boats. It's covered with litter. A little more won't make any difference. I crumple the envelope and throw it as far as I can. I watch it, bobbing on the surface, finding its place in the crowd of refuse.

I continue walking toward the sea until the jetty ends at some rocks and I can't go any further. I sit on one of the rocks, not really seeing anything, not really thinking of anything. There's a thick layer of sound behind me as the docks go about their normal business. There's something comforting about it. Life goes on, time goes by. Whatever I do, whatever happens to me, is just a minor beat making up the rhythm of the world.

In the distance I hear a slow *whomp whomp whomp*. It's blended into the background noise. It grows more distinct, gets closer. I look up and my eyes are skewered by the sun. I shade them with my hand.

There's a flock of hornbills heading out over the water on their way to the jungles of Borneo. I can see the slow, steady beating of their wings. I can make out their colors. I wish I was with them. I shrug my shoulders. If I had wings and could shrug my shoulders fast enough, maybe I could catch up to them.

But I don't have wings. And the *whomp whomp whomp* grows ever more distant, blending now into the salty breeze. And finally I lose them, behind white, pillowy clouds edged with the glow of the sun.

ERIC STONE worked as a writer, photographer, editor, publisher and publishing consultant. He is the author of the novels *Living Room of the Dead* and *Grave Imports,* the first two titles in the Ray Sharp series. Additionally, he wrote the non-fiction book *Wrong Side of the Wall.* He lives in Los Angeles.

As a journalist in Asia, Eric Stone knew the Bre-X scandal firsthand. He spent a lot of time in all the real-life places that feature in *Flight of the Hornbill* and the other books in the Ray Sharp series. Visit him at www.ericstone.com.